DEADLY INTENT

GHOST SQUADRON
2

AUDEAMUS

ERIC THOMSON

Deadly Intent

Published in Canada
By Sanddiver Books Inc.
ISBN: 978-1-989314-31-9

Sanddiver
Books

— One —

Ariel's sun was kissing the horizon when Warrant Officer Miko Steiger entered the ill-kept public park in a suburb of Andersen, the star system's capital. Tall, muscular, with short platinum hair, a square jaw, and watchful eyes, she looked nothing like an officer of the Commonwealth Armed Services.

Most people would take her for one of the vicious so-called activists who bedeviled Andersen and Ariel's other major cities. A Naval Intelligence undercover operative, she wore their characteristic black clothes, heavy boots, and fingerless street-fighting gloves.

She saw her contact sitting alone on a park bench, arms thrown over its back, legs outstretched, ankles crossed. Marine Corps Captain Washburn Tesser, officer commanding Ghost Squadron's Keres Company, was, if anything, scruffier than Steiger, though he looked more like a wharf rat than a rioter. Still, anyone paying close attention would notice the watchfulness in his dark eyes along with neck muscles hinting at a powerful physique beneath the faded work clothes. He appeared entirely at ease, chewing on a blade of grass, but Steiger knew Wash could become a deadly fighter at the drop of a hat.

Steiger walked around the park once, making sure no one could overhear them, then dropped onto the bench beside Tesser.

"And?" He asked without looking at her.

"They're slowly assembling for another night of political mayhem — same compound as before. I saw plenty of illegal weaponry — blasters, plasma carbines, needlers, and explosives this time. It means they plan on ratcheting up the violence by several notches. A couple of cops are watching them from a distance, but even if the Andersen police department turns out in force, they'll be overwhelmed unless they open fire. It might be enough to make the prime minister panic and call for martial law, which would mean blood running in the streets."

"That's what the buggers want."

"And it means tonight's the night." She glanced at him.

"Yep. Time to kill a few *pour encourager les autres*, and let their off-world backers know playtime is over."

"When are you going in?"

"As soon as we're done here, I'll deploy the company into the battle positions we prepared. When they come out of their lair, chains swinging and chanting their idiotic revolutionary slogans…"

Tesser let his words hang between them. Ariel wasn't their first cleanup operation in recent months. Extremist groups seeking to destabilize democratically elected governments were sprouting up in many vulnerable star systems.

They were the newest phenomenon in the Commonwealth-wide secret war waged by Centralists wanting a more powerful Earth exercising greater control over her former colonies. Standing against them were the sovereign star systems, independent entities within the broader human federation. Though nominally neutral, the Fleet had long ago decided humanity's future was with the latter.

Steiger stood.

"I won't stick around for the main event. See you at the pickup point."

"Cheers."

The activists, who belonged to the Ariel branch of a newly formed umbrella group calling itself the United Commonwealth Front, had taken over a rundown part of Andersen, near the waterfront, and created their own no-go zone. The authorities, fearful of a bloodbath that would inflame public opinion across the Commonwealth, had kept the police away from UCF turf for the last few weeks, hoping the movement would burn itself out. But it wouldn't, because interstellar corporate interests with deep pockets provided funding, which was why the Fleet had secretly dispatched one of its elite direct action units.

Tesser left a few minutes later, after making sure no one was shadowing Steiger, and slipped through the lengthening shadows to the warehouse Keres Company had taken over as its staging area. The trooper standing guard inside the doorway nodded at him.

"Everything is quiet."

"Good."

Once inside, Tesser looked for his first sergeant, Antanas Gade, among the hundred or so Marines variously snoozing, playing cards, or cleaning already spotless weapons. Most sported beards of varying lengths, haircuts that would break a regimental sergeant major's heart, and wore clothes just one step above those generally associated with vagrants.

Keres Company had arrived a few days earlier aboard one of the Navy's Q-ships and landed in small groups, bit by bit, to stay inconspicuous. From the spaceport, they'd made their way to the abandoned warehouse identified by Miko Steiger as the best hide and staging point for an attack on the UCF compound.

Steiger herself landed a week before Keres Company, dispatched by Captain Hera Talyn, chief of staff of Naval Intelligence's Special Operations Division, the Fleet's top-secret espionage, subversion, assassination, and sabotage unit. But unlike the Marines, she'd traveled aboard a Navy aviso disguised as a commercial courier ship. Avisos, smaller than sloops but with a frigate's hyperdrives, could reach the highest hyperspace bands where the universe became an eerily strange place, and cross interstellar space at more than twice the speed of larger starships.

Gade, upon seeing his CO, put down the cards he was holding and stood.

"Is it on?"

"We move out at last light."

"Good. It's time we taught those worthless punks a lesson they'll never forget. At least those who'll see the next sunrise."

Gade, along with most of Keres Company, named after the Greek goddesses of violent death, had watched the UCF rioters turn downtown Andersen into a battle zone several nights running. By now, they were impatient to show the galaxy how cowardly the revolutionaries really were.

With orders already given, firing positions prepared, and the extraction route scouted out, Keres Company was ready and raring to go in no time. Once they'd packed their gear, Tesser and Gade inspected the warehouse and made sure they left nothing behind that might identify them as Fleet.

After one last verbal run-through of the operation, E and F Troop headed for their firing positions, disassembled weapons hidden in backpacks. G Troop deployed behind them to secure the withdrawal route, and H Troop moved off to the assembly point, where trucks waited. Tesser, Gade, and the Marines from company HQ took an observation post overlooking the UCF's no-go zone.

The moment he slipped in behind a broken upper floor window, Tesser saw the rioters getting ready by shouting revolutionary slogans and brandishing improvised weapons. There were several hundred of them, many from off-world rather than Ariel citizens, yet the destruction they'd wrought and the political crisis they were precipitating belied their small numbers.

But then, history proved over and over that it takes just a handful of determined, ruthless, ideologically motivated psychopaths backed by wealthy financiers to ruin entire societies. Of the power weapons and explosive devices Steiger mentioned, there was so far no sign. But if the rioters were working off the usual playbook, those would be in the rear ranks, hidden by the black-clad mass, ready to cause further confusion and frighten both the police and local politicians.

Tesser glanced at his timepiece. E and F Troops should be in position by now, silent, sniper-grade railguns assembled and ready. He studied the rioters' front ranks again, trying to identify the leaders. But with most of them masked, the task proved well-nigh impossible. And by design.

United Commonwealth Front members were, in everything but name, insurgents, enemies of star system governments. Grand Admiral Larsson, supreme commander of humanity's ground and naval forces, had issued secret orders designating them as such, meaning for Keres Company, they represented legitimate targets in a counterinsurgency war.

The amorphous mass began spilling through the wide gates of the UCF compound, headed for downtown Andersen and another orgy of destruction, this one worse than before. Tesser saw police in riot gear standing at a distance instead of moving in to block them. When the rioters were half in, half out of the compound, he raised his communicator to his lips and spoke a single word, invoking the mother of the Keres.

"Nyx."

Almost immediately, two dozen rioters in the front rank collapsed, shot through the center of mass with ten-millimeter slugs. At first, the ones behind them couldn't absorb what was happening, and another two dozen fell to the ground, dead. The shouts died away, replaced by screaming, and the mob broke apart, each rioter running for his or her life, exposing the armed faction that was hiding in their midst.

The way they looked around for snipers and held their weapons told Tesser these weren't spoiled, middle-class kids masquerading as wannabe revolutionaries, but trained troops. Yet even that training wouldn't save them. Armed rioters were a priority target, and the Keres Company snipers changed their aim.

Sirens lit up, competing with the screaming and shouting, and Tesser smiled as the Andersen cops finally got into gear, blocking off the main avenue and side streets, and intercepting terrified would-be rioters. The police chief must have found her spine and told both the mayor and the prime minister it was over.

"You're welcome," he muttered before raising his communicator to his lips again. "Extract."

He took one last look at the carnage and estimated his people killed or wounded over sixty UCF goons. The police would take care of another bunch, while those who escaped altogether would burn their masks and black garments and pretend they never took to the streets. UCF members in other cities across Ariel would count themselves fortunate and slink away, never to riot again. But if they did, Keres Company or another unit from the 1st Special Forces Regiment would return and make sure the lesson stuck.

Keres Company's escape, with each troop using a different route, went unnoticed in the confusion. The trucks they'd rented were in the expected locations away from the waterfront, with Marines from H Troop guarding them. They climbed aboard and left Andersen for an abandoned airstrip where they met Warrant Officer Steiger, who informed Tesser shuttles from the Q-ship *Thespis* were on their way.

Two hours later, Keres Company, along with Steiger, stepped aboard the ship, currently masquerading as the Merchant Vessel *Orpheus*. Thirty minutes after that, *Thespis* broke out of orbit while Tesser composed a subspace message informing Captain Talyn of the operation's success.

When he'd done so, Tesser joined his company for a hot wash, followed by an issue of cold beer on the hangar deck. At Steiger's suggestion, they watched the Ariel newsnets on the primary display while enjoying their drinks.

"Those overgrown babies won't be trying shit like that again," First Sergeant Gade said after the newsies tallied UCF casualties and arrests. "Although massacre isn't the proper term. We simply took out the garbage."

Tesser slapped him on the shoulder. "Damn right, Top."

— Two —

Lieutenant Colonel Zachary Thomas Decker's secure office communicator lit up with a call, and he dropped his reader, happy for an interruption. Headquarters came out with new orders, directives, and recommendations seemingly every hour of every day. As Ghost Squadron's commanding officer, he had no choice but to read them, in case something miraculously applied to humanity's foremost Special Operations unit.

"Decker."

"It's me, Zack." Captain Hera Talyn's face materialized on the screen. She was a slender brunette whose smooth features belied her long years as an undercover field operative. Talyn was in her office as well, but at Fleet HQ, several hundred kilometers east of Fort Arnhem, the Special Forces and Pathfinders' home station.

He grinned at her.

"Are you calling because you miss me?"

"You're never away long enough these days for me to miss you. I heard from both Erinye and Keres Company. They report operations carried out successfully within expected parameters. They extracted as per plan, unseen, and are by now in interstellar space. Miko Steiger is coming back with Keres, and Caelin Morrow sends us her best, along with thanks for Curtis' help. There's more to the story, but I'll let him tell you. The newsnets will be interesting in the next few days, once word of events on Mission Colony and Ariel spreads across the Commonwealth."

Decker's grin widened. "Good. It's about time."

"We'll open a bottle of champagne and watch them together when you visit this weekend."

Decker gave his partner a wink.

"Temptress. But you forgot I prefer Shrehari ale. Champagne gives me headaches."

"Another thing, I received warning the Senate is about to summon Grand Admiral Larsson for the quinquennial defense budget hearings. Under the circumstances, he'd like a company from Ghost Squadron instead of his normal escort and close protection detail."

"When?"

"A few weeks from now. Enough time for Erinye and Keres to return home and recuperate."

Ghost Squadron's third company, Moirae, was preparing for a mission, leaving him with a choice between Curtis Delgado, who led the Erinyes, and Washburn Tesser as escort commander.

"If it makes the choice easier, whoever is in charge should be a major, even if it's only on an acting basis."

"Then we're talking Erinye Company. Curtis has seniority in rank over Wash."

"I'll let the admiral know. Talk to you tonight, Big Boy." She blew Decker a kiss. "Talyn, out."

Her image vanished before he could return the kiss. She still enjoyed teasing him, even after their many years together. As relationships went, theirs was more unusual than most. But Decker couldn't imagine being with anyone else, even though they only saw each other in person on weekends and days off. Or when Talyn flew up to Fort Arnhem so she could personally deliver a mission briefing.

Decker reached for the secure communicator, then decided he might as well stretch his legs and see the regimental commander in person to tell him Erinye and Keres were on the way home. Though he'd rather be out there with his Marines, fighting the good fight, Decker understood his days as a Special Forces commander in the field were almost over, and not just because of age. The operational tempo meant they no longer enjoyed the luxury of sending an entire squadron on a given operation if a single company was sufficient. Of course, the addition of a fourth troop to each company shortly after the Arcadia strike gave them more strength and staying power than ever.

Colonel Kal Ryent, a career Pathfinder and the 1st Special Forces Regiment's commanding officer looked up from his desk when he heard Decker's knuckles rapping on the door frame. Light-haired, with clear blue eyes and rugged features, Ryent, a product of the Commonwealth Armed

Services Academy, was several years younger than Decker who'd climbed up the ranks from private. But they respected and liked each other.

Decker considered Ryent a bit like a younger brother who'd done well, instead of always getting into trouble like his elder. They'd worked together often when Ryent commanded the 251st Pathfinder Squadron, and Decker was crisscrossing the Commonwealth with Hera Talyn, righting wrongs, and terminating enemies.

"What's up, Zack?" Ryent gestured at a chair in front of his desk.

"Hera just called. Erinye and Keres Companies reported success and are on their way home. Keep an eye on the newsnets. Apparently, what my troopers did on Ariel might shake things up."

"Excellent. It's well past time we make our enemy follow their own rules. Too bad you and I aren't younger and more junior in rank. We could make up for the opportunities we missed during the years our beloved Fleet was too timid."

"Yep. Hera also warned me Larsson is heading to Earth in a few weeks and wants one of my companies under an acting major as escort instead of his usual. I'll be sending Curtis Delgado and his Erinyes."

"Can't say I blame the Grand Admiral. Plenty of people want his head for letting slip the dogs of war without permission."

"Thank the Almighty he did. Otherwise, Ariel would circle the drain right now. Violent revolutionaries, spineless politicians — not exactly a match made in heaven. Without Larsson's orders, this crap would have spread to most of the outer star systems by now, my ancestral home of Mykonos included."

Ryent made a face.

"Until we go after the people financing this alphabet soup of radical revolutionaries, we'll be playing catchup while honest folk lose faith in their elected leaders."

"With any luck, Hera and the Naval Intelligence brain trust in Sanctum will cook up an actionable plan soon. My squadron's operation taking out Elize and Allard Hogue caused a lot of positive downstream effects and offers a decent blueprint for future strikes against the financiers of chaos." Decker paused for a few seconds, then a broad grin split his square, honest face. "You know, I just experienced a brain fart. We can take away the financiers' own action arm by dusting off Grand Admiral Kowalski's playbook. I wonder why Hera hasn't thought of it yet."

"You mean wiping out the *Sécurité Spéciale* just like Kowalski erased the old Special Security Branch last century? Hera probably hasn't raised the idea yet because she, just like us, is too busy putting out fires before they destabilize entire star systems."

The *Sécurité Spéciale*, which didn't officially exist, was the Secretary-General of the Commonwealth's own covert security intelligence agency, answerable only to him and funded through the executive budget.

"Maybe it's time, what with the 2nd Special Forces Regiment coming online soon. The Fleet Pathfinder

Squadrons can round out our strength, and they come with their own transport. I'm sure Jimmy Martinson would love blooding his division by taking out the biggest trash in the Commonwealth." When he saw Ryent's dubious expression, Decker said, "We didn't start this crap, but we will end it, Kal. Might as well think big right away."

Ryent smiled at his friend.

"You'll never change, will you?"

"Nope. There's nothing the judicious use of high explosives can't solve. Our motto ought to be 'do it with a bang,' don't you think?"

"Nice double entendre, but we'll stick with *'Audeamus'* if you don't mind. Your Marines might look like vagabonds when they're carrying out operations, but we should still keep a modicum of dignity."

"Dignity is vastly overrated. I should know — I lost mine often enough, but here we are, doing the Almighty's work, nonetheless."

"Yet if you hadn't tried so hard to lose it, you might sit in my chair right now, and I'd be sitting in yours."

Decker winked at Ryent.

"Sure, but then I wouldn't have met Hera."

"Will you two ever make it official?"

"Why? I ended my roving days a long time ago, and she had eyes for no one before me. Now she has eyes for no one else. Or are you looking for an excuse to throw the biggest party in Fort Arnhem's history?"

"The union of the most infamous Special Forces officer with the most famously dangerous former Naval

Intelligence Liaison Officer? It would be a gala for the ages."

Decker gave him a suspicious look.

"Or is the Pegasus Club in need of replacement, and you want to blame its destruction on a party that spiraled out of control?"

"Don't even joke about that, Zack. The Pegasus is sacred. When we build a new club, the old one will become a museum."

"If you say so. But back to your original question, the answer is no. Hera doesn't need an uncouth Marine at her side in an official capacity while she climbs the flag officer ranks. She'll be Chief of Naval Intelligence one day, mark my words."

"That, I believe. Though the way things are going, you and I could become general officers ourselves."

"Pass. I'm not interested in becoming a uniformed politician."

"All the more reason for a few stars on your collar, so you can tell the uniformed politicians how it is in the real universe without risking another court-martial."

Decker scoffed. "I doubt the Corps is that hard up for combat-experienced colonels it can promote."

"Stranger things happen."

**

Later that evening, Decker mentioned his idea while he and Hera Talyn spoke over a secure link, something they did most days when they were on Caledonia, but apart from each other.

"A tall order. Kowalski had the full force of the Armed Services Security Branch at her disposal. She turned most of it into the Constabulary afterward, remember."

"Take out the command-and-control nodes, then roll up the field agents at leisure. Surely your lot knows where the former are by now."

"We'd need Grand Admiral Larsson's sign-off on something of that magnitude, and I don't think we'll get it just yet. The political situation isn't quite as fraught as it was in Kowalski's day."

"But we're well on our way. Give it a few more months or perhaps a year. And since Josh, Squadron HQ, and I are nothing more than administrators these days, we have plenty of time for contingency plans. Send me your data on the *Sécurité Spéciale* command-and-control nodes, and we'll war game scenarios."

"My, my, you are getting bored."

"The thought of relinquishing my current rank so I can return to field operations crosses my mind daily."

"That won't happen. We have plans for you, my dear." She blew him a kiss.

"Don't I know it. Kal was talking about stars on my collar earlier today." Decker raised his whiskey glass. "Here's to those plans."

The next morning, at the weekly operations meeting, he announced Ghost Squadron HQ would study taking out the *Sécurité Spéciale* with the help of the entire regiment and selected Fleet Pathfinder Squadrons. Major Josh Bayliss, Decker's second in command and like him, commissioned from the ranks, chuckled with undisguised amusement.

"You want to one-up Grand Admiral Kowalski and be more than a footnote in history? I guess you reached peak boredom, Zack."

"And you haven't?"

"I've been jumping with the School's current trainees every few days. It keeps me young and happy. You should try it."

Bayliss, formerly the Pathfinder School's regimental sergeant major, was a powerfully built, dark-complexioned man with silver-shot black hair. He and Decker had been close friends since they were buck sergeants.

"The only reason you can play is because I handle most of the administrivia," Decker growled.

"And we're grateful for your selfless sacrifice, Oh Wonderful Commanding Officer."

Bayliss' quip and Decker's glower, a routine they'd perfected over the years, earned them grins from the others around the table.

"If we're done with the persiflage, perhaps we can toss around a few ideas. I'm not sure taking out the *Sécurité Spéciale* will ever happen, but I'm convinced they're the link between Centralist financiers and the so-called activists. Short of doing unto the bankers what we did to the Hogues, it's the best way of ending the current, wholly manufactured unrest for good."

"No arguments here, sir," The operations officer, Captain Jory Virk, said. "Planning a campaign like that will be an excellent intellectual exercise."

— Three —

Hera Talyn and Rear Admiral Konstantin Ulrich, the head of Naval Intelligence's Special Operations Division, met the Chief of Naval Intelligence, Admiral Kruczek, in the antechamber to the latter's office.

"Kos, Captain." Kruczek, a lean, silver-haired man with a seamed face, nodded in greeting.

"Sir."

"Ghost Squadron kicked off quite the firestorm on Ariel. The newsnets are beside themselves." He gestured toward the hallway. "Shall we? Grand Admiral Larsson is no doubt watching the subspace feed from Ariel at this very moment."

As they walked along the carpeted corridor toward the office of the man who commanded the mightiest military force in human history, Kruczek allowed himself a chuckle.

"The rampant speculation is its own entertainment. Someone is even floating theories of paramilitary death squads charged with eradicating peaceful activists whose only goal is a better life for everyone."

"That would be me, sir," Talyn said. "Among other rumors. Confusing the enemy is one of my favorite hobbies."

"Ha! Why am I not surprised?"

"But the Ariel arm of the United Commonwealth Front is a spent force. Ghost Squadron killed its leadership and armed support in Andersen. That destroyed morale almost completely while shocking the police and government into action. I don't think we'll worry about Ariel for the next few years."

Larsson's senior aide, a commodore in Navy blue with the gold aiguillettes of her office on the left shoulder, stood as they entered the executive suite.

"Please go right in. The Grand Admiral is expecting you."

Kruczek gave the aide a pleasant nod. "Thank you, Ruth."

They entered the spacious corner office overlooking the Fleet HQ spaceport and halted a regulation three paces from Larsson's desk. The latter, a tall, lean, fair-haired man in his early seventies who'd been watching a video feed of the brief, brutal street fight in Andersen, turned toward his subordinates and gestured at the chairs facing him.

"Please sit. When you asked me several weeks ago to, and I'll quote Captain Talyn's exact words, cry havoc and let slip the dogs of war, I didn't expect such thorough havoc. Ghost Squadron's Marines are exceedingly ruthless and precise. What are the odds they'll blame us?"

Kruczek gestured at Talyn. "Since eradicating violent radicals is Hera's brainchild, I'll let her comment."

"Sir. We planted several rumors assigning blame. Among them are paramilitary death squads, cartels tired of business disruptions, mercenaries hired by commercial interests, and Ariel citizens taking the law into their own hands. The railgun slugs fired are of a commonly available type, and the strike force both infiltrated and exfiltrated unnoticed.

"Of course, the *Sécurité Spéciale* will likely suspect us and spread their own rumors, but without evidence. By and large, the citizenry and governments across the OutWorlds will breathe a sigh of relief now that someone is taking on the radicals, though overtly, they will deplore the degree of violence used. Ghost Squadron's Moirae Company is heading for Merseaux aboard *Sorcerer* the moment it arrives with Erinye Company in a few days. There, it will carry out a similar operation against the Merseaux Justice Alliance, another United Commonwealth Front offshoot funded by the usual suspects and organized by the *Sécurité Spéciale*."

"Let's hope two such strikes at opposite ends of the Commonwealth within the space of a few weeks will send a message to the opposition."

Talyn grimaced.

"Doubtful. I expect the opposition will double down and increase the pressure. This, for them, is a slippery slope, though most on Earth don't realize it yet. The more radical Centralist elements will take control of the movement, pushing the moderates aside, which means more upheaval, disruption, and political violence." She paused for a moment. "I think we are finally witnessing the beginning of the end for the Commonwealth in its present configuration. The trick now is pushing it over the edge and forcing a realignment before we face a real civil war."

"Any ideas how we could manage such a feat?"

"Colonel Decker raised one a few days ago. He suggested we copy Grand Admiral Kowalski and take out the Centralists' action arm. Cut the organizing link between the money and the street thugs, and it peters out. I'd been mulling much the same thing, but him discussing it with me brought the urgency into clearer focus. Great minds and all that, I suppose, sir."

"Doing so would place us on the slippery slope of no return as well, Captain."

"We're already on it, sir. The dogs of war can't be recalled until they win or are put down. And the latter isn't an option."

"I suppose you're right, and I'd rather we win. War game a Kowalski solution, under a top-secret special access designation, but do nothing further until I return from Earth."

"Yes, sir. Colonel Decker has already begun with his headquarters staff, based on the idea we would use the full resources of the 1st Special Forces Regiment and the independent Pathfinder squadrons. I've classified his planning exercise under the special access designation Long Knives."

"Isn't that a bit too much on point?"

"If you wish, I can change it. Colonel Decker selected the code words. As you might recall, he's something of an amateur historian, especially of the pre-diaspora era."

"No, let it be. If the opposition hears of a TSSA codenamed Long Knives, they might worry enough to spoil their aim. Now, the Earth visit. What's the word on my escort?"

"Colonel Decker selected the company commanded by Captain Curtis Delgado. He'll be appointed acting major for the occasion. Delgado just led his Marines through two successful, back-to-back operations, one beyond Commonwealth space and the other an opportunistic strike to support our Constabulary cousins on Mission Colony. The latter probably saved us from going there in force next year or the year after, with all the additional risks and visibility. You'll be as well protected as humanly possible."

"I'd like to meet Acting Major Delgado ahead of time."

"Certainly, sir. They should land early next week. Perhaps that Friday?"

"See Ruth on the way out and ask her to block off half an hour in my calendar."

"Yes, sir."

"Are there any more items of business?"

Kruczek shook his head. "No, sir."

"In that case, shall we go ahead?" Larsson tapped the screen embedded in his desktop. "Ruth, it's time."

The commodore appeared moments later, a camera drone floating in her wake. She dropped something into

Larsson's extended hand, and he pointed at the flag stand behind his desk.

"Let's use this as a backdrop."

Kruczek, Ulrich, and Talyn came around the desk where the aide positioned them, Larsson and Talyn in the middle, Ulrich on Talyn's side and Kruczek on the other.

"Attention to orders. Captain Hera Talyn, Commonwealth Navy, is hereby promoted to the substantive rank of commodore effective today and appointed Deputy Head, Naval Intelligence Special Operations Division."

Larsson reached out and pulled the metallic Navy captain's rank insignia from her collar.

"Hand."

She held it out, and he placed it in the center of her palm. Then he affixed a single silver star in its place.

"Congratulations, Commodore. Welcome to flag rank. We decided we'd advance your promotion and create a temporary deputy head position to help with the transition, considering the pace of events."

"Thank you, sir."

"You can decide on who'll be your chief of staff and fill that seat as soon as possible," Ulrich said.

They posed for pictures, toasted her star with a dram of Glen Arcturus, then left a thoughtful Larsson as he returned to the video feed from Ariel's newsnets, wondering what he'd unleashed on an unsuspecting Commonwealth.

That evening, when she posed for Decker with the shiny new star on her collar, he said, "You should come up here for happy hour tomorrow and wet that beautiful little piece of silver."

"In a Pegasus Club with standing room only? The pay increase from captain to commodore isn't that generous."

"Hey, you only become a flag officer once in your career. Just put a cred chip on the bar and let it run out. Those who get there too late can buy you one instead."

A big part of her wanted to celebrate with the only family she knew, but habit demanded a rebuttal before giving in.

"You can become a flag officer more than once. Admiral Dunmoore made commodore near the end of the war, went back to captain when they reduced the flag ranks after the armistice and rose to become a four-star."

Decker glowered at her.

"Fine, if you want to be pedantic, celebrate with the rest of the stuck-up snobs in the Sanctum Officer's Mess. We'll just enjoy a quiet Friday night by ourselves. Navy officers with Pathfinder wings make flag rank all the time, so it's not really a special occasion." He let the sarcasm drip from his words.

"You're not coming to Sanctum for the weekend?"

"If you won't come up and party with your jump buddies, then no."

Talyn narrowed her eyes and scowled.

"I'll be there at seventeen hundred hours."

"And bring the entire contents of your savings account."

"Just make sure there's fresh linen on the bed."

He gave her a mock salute.

"Yes, sir, Commodore, sir."

That Friday's happy hour in the Pegasus Club became one for the books as both Regiment and School celebrated the Special Operations community's most distinguished NILOs, one of the few in the Fleet's entire history to reach flag rank. Decker and Talyn spent a quiet weekend recovering before the latter returned to Sanctum in the wee hours of Monday morning.

— Four —

Decker stood at the edge of the parade square and watched *Sorcerer*'s shuttles land in orderly packets under the direction of Fort Arnhem's ground controllers on a gray, humid morning smothered by thick clouds promising a downpour. Since he no longer went out into the vast galaxy after coming home from the raid on Arcadia, Decker always saw his companies off and greeted them when they returned, no matter the hour of the day. It was the closest he came to living his old life as a Special Forces field commander.

His communicator buzzed insistently, and he glanced at its display. Hera Talyn.

"What's up, Commodore, sir? I'm about to greet the returning heroes of Erinye Company."

"In that case, my timing is superb, as usual. You can let Curtis Delgado know Caelin Morrow was promoted a few days ago and will join the Political Anti-Corruption Unit on Wyvern as a team leader."

"Good for her. Is that your doing?"

"In part. The PACU will take on a greater role in the overall scheme, though the Constabulary doesn't know it yet, and having a friend on the inside will help."

Decker chuckled.

"You missed your true calling."

"Which is?"

"Career manager."

"Perish the thought. If Admiral Ulrich hadn't rescued me from the regular Navy decades ago, I'd likely have shot mine after he or she posted me to yet another useless staff job, working for some self-important four-ringer. Say hi to Curtis and his troopers for me. I'm working on an appointment with Grand Admiral Larsson so he can meet the commander of his escort."

"Will do."

"Talyn, out."

Decker tucked his communicator away in time to watch Delgado's Marines, wearing their unmarked, armored battle suits and carrying both weapons and packs, form up in three ranks under First Sergeant Hak's orders. Delgado himself headed for Decker, helmet visor up. A relaxed grin split his neatly trimmed, reddish beard.

"How are they hanging, Curtis?" Decker asked when the younger man was within earshot.

"Same old, same old, Colonel. You want to speak with the troopers?"

"Yep. Two missions in one deserve a quick word of appreciation. By the way, I was just on the link with Commodore Talyn. She said Caelin Morrow came out of the Mission Colony business with a promotion and a transfer to the most fearsome Professional Compliance Bureau outfit of them all, the Political Anti-Corruption Unit, as one of the team leaders."

"It means Commissioner Sorjonen liked what he saw of her work when he arrived. Good. She deserves it after tackling that cesspool of corruption." Delgado noticed First Sergeant Hak raising his fist out of the corner of his eyes. "They're ready for you, sir."

"After I do my thing and you climb out of that tin suit, you and I need to talk next mission. It'll differ from the usual."

"Should I worry?" Delgado asked as they stepped off toward the waiting Marines.

"No. The mission comes with an acting, while so employed, promotion to major."

"And just like that, I am worried."

Decker, tailed by Delgado, stopped in front of Erinye company and gave them one of his short, to the point, congratulatory speeches for a pair of jobs well done. Then he dismissed them to stow their gear and head off on two weeks of well-deserved leave.

Delgado, in black battledress uniform, appeared at Decker's office door less than an hour later.

"I'm ready for the bad news, Colonel."

"Sit." Decker pointed at a chair across from his desk. "Is there anything I should know that you didn't include in your mission report?"

"No, sir."

The answer didn't surprise Ghost Squadron's commanding officer. His officers knew him well enough by now and made sure their reports were comprehensive, warts and other uglies included. But he asked anyway, just in case Delgado held something back because he wanted to discuss it in person.

"Then let's talk about your next job, the one with the acting promotion."

Delgado grimaced. "I suppose I can't evade it."

Decker grinned at him, knowing his air of reluctance was wholly feigned.

"Not even if you could travel between dimensions. Grand Admiral Larsson has been summoned to Earth by the Senate for the quinquennial defense budget debate. He wants a company-sized Special Forces escort instead of his usual close protection detail, for obvious reasons, and Commodore Talyn tapped me on the shoulder. Since you're the senior company commander, the Erinyes get the job, and you'll wear an oak leaf wreath around that first and soon to be single pip."

"Then I suppose the order of the day is once more unto the breach, dear friends, once more."

Decker's grin widened.

"That's the spirit. What'll happen next is Commodore Talyn will arrange a meeting with Grand Admiral Larsson since he gets the final say on who commands the escort. The Commodore and I will be there as moral support, but it's up to you. Make an impression, and you're a major.

Disappoint me, and you might wonder why the promotion board no longer returns your calls."

"Losing the promotion board's love is a tempting offer. I'm sure there are worse things than becoming a captain for life."

"Yes, there are, and I can arrange for them just like that." Decker snapped his fingers.

Delgado sighed.

"I'll make sure my dress uniform is up to Regimental Sergeant Major Vanleith's high standards."

"Good man."

"Will we go in wearing the winged dagger, or masquerade as regular regimental troops?"

"That's still up in the air. I suspect Grand Admiral Larsson will make the final decision, based on Commodore Talyn's advice. And that's it; off on leave with you. If we're summoned to Sanctum before it's over, I'll call. Otherwise, see you in two weeks."

**

"How did Curtis react?" Talyn asked when they connected over the secure link that evening.

"Like a hunting dog straining on his leash. He tried the old 'if I'm volun-told, then so be it' routine. But beneath the world-weary facade, our Curtis is tickled pink. If the mission goes well, I wouldn't mind the acting promotion becoming substantive."

"That's in the cards, darling."

Decker snorted with amusement.

"Again, with the career mangling."

"Call it moving the pieces where they'll be ready for opening night. But I'm glad Curtis is raring to go. The general mood on Earth is getting uglier by the day. Massive, occasionally violent protests to support the revolutionaries your people terminated on various OutWorlds in recent weeks are multiplying across the planet. They're accompanied by demands the SecGen punish those responsible for the outrageous acts of suppressing legitimate dissent. Never mind the dissenters in question were murderous thugs whose goal was overthrowing legitimately elected star system governments."

"Centralist street theater."

She nodded.

"Bought and paid for by their corporate backers. They know we're eliminating their foot soldiers but don't feel confident enough to denounce us, so they're raging and howling, but far away from Geneva. Embarrassing Brüggemann at this juncture wouldn't advance the cause."

The Secretary-General of the Commonwealth, Brodrik Brüggemann, was a career politician, with a politician's instincts. Both Decker and Talyn knew he would prevaricate until the very last moment hoping to retain his grip on power.

"Where's the *Sécurité Spéciale* in all this?"

"Busy keeping the street theater away from Geneva since it's only for show on Earth. These things spiral out of control easily enough when activists believe themselves above the law."

"Or a law unto themselves. Are you sure we shouldn't send the entirety of Ghost Squadron to escort Larsson?"

"If one company of your finest can't protect him, then the three of them won't be enough. Best keep a reasonable profile and carry live ammunition. If the opposition tries anything, it won't be by unleashing a paid mob of radical agitators on the Palace of the Stars or suborning the 1st Marines into carrying out a coup against its own supreme commander. If it makes you feel any happier, I plan on sending Miko Steiger ahead as the liaison. She'll tap into our network there and make sure Curtis is kept aware of developing threats."

"Excellent plan. Miko's been amazingly helpful since I brought her in from the cold."

Decker gave Talyn a knowing smirk. She hadn't been keen on Steiger when they first met years earlier, during an intelligence mission, not least because the latter caught Decker's roving eye at the time and on another occasion later.

"Without a doubt. When do you expect Keres Company?"

"They called from the heliopause a few hours ago, so sometime tomorrow."

"Can you arrange an aircar for Miko? I'd like to see her as soon as possible, so she can take a few days off before heading to Earth."

"Consider it done."

— Five —

The next day, late in the afternoon, an aircar bearing Fort Arnhem markings swooped in for a landing by the main gate leading to the sprawling Armed Services HQ complex on the outskirts of Caledonia's capital. The automated guard post scanned the credentials of the passenger and driver, comparing them to their faces and the biometric data on file, then allowed the car through.

It stopped in front of the vast main building's front entrance and the passenger, a tall, strong-faced blonde woman in her forties, climbed out with a travel bag in hand. She wore a silver-trimmed Marine Corps warrant officer's black garrison uniform and a blue beret with the Intelligence Branch cap badge — a silver compass rose on a circular scarlet and green background surrounded by stars.

Although Warrant Officer Miko Steiger was once a senior Army noncom, she'd transferred to the Corps after accepting Hera Talyn's offer of becoming one of Naval

Intelligence's black ops agents. Marines roaming across the Commonwealth attracted fewer questions than Army personnel usually tied to a single star system.

Steiger thanked the driver, who gave her a quick salute before heading home to Fort Arnhem. For Steiger, the HQ complex was home. She had a small apartment in the warrant officers' block where she stayed between off-world missions.

After the automated security station immediately inside the door accepted her credentials, she made her way through what felt like kilometers of corridors until she reached the wing occupied by Naval Intelligence's own headquarters.

The antechamber to Commodore Talyn's office was empty, though her door stood wide open.

"Come in, Miko." Talyn's voice reached her ears before Steiger could rap on the door jamb.

She stopped a regulation three paces in front of the desk and saluted.

"Warrant Officer Steiger reporting to the commodore as ordered."

"At ease and sit. What did I tell you about formalities around here?"

Steiger dropped into one of the chairs and grinned at Talyn.

"You wear a flag officer's star now, Commodore. There's no avoiding a modicum of formality. It comes with the territory."

Talyn knew Steiger was teasing her, so she let it pass.

"Good job on Ariel."

"Thank you, sir. I took a lot of long hot showers aboard *Thespis* to wash off the radical stench." Steiger shook her head. "I've never seen the like before. Most of them were mindlessly evil garbage who enjoyed wreaking havoc, no matter the human cost, simply for shits and giggles, but their leaders? Depraved doesn't begin to cover it."

"A good chunk of the leadership died at Keres Company's hands or is in police custody now that the Ariel government found its spine. The locals are hunting those who survived and are on the run."

"Good. That sort of trash shouldn't be suffered to live."

"Unfortunately, there's always more willing and able. That's why cutting off funding will be vital as we trace it upstream. In any case, the Centralists, via the *Sécurité Spéciale*, are even using their foot soldiers on Earth as the newest source of street violence to support OutWorld UCF groups. Normally, we wouldn't care about Earthers trashing their own star system. But Grand Admiral Larsson is headed there soon for the defense budget hearings in the Senate, and violent activists can escape *Sécurité Spéciale* control, given the right circumstances."

Steiger winced.

"The timing could be better."

"It's excellent as far as the opposition is concerned. That's why Erinye Company will take on the job as Grand Admiral Larsson's close protection detail. You're going ahead of time as Curtis Delgado's liaison with our local network, but not before you take a few days off. I'll arrange for a business class cabin on a liner. You'll operate under a cover identity only Curtis and his command team, as well as the lead agent on Earth, will know. I've already alerted him to search for threats against Larsson. I'll give you the contact instructions before you leave."

"What will the identity be?"

A smile tugged at Talyn's lips.

"You'll enjoy this — Britta Trulson, one of the Deep Space Foundation's leading intelligence operatives."

"Kinky."

The Foundation, ostensibly a charitable organization, had spent years spreading disinformation and subversion on behalf of Centralist interests and their financiers to undermine the sovereign star systems principle at the heart of the Commonwealth constitution. After Naval Intelligence assassinated its founder and the man who ran it, Hera Talyn's operatives had infiltrated and subverted it. The Foundation was now an arm of Naval Intelligence, used for the blackest of black ops, though most employees didn't know about the change of ownership.

"I'll arrange things so that you seem to be traveling directly from Cimmeria, using a trick I developed well before we made the Foundation one of our covert subsidiaries. And I've arranged matters so that Madame Trulson can call upon Senator Nerys Annear's office for assistance. She owes us a few courtesies."

"What are my parameters?"

"You'll enjoy full freedom of action to do as you see fit. Your primary mission is helping Erinye Company protect

Grand Admiral Larsson. However, considering the circles in which they'll be operating, you may take on targets of opportunity that help us weaken the opposition in the long term. Be prepared for a lengthier outing this time."

Steiger grinned at her superior.

"As they say, no rest for the wicked, and I qualify in spades. Mind you, if I wanted a job where I could watch my behind grow wider than an office chair, we wouldn't be talking. Oh, by the way, Zack wanted me to give you something on his behalf, but I told him a warrant officer kissing a commodore on the mouth wouldn't be a good idea. So, consider me passing along the sentiment instead of the act."

Talyn rolled her eyes. That was her partner. A man with a questionable sense of humor who'd done more than just kiss Steiger in years past. Maybe she should turn the tables on those two jokers and accept. Still, the possibility Steiger would enjoy it too much after their earlier and more difficult relationship made the notion seem less than ideal.

"A wise choice. And I'll chat with Zack about suborning my agents. Anyway, that's it. Go home, stow the uniform, and spend a few days enjoying yourself."

**

"Tell me you didn't actually plant one on Miko's lips, Big Boy."

"Please. I know better than that. But I suggested she try to prank you. If that means I committed an offense against a flag officer, I'll stand by for the punishment of your choice." Decker leered at Talyn.

"You'd enjoy that too much." When he put on an air of disappointment, she sighed. "Figures. For a moment, I contemplated forcing her into carrying it out, just so I could teach you both a lesson."

His leer grew. "Now, you're the one teasing me."

"Come to Sanctum after work on Friday, and we'll see about who's doing what to whom. I can't be far from a TSSA terminal these days."

"We have those up here as well, you know."

"But not for the special access codenames I'm working with nowadays."

"Ah. Anything that might involve my trained killers?"

"When it's time, you'll find out. And that won't be for a while yet."

"What about presenting Curtis to the Grand Admiral?"

"I should know in a day or so."

"Make it a Monday, and I'll spend the weekend with you. Curtis can find his way to the transient officers' quarters on Sunday night."

She gave him an exasperated look.

"You do remember that I can plan things rather well. Yes, I'm aiming for either a Monday or a Friday. No point ordering you here in the middle of the week. It's not efficient for anyone."

"While I'm in the Grand Admiral's office, any chance we can discuss my proposal to pull a Kowalski? We've come up with a few amusing scenarios that might, coincidentally, give the rioting rats they're hiding behind a good swift kick in the ass."

"If Larsson has time and doesn't want to play the plausible deniability card." She paused for a few moments. "On second thought, perhaps it's best if we don't discuss that subject any further until he returns from Earth."

"You expect trouble on the cradle of humanity?"

"Just being my usual paranoid self."

"I prefer paranoid you to a hundred complacent flag officers. Worry away."

"But we can discuss options, and by we, I mean you, me, Kal, and Admiral Ulrich. We should whittle them down before briefing the CNI on a proposed course of action." A chime sounded on Talyn's end of the connection. "Hang on. Looks like the Grand Admiral's office is working overtime. Larsson will see us next Monday at oh-nine-hundred. Bring your service dress uniform when you come on Friday and make sure Curtis does so as well. Travel together for all I care. But he should understand he's on his own when you arrive."

Decker winked at her. "Make sure the linen's fresh."

— Six —

The following Monday, Talyn flagged one of the automated shuttles continuously circulating through the warren of corridors beneath the vast, half-buried Armed Services HQ complex. Curtis Delgado had joined her and Decker at the senior officers' apartment block station moments earlier.

"Did you ever visit Earth, Curtis?"

"No, Commodore. You?"

She climbed aboard, and Decker dropped onto the bench beside her, nodding politely at the Marine Corps master sergeant sitting across from them. Delgado followed suit.

"Once, on a mission, long before the colonel and I hooked up."

The master sergeant's eyes widened slightly at Talyn's choice of words, and Decker gave her a wink.

"Is it worth the trip?" Delgado asked.

"If you like museums, nature preserves, old buildings, and condescending snobs, sure. Otherwise, if it weren't for duty travel, I'd give it a pass. You might end up with terminal disappointment at the cradle of humanity."

Decker grinned at the younger man.

"Since you're probably going to witness how they make sausages, figuratively speaking, when you traipse after the boss on his rounds of the government bazaars, take terminal disappointment with Earth as a given."

"Noted, Colonel."

Ten minutes before the appointed hour, Commodore Talyn, Lieutenant Colonel Decker, and Captain Delgado entered the Grand Admiral's office suite. Decker and Delgado were resplendent in silver-trimmed black Marine service dress uniforms with maroon Pathfinder stripes on the outside seams of trousers tucked into shiny, calf-high boots and maroon patches backing the miniature insignia of the 1st Special Forces Regiment on either side of the tunic's high collar. Both wore their rank insignia on silver-edged epaulets and enough ribbons, qualification badges, and other devices to open a museum. By contrast, Talyn seemed almost monastic in her dark blue naval uniform with gold braid and a broad stripe on the cuff, complete with executive curl. However, she also wore Pathfinder wings above an impressive collection of ribbons.

Grand Admiral Larsson's junior aide, a natty Marine Corps lieutenant colonel with recruiting poster good looks and an intricately woven gold cord looped around his left shoulder, rose from behind his desk. The work surface was so bare it reminded Zack of another aphorism about clean desks and sick minds, but he figured only Delgado would appreciate the humor in this hallowed corner of the main HQ building.

"Commodore, Zack, Captain Delgado, welcome." He turned to the latter who'd not met him before. "I'm Anson Hisk. Admiral Larsson's schedule is running on time, a rare occurrence." He gestured toward a settee group to one side. "Please take a seat. Coffee, various teas, water, and juices are available on the sideboard."

Decker nodded.

"Thanks, Anson. But with my luck, one minute before you usher us into the admiral's office, I'll spill something down my front."

Hisk snorted. "Are you sure you've never served as an aide-de-camp?"

"The sad thing is," Talyn said to Delgado in a conversational tone while settling on a well-cushioned sofa, "Colonel Decker's not kidding. He develops this tic when he's about to meet senior officers who aren't proper Pathfinders."

"True story." Zack dropped into an equally plush chair across from them. "And the bane of my life. It always gets me into more trouble than a squad of privates on their first shore leave."

Hisk shook his head, smiling, and slipped back into his seat behind the obscenely clear desktop. At exactly oh-nine-hundred, he stood again and, with a sweeping motion, invited them to approach.

"The Grand Admiral will receive you now."

Hisk opened the oak-paneled door, stepped in, and with a tone more suited to the parade square than a luxurious office, announced, "Commodore Talyn, Lieutenant Colonel Decker, and Captain Delgado, sir."

Then he stepped to one side.

As he entered, Delgado's first, and somewhat irreverent thought was that the Grand Admiral's office could host a grav ball tournament with space left over for the after-game party. Military artifacts from centuries past covered walls paneled in amber-colored wood. A desk large enough for the after-after-game party dominated the far end, complete with the obligatory stand of flags behind it. Two expansive windows allowed the afternoon sunlight to spill across an intricate marquetry floor. They afforded a splendid view of Sanctum and the mountains beyond.

A tall, thin man in his seventies, standing by one of the windows, hands clasped in the small of his back, turned to face them. Delgado recognized Larsson from his official portrait in what he privately called the rogue's gallery — images depicting the chain of command from the Grand Admiral to Colonel Ryent hanging in the regimental HQ main lobby. What the portrait didn't show was a fruit salad with enough ribbons and devices to rival even Lieutenant Colonel Decker's impressive collection. Larsson watched them approach with a gaze that struck Delgado as chillingly intense.

They came to a precise halt three paces from the desk and saluted in unison. Larsson, bareheaded, returned the compliment with a brief nod and examined them for a few seconds longer, then said, "Please stand easy."

He waved toward a cluster of leather-clad sofas surrounding a low teak table and said, "Why don't we take our ease. Can I offer you some refreshment? Coffee or tea?"

"Thank you, sir, but we're fine," Talyn quickly replied before Decker could suggest something more potent, even though it would be in jest.

As they sat, Larsson rested his eyes on Delgado.

"I'm told Commodore Talyn and Colonel Decker think highly of you, Captain. Your record of service, the one marked top-secret, not the one held by the Marine Corps career managers, is impressive. And the commodore briefed me about your last two operations, the planned one and the impromptu intervention on Mission Colony. Well done."

Delgado inclined his head.

"Thank you, sir."

"Captain Delgado is aware of the reasons you requested a Special Forces escort instead of the regular close protection detail, sir," Talyn said. "And he didn't hesitate to step forward when Colonel Decker offered him the assignment. His command, Erinye Company, is among the most effective and deadliest in the Commonwealth Marine Corps' history."

Larsson frowned.

"Erinye Company? What an unusual name."

"Sir, when I took command of the squadron," Decker replied, "I decided we would give the companies unofficial titles instead of numbers, and my Marines chose classical mythology as the source. Number One Company took the name Erinye, as the Furies of old were known in Greek."

"I see. How interesting. And your other companies?"

"Number Two Company took on the name Keres, after the Greek death-spirits and Number Three Company, Moirae, the incarnations of destiny."

"I see a theme in your nomenclature, Colonel." A wintry smile briefly relaxed Larsson's features. "And I approve. They're apt names for Ghost Squadron."

"The practice is spreading across the 1st Special Forces Regiment, sir. Each squadron is basing theirs on different mythologies."

"Considering how many of them evolved throughout our species' history, I know there will be enough for the 2nd and 3rd Regiments when they stand up." Larsson turned his gaze back on Delgado. "I wanted to meet you in person before deciding whether you'll be a good fit, Captain. Perusing a personal file only goes so far, and I pride myself on possessing a good instinct for people. Tell me about yourself. Start with your earliest childhood memories."

For the next ten minutes, Delgado, initially a bit nervous, spoke of his life with growing self-confidence. Larsson then asked several pointed questions about the missions he'd undertaken since joining the Special Forces, proving he had not only read Delgado's top-secret service record but remembered the details. When the latter finally fell silent, Larsson glanced at Talyn and nodded.

"He'll do. And I believe a promotion comes with the appointment."

"Acting, while so employed, as a major, sir," Decker replied.

"If you brought the hardware, I'll be happy to pin on Major Delgado's new rank insignia and see that Anson takes pictures."

Decker reached into his tunic pocket and produced a pair of oak leaf wreaths. At an unseen and unheard signal, Lieutenant Colonel Hisk entered the office, trailed by a video drone.

"Let's do this in front of the flags." Larsson stood with surprising energy and led them around his desk.

While the drone recorded the events for posterity, Larsson and Decker removed two of the three captain's pips from each epaulet and pinned an oak leaf wreath around the remaining one. Then, Larsson, Talyn, and Decker, in turn, shook hands with the newly minted field grade officer.

"Welcome to my personal staff, be it an ever so temporary assignment, Major Delgado," Larsson said once they were back in their seats. "You've already met Anson, my junior aide. He'll be coming with us, as will my senior aide, Commodore Ruth Lee. I'll make it clear to them and the rest of the delegation that on matters of security, yours is the final say, rank be damned."

"Who is part of the delegation, sir?" Talyn asked for Delgado's benefit since she'd already seen the list.

"Admiral Enya Christophe, the Fleet's chief financial officer and General Jerrold Pihl, head of procurement.

Both are bringing staff along with them. I'm afraid that you'll be the most junior officer present, Major."

"As long as no one makes me fetch coffee while I'm supposed to be watching your back, sir."

Larsson chuckled.

"I'm sure someone with more self-importance than common sense will try. You may refuse with my blessing, but politely, please. Special Forces officers enjoy a reputation for telling puffed-up jackasses where they should go, and as much as we try, a few of the latter always find their way into important delegations such as this one. However, as I said, I'll speak to everyone."

"Uniforms, sir?" Talyn asked.

"Right. There will be many formal events, so please bring full dress uniforms. You and your command noncoms should also pack mess uniforms. On Earth, appearances matter more than substance in many things, and the defense budget hearings will include the usual amount of chest-puffing and strutting around. The one question I've been pondering is whether you should wear the winged dagger or insignia identifying you as coming from a line regiment. Opinions, Commodore?"

"Best you let everyone openly see hardcore operators, sir. It might be enough of a deterrent if ever the Centralists and their allies become frisky and decide you're personally responsible for wiping out their jackbooted armies on the OutWorlds."

"The winged dagger it is."

"Yes, sir." Delgado was pleased with the decision to send a powerful message. "That'll make our lives easier. If I may ask, what ship are we taking?"

"The entire delegation is traveling in *Terra*. You're familiar with her, Major?"

"I've heard the name, sir, but that's it."

"She's the last of the Colonial-class star carriers, turned into a space control ship when the Fleet ditched the whole carrier business. Her name is probably familiar because she took the armistice delegation to Aquilonia at the end of the Shrehari War." When he saw the surprise in Delgado's eyes, Larsson nodded. "Yes, she's that old, but she spent thirty of the intervening years mothballed in the Fleet Reserve. *Terra* is outfitted as a flagship, and that means she has plenty of spare room for passengers along with a hangar deck capable of handling more than enough armed shuttles to convey and escort the delegation in style."

"Which means a hangar deck big enough to train on," Delgado said. "That's good. My Erinyes won't be sitting on their thumbs during the trip."

"I suppose you'll be issuing SOPs before we leave?" Larsson asked.

"We will," Talyn replied. "Once you're aboard *Terra*, Major Delgado will brief the entire delegation in detail."

"Good."

The Grand Admiral climbed to his feet, signaling the end of their meeting. Talyn, Decker, and Delgado followed suit.

"Thank you for coming. Please discuss any preparatory matters with Lieutenant Colonel Hisk or Commodore Lee. They'll pass on anything I need to know. We shall see each other again at the spaceport."

By common accord, the three came to attention.

"With your permission, sir?" Talyn asked.

"Dismissed, Commodore."

— Seven —

*T*erra's main conference room, in keeping with her impressive size, boasted enough chairs around the oval table for the entire delegation, aides included, with plenty of extra space, and a podium big enough for Delgado and Erinye Company's command team. He and his sergeants studied the admirals, generals, and sundry staff officers as they filed in a few minutes before the time set by Grand Admiral Larsson's senior aide, Commodore Lee.

Both four stars, Admiral Christophe and General Pihl, had brought several rear-admirals, commodores, major generals, and brigadier generals. A bevy of Navy captains and Marine Corps colonels along with lieutenant colonels and commanders wearing the woven gold cords of aides-de-camp trailed each of those.

The senior officers and their retinues, in turn, examined Delgado, First Sergeant Hak, and the command sergeants leading Erinye Company's four troops. Unlike the delegation, whose members wore the standard service uniform adorned by ribbons, badges, and devices collected over long careers, the Special Forces operators were in battledress with holstered sidearms. And their stark, black combat tunics were embellished with nothing more than Pathfinder wings and rank insignia.

Commodore Lee, who'd remained by the door, stiffened to attention.

"Grand Admiral Larsson arriving."

Those who were sitting stood, while Delgado and his sergeants snapped to attention.

"At ease," Larsson said, his long stride taking him to the podium. "Please take your seats."

He climbed up beside Delgado and faced the assembled delegation.

"As you know, the growing unrest across the Commonwealth has raised the threat level against senior officials, especially those in the Fleet, thanks to certain factions claiming we're responsible for said unrest. At the behest of the Chief of Naval Intelligence, I have placed our security into the hands of a highly experienced Special Forces officer and his company from the 1st Special Forces Regiment. Please listen carefully when he speaks. His instructions may save lives if we are indeed walking into a hostile environment on Earth.

"Don't let his relatively junior rank or the fact that he might, from time to time, be wearing aide-de-camp aiguillettes when in service uniform, distract you from his main purpose. In matters of security during this trip, consider anything he and his command team say as coming from me. And on that note, I'd like to introduce Major Curtis Delgado, officer commanding the 1st Special Forces Regiment's Erinye Company."

Delgado was surprised and pleased at Larsson using his unit's unofficial name instead of its more prosaic designation as Number One Company.

"Sir." Once Larsson took his seat at the table, Delgado stepped forward. "Good afternoon. I trust you had the chance to read the information packages we left in your quarters. As you might have noticed, what little we know about potential threats is rather vague, meaning we've developed protocols encompassing most of the higher-order probabilities. They will entail restrictions on your movements once we arrive at our destination and will most certainly result in regular last-minute changes of plan to throw off any ill-intentioned people. We ask for your patience, forbearance, and cooperation. Any instructions we give you will be to ensure Grand Admiral Larsson's and your security."

He paused and let his eyes roam around the table, seeing mostly interested if guarded expressions.

"My executive officer is First Sergeant Emery Hak."

The latter came to attention. "Sir."

"First Sergeant Hak speaks with my voice. The non-commissioned officers with him are the troop leaders, Command Sergeants Painter."

"Sir."

"Bassam."

"Sir."

"Dyas."

"Sir."

"And Saxer."

"Sir."

"My Marines are the best in the business, bar none. If they cannot stop a threat, then no one else in the known galaxy can. If any of them ask you to duck, step back into your quarters, run for cover, or otherwise do something you neither expect nor understand, it will be because they've detected a threat. They probably won't have time to explain or follow the usual military courtesies. Don't argue. Obey their instructions and do so instantly. The margin between survival and a plasma bolt through the forehead is often only a fraction of a second.

"If you have issues or concerns with my Marines or their activities, please speak with me, but do not interfere with their duties. Their job is ensuring we're back on Caledonia unharmed in a few weeks. That means they don't carry luggage, fetch coffee, run errands, or drive staff cars, even if you do see them in service uniform from time to time, rather than battledress or civilian attire. You may assume that they're armed twenty-four hours a day, without necessarily seeing their weapons."

Delgado let his words sink in, knowing that more than a few of the senior officers were silently bristling at his tone and at what his statement implied. He met a few resentful stares, though he kept a stony expression. With the Fleet's supreme commander present, none would dare speak out, but he wouldn't be surprised if one or two of the colonels buttonholed him later.

A few of them exuded the self-important REMF aura that stemmed from spending careers in various headquarters instead of frontline regiments. But he doubted any of the Navy officers would try him on. For most of them, the mind of a Marine was a strange and frightening thing, and that of a Special Forces operator even more so.

"I'll now take you through the security standard operating procedures Grand Admiral Larsson approved and which form part of the information packet you received." Delgado knew that perhaps only one in three of the officers present had bothered reading the instructions. "Feel free to ask questions or request clarification as we go along. I'd like everyone on the same wavelength when this meeting ends. Misunderstandings can cost lives."

By the time he was done, Delgado knew he hadn't made many friends. Senior officers enjoyed having restrictions placed on their movements even less than being told they couldn't use enlisted Marines for general duties. Especially when they heard it from an acting major who started his career as a private and hadn't so much as seen the inside of the Armed Services Academy.

After Grand Admiral Larsson thanked them and left, and Commodore Lee dismissed the assembly, a tall, rangy, middle-aged Marine major general approached Delgado before he could discuss the duty rotation with Lieutenant Colonel Hisk. He was the only one besides the Erinyes wearing Pathfinder wings on his chest.

"I know Special Forces officers enjoy a reputation for speaking plainly, Major," the general said, an amused smile playing on his lips, "but I didn't know your lot could be that direct. Ionas Veitling, by the way, Director, Priorities and Planning in the Office of the Strategic Joint Staff." He held out his hand. "You irritated a fair number of the palace guard, I shouldn't doubt. Being included in this quinquennial excursion to the fleshpots of Earth is supposedly a sign of one's superiority within the confines of the bureaucratic shark tank at HQ. Having a mere acting major talk down to them isn't part of the plan, especially when one or two of them looked like idiots because they asked questions your SOP packet already answered, proving they didn't bother reading it."

"And you're not a member the palace guard, I take it, sir?"

"We're all part of it, whether we want to, you included for the duration of your mission, but I still think of myself as an honest Marine, even if I lost my jump status twenty years ago. There's not much call for a logistician to play commando once promoted beyond the rank of captain."

One of those who asked a dumb question, a colonel whose arrogant demeanor was inversely proportionate to the paltry collection of award ribbons on her chest, gave Delgado a dirty look over General Veitling's shoulder before walking out. It promised retribution at a later date, but he mentally shrugged. There was nothing a staff colonel could do to harm him.

"I may be long removed from field operations," Veitling continued, "but I'm probably one of the few who understands the sheer amount of competence you and Erinye company bring to the table. If you hadn't warned the assembly about not mistaking your Marines for the hired help, I don't doubt a few would have confused them with servants. In fact, I wouldn't be surprised if someone tries. Your first sergeant is giving us a significant look, so I'll leave you to it. If you need a bit of insider help to deal with some of the palace guard's more egregious members, please reach out, one honest Marine to another."

"Thank you, sir."

"And one of these evenings, I'll buy you a beer in exchange for the story behind your company's unusual name." With a last nod, Veitling joined the exodus of delegation members leaving the conference room.

"What was that about, Skipper?" Hak asked in a low voice.

"A member of the palace guard warning me about the palace guard," Delgado replied in the same tone. "Major General Ionas Veitling, of the Strategic Joint Staff. Said we should reach out to him if we get static from anyone in the delegation."

"According to the dossier Commodore Talyn gave us, he's one of the least political flag officers on this trip, so I'd take the offer as genuine. Not everyone who spends years at HQ forgets where they came from. Besides," he added, nodding at the wings on Delgado's uniform, "he knows the secret handshake, or at least he did in his younger days. The society of crazy people who jump out of perfectly good shuttles might come in handy if people like Colonel Wynne decide we offended them."

"She would be the one who showed her inability to read and then gave me the stink eye on her way out, right?"

"Correct. Word of advice — restrain any temptation at baiting the good colonel if she decides carrying a grudge will salve her wounded pride. Wynne's dossier mentions she's extremely well connected for an officer with a career mostly spent working in the shadow of various generals. Young for her rank, too."

"Let me guess, you memorized the dossiers of everyone in this delegation, didn't you?"

Hak nodded once.

"Of course. One of us always looks inward, and since your job is concentrating on the outer perimeter, that's part of my job. We should do the rounds and check on the deployment of our folks around the flag quarters."

A lazy smile lit up Delgado's face.

"*Terra*'s captain will be thrilled that part of his ship is off-limits to most of the crew, except by permission."

"He's already aware of the security arrangements. Commodore Lee warned him when she came aboard with the advance party last night."

Delgado's stomach chose that moment to make its existential weariness known in a way that amused Sergeant Hak.

He chuckled. "The rounds and then food, I think."

"It's a shame I can't eat in the enlisted mess," Delgado said as they left the now empty conference room. "The company would be more congenial."

"Can't violate every naval tradition, now can we. You made friends with a two-star who passed through Fort Arnhem as a youngster, so it won't be all bad."

"Actually, I figure they'll expect me to sit with Commodore Lee and Colonel Hisk. You know, the happy five-star dog robbing family," Delgado said, referring to the aide-de-camp insignia he would soon wear. It was a small black shield showing the number of silver stars worn by the flag officer he served, which meant Grand Admiral Larsson's five.

"Hisk is okay, Skipper. He doesn't strike me as the chickenshit sort, and he's been polite from word one. Lee seems to be pretty much the same. I'll bet anyone gives us problems, she'll sort them out. Those two are more concerned with the Grand Admiral's safety than the niceties of protocol. Besides, you need to speak with them at least once a day and make sure we're synced. Doing it around a plate of bacon and eggs isn't a bad way."

"Always the voice of reason," Delgado muttered. "This trip will be a laugh a minute. I'm beginning to regret ordering us dry for the duration. Heck, I'll be stunned if no one's charged me with insubordination by the time it's over."

"That's what I like about you, sir. Always the optimist."

"Which is why I keep you around as a counterbalance."

Hak gave his commanding officer a hard look. "Are you saying I'm a pessimist, Skipper?"

"No. A realist."

— Eight —

Delgado was proved right. Commodore Lee, who sat with Lieutenant Colonel Hisk at a round table in one corner, waved him over when he entered the mess set aside for the delegations' officers.

"Everything is well?" She asked once he'd made his way through the buffet line and taken a seat across from her.

"Yes, sir."

"That was an interesting performance at the security briefing earlier, Major," Lee gave Delgado a faint if wry smile. "I doubt the attendees will forget it anytime soon, which I suppose was your goal. Your bluntness amused the Grand Admiral."

When Delgado glanced around to see if he could spy their supreme commander, Lee shook her head.

"Admiral Larsson is dining in his quarters with General Pihl and Admiral Christophe, which I suppose will be a frequent occurrence so they can discuss strategy without the staff overhearing." She paused. "May I propose that since you've made your point about the seriousness of the security situation, you adopt an aide-de-camp's accouterments? There's something to be said for wearing the five-star shield when suggesting senior officers should heed the standard operating procedures."

Delgado inclined his head.

"Understood, sir. I will do so, but I'm damned if I know where to dig up proper aiguillettes for uniforms other than service dress."

Hisk gave him a half-smirk.

"I thought you might say that. Fortunately, those of us who've been in the aide-de-camp business for more than twenty-four hours picked up a thing or two about finding the proper pieces." He reached into his pocket, produced a simple knotted gold cord, and dropped it on the table beside Delgado's plate.

"Did you need help to put it on, or will you be okay?"

"Well played, Colonel, and yes, I can put it on by myself, thank you." Delgado, knowing when he was beaten, demonstrated that fact by correctly slipping the cord over his left shoulder and affixing it at the right angle. He then pulled a small enameled shield sporting five stars from his battledress tunic pocket and pinned it over his name tape. "There. Now I need a dog to rob. Do you think *Terra*'s captain has a pooch? I hear space beagles are all the rage these days."

Hisk let out an amused snort while Lee shook her head at Delgado's rueful expression.

"The first rule of being a dog robber," she said, "is we don't talk about robbing dogs."

"Indeed," Hisk added with mock seriousness. "We just do it. Although I wouldn't try my luck with the captain's terrier. I understand the little fellow is rather fierce and known by the crew as Kodo the Terror. You might have noticed him on the hangar deck when we arrived. A little ball of black and tan fur staring intently at us as he sat beside a bosun's mate by the airlock."

"Now that you mention it, yes. I'll keep my distance."

Hisk chuckled. "The nickname was bestowed with the sort of irony spacers enjoy. The only risk when approaching him is getting licked to death."

**

In the end, no one bothered a five-star shield and aiguillette-wearing Delgado during the trip, not even Colonel Wynne. However, he found that few of the delegation's officers besides Hisk and Lee were willing to socialize with him. The Marine figured word getting around about Grand Admiral Larsson joining Erinye Company for daily physical training on the hangar deck probably helped.

That the Fleet's supreme commander did it on Commodore Lee's advice remained a secret, though, by all appearances, he enjoyed creating a tighter bond with his Special Forces escort. Still, when Terra finally entered an overcrowded Earth orbit, most Marines were ready to jump ship out of sheer boredom.

"Somewhat underwhelming," Hak murmured, nodding at the display that dominated the flag CIC, where Grand Admiral Larsson and his immediate staff assembled for the arrival maneuvers. It showed Earth's night side, the surface speckled with millions of lights, but also with conspicuous dark zones on landmass areas where he would have expected more evidence of human activity. "Based on the tales I've heard about the cradle of humanity, I figured we'd see one single planet-spanning metropolis shining brightly in the dark."

"You should listen less to half-drunk canteen conversations and spend more time reading, Top," Delgado replied in the same low tone. "They turned half of Earth into nature preserves, and a lot of areas are still uninhabitable because of radiation left over from the last world war."

"That was almost four hundred years ago. You'd think by now, they would have done some cleanup work."

"No reason to. After sending two-thirds of the surviving population off into the big bad galaxy the moment someone discovered FTL travel, space is no longer at a premium."

The console Delgado appropriated as his workstation emitted a soft chime. He glanced at the screen and grunted with satisfaction.

"At least they're not asleep at their posts down there. We have a security plan from Turenne Base." He touched the control surface. "There, everyone now has a bit of light reading. I'd like opinions and comments in thirty minutes.

That'll give us enough time to fix problems before the Grand Admiral's shuttle launches."

"Can't fault a thing," Rolf Painter said half an hour later when he, Delgado, and the troop leaders convened in the conference room. "They might not be of much use beyond the parade ground, but they seem to understand VIP protection."

"Are you perchance insinuating that the men and women of the 1st Marine Regiment, the oldest and proudest unit in the Commonwealth Armed Services, are nothing more than chocolate soldiers, Command Sergeant?"

"I'm not insinuating anything, sir. That was a statement of fact."

"Which part?" Delgado asked, grinning. "That they're useless beyond the parade ground or that they understand VIP protection?"

"Yes, sir," Painter replied with feigned seriousness.

"You might wish to make sure none of your battle-honed troopers let their disdain show. We're part of the same Marine Corps, and if their job is looking good for the brass and the newsnets, we don't need to, right?"

"No arguments here, Major." The noncom chuckled. "It's not like you or I have recruiting poster looks."

"You got that right. But half of us will try anyway when we land. That means your troop, B Troop, and little old me will be in full fig as the formal escort while the rest of Erinye Company under the first sergeant provides overwatch."

Painter groaned theatrically. "Why me?"

"Because you flap your lips too much, Rolf," Hak replied. "Silence is golden. Didn't your mother teach you that?"

"Didn't I hear you call him a motherless bastard a few weeks ago, Top?" Command Sergeant Saxer grinned at his colleague.

"Oh. Right. Never mind then. Keep talking, Rolf. I'll need volunteers for other fun jobs over the coming weeks."

**

"I wasn't aware you secret squirrels cleaned up so nicely," Lieutenant Colonel Hisk said in a low aside to First Sergeant Hak when Delgado, along with A and B Troops, entered *Terra*'s cavernous hangar deck.

The Marines wore full dress uniforms, although they carried combat carbines along with their daggers.

"They might even give the chocolate soldiers pangs of envy with the impressive fruit salads made up mostly of combat awards rather than participation medals."

Hak was in unadorned battledress with a tactical harness and carried a short carbine along with other assorted weaponry, as did C and D Troops. And while Hisk didn't appear quite as splendid as Delgado, both sported the ornate, formal, heavy gold cords of a five-star admiral's aide-de-camp on their left shoulders.

"The skipper's job is distracting the opposition while the rest of us go in for the kill, sir. He's certainly distracting the palace guard." Hak nodded toward the openly curious officers clustered by a large shuttle bearing the circled five stars of Grand Admiral Larsson's rank. "The only way he could top this is by wearing his rack of full-sized medals and carrying a ceremonial sword, both of which I know are lurking in his luggage by order of Colonel Decker. It's a cruel world, isn't it, sir? You couldn't pay me enough to peacock like that."

Hak's last few words must have reached Delgado's ears because he growled, "What did you just call me, Top? Peacock? I could order you into full dress uniform before we leave."

"And make the 1st Marines feel totally inadequate at the sight of us together? I'd say that comes under cruel and unusual, and is against the regs, Major, sir." Delgado gave him a dirty glare, and Hak snorted. "As Colonel Hisk will corroborate, I was merely telling him you couldn't pay me to play peacock like they're making you do. No insult spoken or intended, although I've developed a theory that your job is distracting would-be assassins while we do the dirty work."

When Delgado's glare didn't waver, Hak shrugged.

"What? Tell me it's not a good idea. You of all people understand how valuable a bit of distraction can be in our line of business." Before Delgado could respond, Hak spied Commodore Lee herding the waiting delegation into the shuttles. "I think we're being told we should prepare for the Grand Admiral's arrival."

"In that case, let the pomp and circumstance begin." Delgado nodded toward the escort shuttles' open aft ramps. "Off you go, Top. See that everyone boards."

Hak snapped off a regulation salute and pivoted on his heels.

"May I assume you're suitably armed?" Hisk asked Delgado when they were alone. "I can't figure out where you'd hide ordnance under that martial elegance."

"If you examine me closely, you'll see that my dagger is in its ceremonial position, hanging from my tunic belt by my left hip. It is, however, a fully functioning hand-to-hand combat weapon. I also carry a ten-millimeter blaster, powered and loaded in here." He patted the shiny, ceremonial holster on his right hip. "It's not my usual caliber, but I suffer from space limitations. How about you?"

"Regular aides don't carry outside of combat zones." When Hisk saw the look in Delgado's eyes, he chuckled. "I carry your blaster's twin tucked into the small of my back and a needler in my right boot. Does that meet with your approval?"

"It'll do, sir." Movement by the hangar deck door caught his eye. "Look sharp."

Two Special Forces operators from C Troop entered through the main airlock, weapons in the low carry position, ready to snap up at the first sign of a threat. Aboard *Terra*, the security detail was mostly for show. But once they stepped off the shuttle in less than an hour, it would be for real.

A few heartbeats later, the Supreme Commander of the Commonwealth Armed Services came into view, his long stride taking him over the threshold and across the hangar deck to where Delgado and Lieutenant Colonel Hisk waited. A second pair of troopers, virtual clones of their leading comrades, trailed Larsson. As one, the officers snapped to attention and saluted.

"Since you're the last not yet aboard, save for my minders, may I infer Commodore Lee has shepherded the rest of the delegation to their seats?" The Grand Admiral asked.

"Yes, sir," Hisk replied. "We are, in every respect, ready to launch."

"And you're happy with the security arrangements, Major Delgado?"

"I am, sir. My advance team, D Troop, under Command Sergeant Saxer, has been on the ground for the last four hours and reports everything is good to go. A and B Troops are aboard your shuttle, while the rest of my Marines are in the escort gunships that will precede us."

"Good." Larsson gave Delgado the once-over. "I do believe you'll set a new standard for recruiting poster looks and give the 1st Marine Regiment's honor guard pangs of jealousy. If there's nothing else, let's be at it."

— Nine —

The whine of the shuttle's thrusters died away moments after it settled on the tarmac at the heart of the Fleet's primary ground installation on Earth, Turenne Base, named after the Commonwealth Marine Corps' first Commandant, General Piotr Turenne. Nestled at the foot of the Jura Massif's southern end, southeast of the River Rhone and a few dozen kilometers from the capital, Geneva, the base hosted the planet-side half of the Home Sector Headquarters. The naval part of Sector HQ was aboard Starbase One in geosynchronous orbit overhead.

Thus, it came as no surprise when a Marine flag officer, accompanied by a pair of aides, a lieutenant colonel, and a captain, approached the shuttle's descending aft ramp to greet Larsson instead of Sabine Bavadra, the four-star admiral in command of the Home Sector.

Lieutenant General Tasha Bowen was a striking woman in her own right, with haughty patrician features framed by shimmering silver hair. But Delgado's eyes, the moment he emerged into the watery morning sunlight, were drawn to the Marine captain wearing the accouterments of a three-star flag officer's aide-de-camp standing a pace behind Bowen.

The last time he'd seen her, she was wearing the regimental insignia of the 22nd Marines when both were buck sergeants assigned to its 3rd Battalion. Judging by the badge now adorning her beret, she'd wangled a transfer to the 1st Marine Regiment and a job as dog robber to the top Marine on the planet. Some things never changed.

He led A and B Troops out onto the tarmac, boxing Larsson in, then spread them out in three ranks on either side. Larsson and Bowen exchanged salutes, then a handshake while the aides sized each other up. Behind the reception committee, the honor guard, a full battalion of the 1st Marines, shouldered arms to prepare for the traditional ruffles and flourishes to greet the Supreme Commander of the Commonwealth Armed Services with ceremonial formality. At first, Delgado saw an air of passing curiosity briefly light up the captain's countenance as she studied the officer standing a pace behind the Grand Admiral.

Then, she recognized him and blanched while an expression of horror replaced the earlier curiosity. Delgado was saved from fighting off an irresistible urge to wink by Bowen leading Larsson toward the reviewing stand, forcing the aides to follow. The latter lined up behind the dais in order of rank while the two flag officers climbed onto the raised platform. Delgado, as the second most junior officer, stood beside the captain. This time, he didn't bother with self-restraint.

"Fancy meeting you here," he whispered to his neighbor as the band struck up the general salute. "Who'd have thought a scheming backstabber like Claressa Mori would land a job robbing dogs for a three-star. But if it keeps you away from actual fighting Marines, I suppose I shouldn't complain. And yes, as you can see, I now outrank and out dog-rob you. Funny how life turns out, isn't it, Captain?"

The music died away, and Delgado glanced at his erstwhile fellow squad sergeant, the woman who screwed him out of a chance to become an officer years ago. In the end, the commanding officer of the 22nd agreed he'd been hard done by, but the damage to his reputation within the regiment was done, and Mori escaped retribution. However, instead of dwelling on his misfortune, Delgado volunteered for Special Forces, passed the rigorous selection process, and found his true calling.

"I believe," Delgado continued in the same low tone, "the expected answer is yes, sir, life sure is funny, sir."

"No, sir," Mori hissed through clenched teeth, eyes fixed on the two flag officers heading for the battalion's right flank to inspect the guard. "Life is not funny, sir."

"Still no sense of humor, Claressa? Sad. Don't worry, I haven't lost mine, and I'm enjoying every second of this tearful reunion." Hisk, standing on Delgado's right, nudged him with his elbow, a signal he should stop whispering. "I'm sure we'll continue this conversation later."

Consigned to silence, Delgado amused himself by looking for the covert surveillance detail from D Troop, aware of the delegation disembarking quietly behind them, the senior officers spreading out instinctively in a single rank on either side of the dais.

Unable to detect Command Sergeant Saxer's people, his eyes settled on the men and women of the 1st Marine Regiment standing stiffly at attention while Larsson and Bowen walked through the ranks. Though beautifully turned out, with the ornate uniforms he expected from chocolate soldiers whose principal mission was ceremonial guard duty, Delgado nonetheless spotted more than a few combat-related awards and ribbons pinned to silver-trimmed black tunics. They proved the unit mustered a few veterans of the rough and tumble guerrilla warfare endemic on the frontiers.

The Grand Admiral and General Bowen stepped onto the reviewing stand again. Ruffles and flourishes sounded as the soldiers presented arms, ending the ceremony. In the ensuing silence, five vehicles — a troop transport followed by three spacious ground cars, one bearing a dark blue plate with five silver stars, followed by another troop transport — pulled up. A quick glance at the drivers told Delgado they were from D Troop's advance party.

While Commodore Lee and Lieutenant Colonel Hisk ushered Larsson aboard his car, Delgado made sure A and B Troops climbed into the transports before joining the Grand Admiral's party. His last glimpse of Captain Mori as she called up General Bowen's vehicle was that of a dejected officer, one who figured the past might finally have caught up with her.

**

An entire block of transient officers' quarters had been set aside and cordoned off for Grand Admiral Larsson, the delegation, and Erinye Company. The latter established a security perimeter cutting the rectangular glass, steel, and granite two-story structure off from the rest of Turenne Base. It, in turn, was surrounded by a tight defensive perimeter, including aerospace defense pods capable of destroying threats with extraordinary speed.

The airspace above the base, and indeed above the capital itself, was out of bounds to civilian traffic other than that landing at the Geneva Spaceport. However, Delgado still felt uneasy, thanks to the surrounding hills and low mountains. Some precision direct fire weapons could easily reach the heart of Turenne Base from the nearest of them. And although the building could withstand even a direct hit from a surface-to-surface missile, Larsson would be vulnerable during brief periods as he moved between the front door and his staff car. At least the meals would be catered rather than subject the entire delegation to a full security cordon for the short distance to the officers' mess two or three times a day.

Delgado and his Marines took rooms on the ground floor while the VIPs settled into suites on the second story. Hak brought him up to speed on the dispositions he'd made while Delgado exchanged his service blacks for battledress, happy the opening bit of kabuki was behind them.

"Mind if I get personal for a moment, Skipper?" Hak asked when they finished discussing business.

Delgado grinned at his first sergeant.

"Did my objections ever stop you?"

"No, but I prefer being polite about certain matters. Anything I should know about that 1st Marines captain who seemed really unhappy at seeing you?"

"How did you notice? I can't remember spotting you or any of the perimeter protection detail at the landing strip."

"I was watching Larsson, and you were stuck to his six. Hard not to notice."

"Weren't you tasked with looking for threats, not admiring his Grand Admiral-ness?"

An air of exasperation crossed Hak's usually impassive features.

"You're evading the question, sir. That tells me I definitely should know who Bowen's junior dog robber is in your universe."

Delgado let out a loud exhalation.

"Alright. Her name is Claressa Mori, and she's a galaxy-class backstabbing careerist. We were buck sergeants together in the 22nd Marines when we were younger and dumber. She's the reason I volunteered for Special Forces."

"Then she did you a favor."

"Yeah. I figured that out a few years back when I realized my chances of making command sergeant and then earning a commission would have been a lot slimmer in a line regiment. You could say I was a bit too rambunctious for the 22nd."

"You're a bit too rambunctious for Special Forces, Skipper, but we use your failings for good rather than evil. What happened with this Mori character?"

"It was rather embarrassing at the time."

"Yet here you are, a major commanding an elite unit, and she's tending to a three-star general on Earth, where they haven't heard a shot fired in anger since the twenty-third century. If this tearful reunion might impact your effectiveness, I should know."

Delgado turned his eyes upward and sighed.

"Remember years ago, when regiments were given one or two slots a year on the Officer Training Course for corporals and buck sergeants?"

"Yeah. I'm glad they ended that program. The new one, setting above-average noncoms on the accelerated command sergeant track, then giving them a direct commission once they prove themselves is much better."

"Which is how I became a captain, and I admit I'm better for going the long route. Well, Claressa, me, and a bunch of others competed for the two spots. It really was a competition for one slot because the regiment's top three-striper owned the other. It quickly became just her and me, and at one point, it was becoming obvious she wouldn't make it. So, during one of the final field problems, she set me up to make it look like I cheated as a way of covering her own mistakes. I was too damn naïve at the time and didn't see it coming, but the evaluators removed me from the process for exhibiting questionable judgment, which is an automatic fail. Once I was back on base, I went to the regimental sergeant major, and because he knew Claressa's propensity for manipulating her way up the ranks, he took me to the colonel.

"By then, Claressa had been anointed the second of the two candidates, given her officer cadet stripe and booked on the next transport out. Absent hard evidence that she screwed me over, the colonel wouldn't rerun the final field problems and suggested I try again the following year. Somehow Claressa heard about my complaint and spread rumors I was a whiny little loser who couldn't hack it. Unfortunately, she had enough friends who made my life miserable on her behalf. That's when I decided I would try for Special Forces and trained like a maniac. I aced the selection test and couldn't move off-planet fast enough."

Hak nodded.

"And here you are, years later, an acting Special Forces major. I bet you had plenty of friends who made sure Mori never lost that cheater's stench, which is probably why she didn't return to the 22nd after receiving her commission. Odds are, she ended up here with the chocolate soldiers after OTC, where she can't screw over honest Marines to advance her career. But one thing's for sure, she felt fear at seeing you wearing a major's finery."

Hak pointed at Delgado's dress uniform tunic.

The latter snorted. "You know, maybe she's scared I'll let something about the past slip. Officer promotions in the First Marine Division are based as much on reputation as they are on efficiency. And she's been a captain for an awfully long time by now if I made it to command sergeant before becoming a captain myself."

Hak slapped his commanding officer on the shoulder.

"There you go, Skipper. Advantage Major Delgado. Now let the past go and focus on getting us through this clusterfuck."

—Ten—

"Why a mess dinner on the first night, I'll never understand." Hak wandered out of his room and across to Delgado's open door while fastening a blindingly white mess uniform shirt tucked into black cavalry overalls with twin maroon stripes on the outer seams.

"Earth gets the Grand Admiral's visit every five years, Top. The locals want to make the best of it. Even Admiral Bavadra is coming down from her orbital aerie for this one."

"Bully for Bavadra. As if drowning in senior officers aboard *Terra* for days on end wasn't enough," Hak grumbled, tugging on each shirt sleeve in turn. "We now face doing it around bad wine, worse port, and rubber chicken the cook swears was pecking at the ground two hours before he zapped it."

"No booze for us, remember?" Delgado, also in shirt and overalls, studied his mess uniform tunic to make sure the many miniature devices and medals were in their proper places. The brand new field officer's silver braid on the shoulder boards and cuffs seemed as strange as the aiguillettes dripping from the left shoulder. "Rubber chicken only."

"That means I'll stick to the overcooked vegetables, thank you very much. Or better yet, let me join the perimeter detail, and I can eat a decent meal in the senior noncoms' mess beforehand."

"Can't. You and I are part of the Grand Admiral's close protection detail tonight."

"I thought our job was showing the Special Forces flag, so any tango with delusions of adequacy thinks twice."

Satisfied by his tunic, Delgado straightened and turned toward Hak.

"Six of one, half a dozen of the other."

"Did you figure out how you'll carry a sidearm under that penguin suit?"

Delgado grimaced.

"Shoulder holster, and it'll be damned uncomfortable."

"Visible, too. Then there's the communicator. Tell you what, if Ghost Squadron is tapped for this sort of mission more often in the future, it's time we abandoned cavalry tradition and wore looser mess uniforms. I can barely sit as it is."

Hak wandered back across the corridor just as two sergeants first class from company HQ, Enrique Bazhukov, and Metellus Testo, also in mess uniform, came around the corner, looking more amused than annoyed.

"Hey, Top," Bazhukov, a giant, hairless slab of a man, with a boxer's flattened nose, a square jaw, and intelligent, deep-set brown eyes called out. "Did you try a quick draw from the shoulder holster with the tunic on yet?"

"No."

"It's ugly. We need looser jackets if this is our new normal."

"Funny you should mention that. It's what I just said to the skipper."

Delgado stuck his head out into the corridor.

"Tell you what, find a tailor on this base who can let out our jackets just enough for the next mess dinner, and I'll pay for our alterations from my own pocket."

Bazhukov, the company supply noncom, nodded enthusiastically.

"I'll ask around."

His companion, the operations sergeant, a short, wiry, dark-haired man with lean, angular features made a face.

"Does that mean there will be more command performances, Major?"

"A few, I'm afraid."

"Ugh."

"Considering how much these uniforms cost us, we might as well get some use out of them beyond the annual regimental dinner."

Testo shrugged. "I guess."

"Show the skipper your quickdraws," Hak suggested. "Ready. Target!"

Both sergeants did a creditable job under the circumstances, producing their ten-millimeter blasters faster than Delgado thought possible, though going into a crouch, weapons raised to eye level seemed more of a strain thanks to the tight trousers.

"I'm about to issue an executive order that will horrify RSM Vanleith when he hears of it. Undo the overall stirrups. We won't look as sexy and sleek, and yes, the bottoms will bunch over our boots, but better that than losing speed in an emergency."

Bazhukov let out a heartfelt groan.

"Thank the Almighty."

"He was hoping you'd think of it, sir," Testo said, giving his friend a sidelong look.

Both Delgado and Hak dropped their overalls right there and bent down to remove the stirrups that kept them fashionably straight and unwrinkled. When he pulled his back up, Hak practiced a few crouching maneuvers and grunted with satisfaction.

"Much more comfortable. If Gus objects once we're back home, I'll challenge him to find a better solution. Our job is protecting the Grand Admiral, not looking pretty. That's the 1st Marine Regiment's job."

Delgado, Hak, and the two sergeants met Commodore Lee and Lieutenant Colonel Hisk in the lobby twenty minutes later.

"Everything is ready?" Lee asked.

"A Troop is deployed inside the mess, B and C Troops are covering the path between here and the mess, and D

Troop is deployed around the mess. They've been operating the threat detectors for the last two hours."

It wouldn't be enough for a determined assassin firing from a standoff position. But Delgado figured mentioning that fact might be ill-advised, although he and the other three boxing Larsson in would make the Grand Admiral a smaller, more difficult target.

"Excellent."

They stepped aside as the delegation members, also in mess uniform, flowed past them and out into the balmy evening air, chatting quietly among themselves. Other than Major General Veitling, who greeted them with a polite nod and a smile, no one deigned to notice the Marines, even though each wore an impressive set of miniature medals, most of which were emphatically not of the 'I was there' sort.

Finally, a lonely naval officer in a dark blue uniform with gold braid almost covering the tunic's arms from the cuffs to the elbows, slowly made his way down the stairs, trailed by two Erinye Company troopers in battledress.

At Commodore Lee's whispered orders, they came to attention.

"We're ready, sir."

"Thank you." Larsson examined the four Marines with a critical eye, then nodded. "Nice turnout, Major. You're armed, I presume."

As one, they lifted the left side of their mess jackets to reveal blasters in shoulder holsters.

"Powered and loaded with ammo, sir," Delgado said.

"I wonder how Admiral Bavadra and General Bowen will react when they find out you're carrying weapons into their mess." Larsson waved his words away before anyone could answer. "Never mind. Needs must when the devil drives. Shall we?"

Once outside, Delgado wondered what their little cluster looked like from a distance. Three sergeants and a major in red jackets, surrounding a five-star admiral in blue and trailed by a pair of aides, must make quite a sight.

As they neared the mess, the strains of a military band playing classical music reached their ears. Delgado had heard that if the 1st Marines could boast of nothing else, their band was the best in the entire Armed Services.

The glass doors slid aside at their approach, and he groaned mentally. A reception line, headed by Admiral Bavadra, with Lieutenant General Bowen beside her. Officers of decreasing rank stood to Bowen's left, ending with a Marine colonel who wore the insignia of the 1st Regiment on his mess jacket collar.

Delgado, the aides, and the escort kept to the right, away from the reception line, and let Larsson carry on with the formalities unhindered. The moment he finished shaking the hand of the 1st Regiment's CO, a trumpet sounded, heralding the arrival of humanity's top military commander. The rumble of conversation in the main room died away almost instantly, and everyone present turned toward the entrance. Delgado caught the eye of a battledress clad Command Sergeant Painter, standing by a side door. The latter nodded once. Everything was good.

Before Larsson could step forward, Delgado and Hak slipped in front of him and entered first.

"Officers and honored guests," a disembodied voice announced, "the Supreme Commander of the Commonwealth Armed Services, Grand Admiral Fredrik Larsson."

For the next thirty minutes, Delgado and his men trailed Larsson as he went around the room, shaking hands and exchanging pleasantries with the two hundred or so attendees, Home Sector's most senior military leaders and their aides. Delgado spotted Claressa Mori in the crowd, shadowing her general alongside Bowen's senior aide. Mori's job seemed to be making sure the general never wanted for a fresh drink in hand, which amused Delgado.

If nothing else, no one would make him fetch a glass, even though he was a mere major wearing aiguillettes, and along with Mori and a few others, among the most junior officers in the room. Hak was right. She did him a favor, though neither of them knew it at the time. When their eyes met, Delgado put on a mocking smile and winked at Mori. While she fetched, he was never more than a few paces away from the supreme commander. As ego-stroking went, it didn't get any better.

The evening, as Delgado expected, dragged on through a surprisingly tasty, five-course meal, followed by the usual marches, toasts, and endless speeches. Though not at the head table, he and his wingers sat within a few paces of Grand Admiral Larsson. The other attendees studiously ignored them once they figured out the watchful men with the winged dagger insignia on their mess jacket collars weren't there to enjoy themselves. Especially once they noticed the weapons beneath said jackets.

Toasting the Commonwealth, the Armed Services, the Navy, the Corps, and its regiments, including the 1st Special Forces Regiment, with water instead of champagne, wasn't much of an imposition. Several senior officers in attendance, however, didn't stint themselves and, by the end of the evening, were behaving less decorously than they should. Fortunately, none of them were from the delegation.

Delgado and his Marines felt nothing but relief when the Grand Admiral made his goodbyes and returned to the VIP quarters under a starlit sky. After changing into battledress, he and Hak inspected the perimeter, spoke with the troopers on duty, and checked in on the command post.

"You're saying there'll be more of this, Skipper?" Hak asked when they reached their rooms.

"Consider tonight a dress rehearsal. The fun will start with the Secretary-General's reception in the Palace of the Stars. That won't just be a walk across the park, but a full-blown armored convoy from here to downtown Geneva."

"Oh, how wonderful. I can't wait. Good night, sir."

"Good night, Top."

— Eleven —

"Lovely countryside, lovely city, but one of Earth's great fleshpots it isn't," Delgado said to no one in particular as the staff skimmer came within sight of humanity's capital.

He, Command Sergeant Rolf Painter, Sergeant First Class Testo, and Marines from A Troop were carrying out a reconnaissance of the route between Turenne Base and the Palace of the Stars. Nestled at the heart of the Ariana Park near the western shore of Lake Geneva, the ancient complex once known as the Palace of the Nations, encompassed the offices of the Commonwealth Secretary-General's government and the Senate's assembly chamber.

Meanwhile, the Fleet delegation was spending the day on base recovering from the previous night's mess dinner and preparing for the Secretary-General's reception that evening. The actual work of negotiating the quinquennial Fleet budget wouldn't begin until the following day.

"There's fun to be found, Major," Painter replied with a knowing grin. "As long as you ask the right sort of locals."

"And you have?"

"Some of us didn't spend last night staring at booze they couldn't touch. I chatted with the sergeant major from the 1st Marines in charge of the local guard detail. Turns out we know a few of the same people. He did a twenty-year hitch with the 11th on Cimmeria before coming home to Earth and a second career half without people regularly shooting at him."

Delgado grunted, eyes on the cityscape unfolding before them.

"I hope your friendly sergeant major was talking about clean fun. A government city like Geneva probably has plenty of degeneracy hiding behind the prim and proper facades, and that's not something honest Marines like you and I want. For all that, it seems quaint and well-maintained compared to many places I've seen, almost like a museum."

"Not surprising, sir. Apparently, the powers that be made sure it wouldn't change much outwardly over the last few centuries," Testo said. "It's one of the few major cities in western Europe — heck, the western hemisphere — that didn't suffer partial or total devastation during the ethnic and religious blow-ups in the late twenty-first century. The fleshpots you're thinking of aren't nearly as nice looking, especially the parts they didn't or couldn't rebuild. Remember those unlit nighttime expanses we saw from orbit? Some of them were bright metropolises before things went to crap."

"Devout zealots with mini-nukes leave a mark. Fortunately, that particular strand died out before it could join the fun of the Migration Wars."

"Turning a few holy sites into glass craters that glow in the dark helps take care of said zealots permanently," Painter remarked.

"It's time we joined regular folks on the surface roads," Testo said to the driver, one of A Troop's lance corporals, pointing at the rapidly approaching Autoroute bridge over the Rhone. "They don't allow skimmers on the water past that point, not even military ones."

Delgado let out a grunt.

"At least we're exempt from joining the centralized traffic system. Can you imagine the security nightmare that would cause? Or at least the head-butting I'd face for an exemption?"

"Most of the official vehicles around Geneva are exempt, Major. Do you think the grandees of the Senate or the Cabinet enjoy having a traffic AI take charge of their limousines?"

The lance corporal turned the vehicle to port in a wide, gentle arc that took them over the riverbanks and across a small grassy field before merging smoothly with the sparse mid-morning traffic on the *Route du Bois-de-Bay*.

"Now that I've seen the Rhone in person, I figure if we're running a convoy," Delgado said, "we should probably avoid it altogether."

He called up a holographic map projection.

"After our visit to the *Palais des Étoiles*, we'll take the southbound A1 and get off here at Bernex, then take the *Route de Chancy* back into town. After that, I want to try approaching the *Palais* via every one of the urban bridges, so we're familiar with the alternatives. Chancy is the most direct land road from the base anyhow."

"And if it's compromised?" Testo asked.

"Then we'll take one of the more southerly detours, roads that connect with the northbound highway, and pick up one of the lesser arteries crossing the Arve River." He glanced at his timepiece. "We have six hours before it's time to go back and change. That's enough time for a dry run over three or four alternate routes."

**

"Behold," Delgado said as they climbed out of the skimmer in the shadow of the Assembly Hall, "six hundred years of bloviation, hot air, and bullshit contemplate you." Thorough guards from the Terra Regiment had admitted them into the Government Precinct via the Pregny Gate after scrutinizing their credentials.

"How nice," Testo replied, grinning as they stepped out onto the worn concrete. "Massacring Napoleon Bonaparte's famous quote and insulting our dear Commonwealth government in one breath. Well done, sir."

Painter chuckled. "The skipper has a way with words."

"Something that will come in very handy with that fine specimen of the Terra Regiment's officer corps sizing us up for expulsion." Delgado nodded at a captain wearing a rifle green uniform headed in their direction from the Assembly Hall.

"Or perhaps he's our guide, you know, the one we arranged before leaving the base," Testo said, "seeing as none of us visited this place before. Left to our own devices, we might stumble into a plenary meeting of the Commonwealth Senate by mistake. Imagine how such a display of military boorishness might bugger up the budgetary negotiations."

The officer stomped to a parade ground halt six paces from their car and saluted.

"Captain Anton Zwellig, of the Secretary-General's Guard Battalion at your service. I assume you are from Grand Admiral Larsson's close protection detail here to check the lay of the land?"

"We are. I'm Curtis Delgado, the commanding officer. These are Sergeants Painter and Testo. Sergeant Painter leads A Troop, and Sergeant Testo is my unit's operations noncom."

Zwellig nodded once, replying in his French-accented Anglic, "A pleasure. If you'll follow me, I shall show you where tonight's events and the subsequent days' negotiations will take place."

"Thank you, Captain," Delgado said. "Are you perchance a native of the region? Sergeant Painter is keen on the local attractions."

"Born and bred in the Switzerland District, Major," Zwellig replied with evident pride. "I'd be proud to tell you about the best Geneva offers."

"Well, what do you know," Testo murmured just loud enough for Delgado to hear, "a real Swiss Guard, minus the fancy striped pajamas."

Delgado gave him an annoyed look, then smiled at Zwellig. "We'd be grateful for recommendations, Captain. My Marines will probably find themselves with a bit of time on their hands while the Grand Admiral is in-camera with the Senate."

"I shall arrange for a list of must-see places in Geneva and the surrounding area, sir. Now, may I suggest we take the exact path the Fleet delegation will use this evening?"

"Let's do that."

The Army officer led them into the imposing lobby, pointing out the sights along the way. They met surprisingly few people, and when Delgado remarked on that fact, Zwellig told them the Senate, which held court on the third floor, was in recess until the budget hearings started.

"Here we are." After climbing several flights of stairs, he ushered them into a long, high-ceilinged room brilliantly lit by the morning sun streaming through tall windows. "The *Salle des Pas Perdus* or Hall of the Lost Footsteps, where tonight's plenary reception will take place ahead of the more private supper with select members of the cabinet and Senate. The Senate Assembly Hall is behind those doors."

"Impressive." Delgado's eyes took in their surroundings. Then, in quick succession, he tossed a string of security-related questions at Zwellig, grunting with satisfaction when the latter fell silent, having satisfied his concerns. "And supper?"

"It will be in the Ariana Museum. We will go there momentarily, but along the way, I shall show you where the budgetary discussions will be held — the *Salle du Conseil* on the first floor of this building. It is one of the few meeting spaces that has been renovated to reflect the original early twentieth-century appearance."

"Please do," Delgado quickly replied before Testo could utter the innocently biting observation he saw taking shape behind the operations noncom's oh-so-innocent gaze.

As they retook the stairs, Testo, unable to contain himself, leaned toward Delgado.

"Considering the early twentieth century was a time of assaults against democracy and human rights on the bumpy road to World War Two," he said in a voice pitched for Delgado's ears only. "I wonder whether the SecGen is sending Larsson a message."

"I doubt he or his staff are that subtle, Sergeant. Your fetish for obscure historical facts isn't that widespread."

"Something for which we should be thankful, I suppose," Painter murmured. "Though learning from history is a fine thing, as Colonel Decker would say, politicians have an unfortunate habit of picking up the wrong lessons, hence the rising body count since the first intra-human war to end all wars. You know, the one which, perhaps not coincidentally gave birth to this architectural monstrosity."

"It's not that bad." Delgado gave him a warning look as they stopped at a door opening on a large space with tiered tables and seats arranged in a squared-off half-circle facing a row of raised desks and several tall, curtained windows. Ancient frescoes covered the walls and ceiling, while a spectator gallery higher up offered room for observers.

"It's a bloody museum," Painter replied, "and we haven't visited the actual museum yet."

"Would you care to inspect the room?" Zwellig asked, his eyes showing awareness of the Marines' whispered conversation, if not of its contents.

"Absolutely and thank you."

**

That evening a convoy of armored staff skimmers disgorged the delegation in front of the Assembly Hall. Once more in dress uniform, Delgado, Hak, and the Marines from A Troop formed a loose, not particularly noticeable protective perimeter around Grand Admiral Larsson during the short walk between the unmarked car and the hall's door.

Overhead, Erinye Company's silent, AI-controlled drones, which had escorted the convoy up the Rhone Valley from the base, shifted to a random crisscrossing patrol pattern over the Government Precinct. They fed video and sensor data to troopers of company HQ sitting at consoles in an improvised operations center in the VIP accommodation building's basement. B and C Troops, the flank guards, remained outside the Palace's perimeter, standing watch. One of them would prove the return route a few minutes ahead of Larsson's convoy later, while the other protected their rear.

Commodore Lee and Rolf Painter, who'd arrived earlier with a small advance party, waited in the lobby.

"We're ready," Lee announced the moment Larsson came within earshot. "Everyone save the SecGen is in the *Salle des Pas Perdus*. He'll greet you at the top of the stairs, and you'll enter together."

"We ran a sniffer through the hall and over the canapes, and gave the catering crew a thorough scan," Painter added. "So far, we're clear. I can't vouch for the senators or cabinet members, however." An ironic smile briefly crossed his features.

"I fear you've been spending too much time with Major Delgado, Sergeant," Larsson said, eyes twinkling. He gestured toward the staircase. "Shall we? Perhaps the major and his first sergeant should take the lead. If anyone can part a sea of politicians, it'll be imposing Special Forces troopers wearing more medals than two dozen Home Fleet admirals."

They took the stairs at a sedate pace, lending the procession an air of unhurried dignity. The sound of many voices talking over each other soon reached their ears, and when they came to the third floor, Delgado and Hak came face-to-face with Secretary-General of the Commonwealth

Brodrik Brüggemann. An overweight individual in his sixties, with thick, wavy dark hair, and a fleshy face, Brüggemann could pass for one of Delgado's many uncles, if it weren't for the hard, calculating look in his brown eyes.

Hak and Delgado saluted their head of state, the latter announcing in a formal tone, "Grand Admiral Larsson, sir."

They stepped to one side and let the most powerful politician in human-controlled space greet the most powerful military commander in the known galaxy. The two men shook hands, exchanging meaningless pleasantries, then they entered the hall side-by-side, almost as equals. An instant hush fell over the crowd of senators, cabinet members, and those well connected enough for an invitation. All eyes turned on Larsson and Brüggemann, except for one pair, which passed over the Grand Admiral and the flag officers following in his wake, before settling on Delgado. They belonged to a tall, handsome woman wearing expensive-looking evening clothes.

He nudged Hak and whispered, "If I didn't know better, I'd say that was Miko."

"It is. And she clearly doesn't want us to acknowledge her."

"How the hell did she finagle an invitation?"

"Search me, Skipper."

Larsson, following Brüggemann's lead, headed into the crowd, champagne glass in hand, nodding politely at the select few charged with their species' destiny. Delgado and Hak stepped into the open space created by their wake, as perfectly dutiful aides would, eyes everywhere, searching for both threats and Rolf Painter's Marines.

The lengthy shadow dance between the Fleet and the government for control of the Commonwealth defense funding was beginning in earnest. For a moment, Delgado yearned to be back on Mission Colony, stomping out ComCorp's latest outrage.

He took a canape from a passing salver and popped it in his mouth. Though the security detail couldn't drink, there was nothing wrong with the odd snack. He searched for Warrant Officer Miko Steiger, or rather her undercover alter ego, but she had vanished into the crowd.

— Twelve —

Steiger knew Delgado and Hak recognized her despite the disguise and understood they shouldn't be seen acknowledging each other. Yet the curiosity in their eyes at seeing her in such rarefied company was evident.

"Did anyone ever mention you resemble one of the figures of Norse mythology? Are you perhaps a reincarnated Valkyrie?" A soft man's voice, deep, confident, and perhaps a tad amused, reached her ears, and she detected the faint accent of someone whose first language wasn't Anglic.

Steiger turned and came face-to-face with Andreas Bauchan, the director-general of the *Sécurité Spéciale*. She recognized him from the Naval Intelligence dossiers on leading government figures she'd practically memorized before leaving Caledonia.

Tall, handsome with a square jaw and a mane of silver hair brushed back from a high forehead, Bauchan's eyes held a roguish twinkle that didn't quite mask the emptiness behind them. Though in his seventies, he seemed as fit as a man half his age. Steiger, practiced in hiding her thoughts, gave no sign she was aware of his identity. But then, few in this room would be aware of his actual responsibilities since his official, and more innocuous title was that of Executive Security Adviser to the Secretary-General.

"You would be the first, but I appreciate the compliment. I've always found the women of Norse mythology deeply compelling. My ancestors came from Northern Europe, so perhaps one of the more enterprising men snagged himself a Valkyrie back in the days of the Vikings, and their offspring passed along the genes. I'm Britta Trulson, by the way."

Bauchan bowed his head in a surprisingly formal and somewhat outdated manner.

"An appropriately Scandinavian name. I am Andreas Bauchan." He pronounced his name with a definite French inflection. "I work for the Secretary-General."

"*Enchantée,* Monsieur *Bauchan.*"

"And you speak my mother tongue! How delightful. What brings you to this little gala?"

Steiger understood he really meant who arranged for an invitation but decided she would play coy. Bauchan supposedly had a weakness for verbal sparring and statuesque women.

"Curiosity."

"That makes you a rarity in this splendid assemblage. Most are here so they can be seen among the powerful, when they're not cooking up deals in quiet corners, that is. They do say politics is the second oldest profession."

"And power the ultimate aphrodisiac. How about you?"

"Why am I here?" He took a sip of his champagne while studying her with those unnervingly intense eyes. "To observe, listen, and learn. It's astounding how much one can discover about another's character in this setting."

Steiger smiled at him.

"In other words, you're here out of curiosity as well."

Bauchan inclined his head.

"Yes. Tell me, Madame Trulson, I've never seen you in official circles before, and my memory for names and faces is rather phenomenal. Some even call it legendary."

Her smile widened.

"That's because I'm an off-world visitor. This is my first time in Geneva."

"Ah. And what brings you to our fair planet?"

"I'm here on a research mission for the Deep Space Foundation, my employer."

He nodded.

"I see. Does that mean you're from Cimmeria?"

"Yes. I'm a Cimmerian born and bred."

"It's a lengthy trip from the Rim."

Steiger realized Bauchan would check up on her before the night was out. But he would merely discover that a Britta Trulson, employed by the Deep Space Foundation, had indeed traveled to Earth from Cimmeria. What he wouldn't learn was that the Trulson who crossed interstellar space on the Cimmeria-Arcadia leg wasn't the same one who embarked on a different starship for the final bit between Arcadia and Earth.

"It is, but I go where my employer needs me."

"And how is the Foundation faring these days? I understand there was trouble a while back."

"It is thriving, I'm happy to say. Those troubles are long behind us."

Bauchan took another sip of his bubbly.

"Care to satisfy my curiosity just a bit more, Madame Trulson?"

"Certainly, and please call me Britta."

"How did an off-world researcher finagle one of the most desired invitations in town?"

"Senator Annear's office kindly arranged it at the Foundation's request."

Which was nothing but the truth. Nerys Annear, Cimmeria's senior senator, wouldn't know Britta Trulson from Eve. But after Annear's daughter almost murdered most of the Rim Sector's leading officials, the Fleet could count on her for a little help when certain unnamed people came calling. People such as Commodore Talyn's operatives inside the Foundation.

"Then, your organization is indeed thriving. I wasn't aware Senator Annear supported its activities."

"The change in management and sponsorship helped bring the senator around, Monsieur Bauchan."

"Please, call me Andreas."

Did Steiger see a spark of interest in the man's eyes? If so, how hard should she push? Getting friendly with the head of the *Sécurité Spéciale* wasn't her primary objective. It remained supporting Erinye Company, but she understood that one day, the Fleet would face the need to eliminate Bauchan's organization. Though no one in Naval Intelligence or Special Operations had said so aloud, everybody understood the time would come.

For all Steiger knew, Talyn was already planning its demise. She always seemed five steps ahead of the opposition. Perhaps Steiger attending the reception was a scheme within a scheme, an espionage matryoshka doll, one in which Talyn trusted her agent's sense of initiative. She was an undisputed master manipulator of both people and events.

"Would you like to meet the Secretary-General and the Grand Admiral?" He asked, gesturing in their direction with his glass.

Steiger shook her head. "I prefer observing. As a student of human behavior, this environment fascinates me. Much of what happens tonight has no bearing on anything beyond these walls. How about you, Andreas?"

"I'm much the same. Wielding political power out there, in the real world, even behind the scenes, is preferable to this sort of kabuki theater. Still, I fear our shared opinion puts us in the minority."

Their eyes met again, and she definitely saw something in them.

"I've never experienced difficulties standing apart."

He smiled. "No doubt. Valkyries generally do as they please."

Steiger raised her champagne glass. "So I understand."

She took a sip, eyes locked with Bauchan's, then smiled back.

**

"Why do I think Miko's trying to get lucky?" Hak whispered into Delgado's ears as they followed Larsson and Brüggemann around the room.

"Because the man's a target?" Delgado replied in the same tone. "Whoever he is. It's probably best if we don't pay attention."

"Roger that, Skipper."

The Marines breathed a sigh of relief when Larsson, his host, and a smattering of humanity's top officials left the *Salle des Pas Perdus* for the Ariana Museum and dinner. When they glimpsed Miko Steiger one last time before leaving the din of conversation behind, she was headed for the exit along with the tall, distinguished looking man.

"At least someone might have fun tonight," Hak muttered. "While we're stuck standing around like meat and bone ornaments."

And stand around they did, for three long hours, watching the Commonwealth's elite enjoy a seven-course meal ordinary people could only dream of.

When they finally climbed back into the armored staff car for the return trip, Delgado almost breathed a sigh of relief before reminding himself the job wasn't over until they'd seen Larsson safely to his suite. So far, none of the political unrest on Earth had reached Geneva, but that could change very quickly, especially if Naval Intelligence was right and the *Sécurité Spéciale* was behind the agitation.

Although he was tense, Delgado knew no one in his right mind would attack them. Not with his company in combat cars borrowed from the 1st Marines, cars whose weapons were loaded with live ammunition. He nonetheless felt a minor wave of relief when they passed through Turenne Base's main gate and came under the protection of its aerospace defense dome.

But his evening wasn't over yet. After ensuring the Grand Admiral and the rest of the delegation were tucked away for the night, Delgado assembled the troop leaders and company HQ noncoms in the makeshift operations room for an after-action review and a quick scan of the aerial recordings taken by the drones.

They were watching the latter's record of the return trip when something caught Delgado's eye.

"Stop the playback."

Sergeant Testo at once tapped the controls and looked up at his commanding officer. "Sir?"

"Back it up slowly."

Everyone in the room stared intently at the primary display. Thanks to the drones' night vision sensors, they could see the countryside bright as day.

"There." Delgado tapped the screen with an extended index finger. "What's that?"

"The moon reflecting off something?" Hak suggested.

"Can you zoom in on it?"

Testo nodded, and the glimmer of light in the middle of an otherwise darkened landscape grew. They made out a few shadows in the wood line, but the moon's reflection on what was likely an optical device blotted out the details.

"Let's see where that is." Delgado reached out, and a map of the surrounding area appeared on a secondary display. After a few moments, a red dot appeared as the AI matched the video feed from the drone with the terrain model in its memory banks. "Interesting. On the heights above the Rhone. Good observation and firing position."

"Pretty long range, though. Could be a coincidence," Sergeant Painter said in a dubious tone.

"That's parkland, Rolf. No access road nearby. Why would someone sit on the edge of that drop-off where they can see every route leading from Geneva to Turenne Base at this hour?"

Painter gave Hak a sideways glance. "Point taken. Should I alert a patrol and check it out right away, Major?"

Delgado thought for a few seconds, then shook his head.

"No point going there before daylight. If that was people watching us, they'll be gone by now. We'll send a drone after first light, and if we see traces of an observation post, I'll send a patrol to the spot in case they return."

"Roger that, sir."

They finished with the video review, and after walking the perimeter with First Sergeant Hak, Delgado slipped into bed. The next command performance would be after the midday meal. Senate hearings were apparently an afternoon thing, and that suited him fine.

— Thirteen —

"This is the spot." The drone, under Sergeant First Class Testo's control, hovered over a lip of rock near the top of a low mountain east of the Rhone, sending back real-time video to Erinye Company's operations center. "No one there, but you can see traces of occupation. Broken branches, disturbed ground cover."

"Right. D Troop?"

"Major." Command Sergeant Faruq Saxer, who'd been leaning against a table at the back, pushed himself upright.

"Send a patrol to watch that spot. Circuitous approach, forty-eight-hour autonomy. They leave when ready."

"Rules of engagement?"

"Observe and report, unless they deploy long-range weapons and are preparing to engage the convoy, in which case, take them out."

"Roger, sir."

Saxer came to attention and left the operations center.

"Do you think we stumbled on the bad guys' hide by accident, sir?" Command Sergeant Painter asked.

"Maybe, and it only took one drone veering at just the right angle, so it picked up moonlight reflecting off a lens. In other words, dumb luck." Delgado seemed lost in thought.

"Luck we wouldn't have enjoyed if we hadn't deployed drones in the first place, sir. As they say, luck is when preparation meets opportunity."

Delgado nodded. "True. But surely they're aware we use armored staff cars."

"A standard, portable missile launcher can cover the entire area and send an armored staff car tumbling even if it doesn't punch through," First Sergeant Hak pointed out.

"Also true. It means the Grand Admiral rides in one of the combat cars. A different one each time," Delgado replied, eyes still on the image of the cliff top hide. "I'll explain the situation to Commodore Lee. She'll tell him."

"Not much VIP comfort, Skipper. Want me to see about padding a seat in each of them."

"No. Larsson knows the score, and he's not like some in the delegation who are overly fond of their comforts."

Painter snorted. "Isn't that the truth?"

"Now, we just need to figure out how we load him with no tangos, or the Almighty forbid, insiders, spotting which car he's riding."

"Remove their markings and shuffle them on the way out, Skipper."

Delgado gave his first sergeant thumbs-up. "See that they're sterilized, Top. We can apologize to the 1ˢᵗ Marines when this is over."

"Will do."

"You know, sir," Testo said in a thoughtful tone, "I can't help but think we should write up TTPs around what we're doing in case this level of VIP protection becomes part of our normal job list. By now, we're way beyond the protocols used by military police VIP escorts."

"Are you volunteering?"

The sergeant grinned. "So I can make those TTPs my own and then push them on the MPs? You bet."

Later that morning, Delgado briefed Commodore Lee and Lieutenant Colonel Hisk on their findings. The latter understood the implications right away.

"That didn't take long if it was someone looking for trouble."

"If they return, my patrol will decide whether we're looking at a threat or something totally unrelated. Whoever was there has no reason to suspect we saw them. It was pure chance."

"Still — letting moonlight reflect off a glossy surface is one of the most basic mistakes an observation post can make."

"It happens, sir. And I know from personal experience the people causing trouble on the OutWorlds these days aren't professionals like us. They're mostly disaffected or thrill-seeking amateurs organized and stiffened by undercover operatives."

"I'll speak with the Grand Admiral," Commodore Lee said. "I expect nothing more than an acknowledgment. Besides, now that the ceremonial aspect is over for a while, the news nets won't be breathlessly covering our arrival and departure from beyond the Palace of the Stars' perimeter, so we needn't worry about appearances."

**

"My dear Britta." Andreas Bauchan stood and took Miko Steiger's outstretched hand into both of his. Though his smile was warm, it didn't quite reach his eyes.

"Andreas. Thank you for inviting me to a lovely lunch. This location," she waved at the restaurant's lakefront patio bordering the *Quai Gustave-Ador*, "is enchanting."

"A worthy setting for an intriguing companion."

They'd spent a few hours after the reception walking along the shores of Lake Geneva in the *Parc Barton*, talking and enjoying the cool evening air before stopping for a nightcap at a little cafe in the *Parc de La Perle du Lac*. By the time they went their separate ways, Steiger was sure she had him, if not hooked, then at least deeply interested.

Bauchan ushered her into a high-backed chair facing the lake. "I trust you slept well."

"After a few hours of fresh air and stimulating conversation, how could I do otherwise?" Steiger gave him a brilliant smile.

Before he could reply, a white-aproned waiter approached their table and bowed his head.

"Monsieur Bauchan. *Bienvenue*. The house is always honored by your presence."

"And I'm always happy to be here. This is Madame Britta Trulson, a distinguished visitor from Cimmeria."

"*Bienvenue*. A friend of Monsieur Bauchan is an honored guest indeed. Is this your first visit to Earth, Madame?"

"Yes."

"And you chose Geneva. You will not be disappointed by the beauty of this city and its surroundings." He glanced at Bauchan. "May I offer an apéritif?"

Bauchan turned toward Miko. "The excellent house Chasselas would be a pleasant introduction to local white wine vintages."

"Certainly."

"A bottle, Monsieur Bauchan?"

"Please."

"It's curious," Bauchan said once the server was out of earshot, "but you never told me what you do for the Deep Space Foundation. The title researcher can mean many things depending on the context."

Steiger gave him a coy look.

"And you never mentioned your role in the Secretary-General's office."

A bark of laughter.

"Touché."

"I'm a socio-political researcher. My job is identifying trends, threats, and opportunities."

"You're in the intelligence business then."

"I must confess I'm not particularly fond of that militarized term. Besides, I do more than collect and analyze data. I also propose courses of action so the Foundation can exploit as yet unseen forces that move events or star systems in given directions. And you?"

The waiter returned with a chilled wine bottle and two glasses. They watched him go through the ritual of uncorking and serving in silence.

"Have monsieur and madame consulted the menu?"

Bauchan shook his head. "No. We'll signal when we're ready to order."

The waiter bowed his head again. "As monsieur wishes."

Bauchan picked up his wine glass. "To your health, my dear."

"And yours."

They took appreciative sips, then Steiger smiled again. "Wonderful."

"It is, isn't it? They grow the grapes on the slopes behind us. Now, what line of business am I in? Something like yours. I'm the Secretary-General's Security Adviser and responsible for many of the things you just mentioned." Bauchan settled back in his chair, eyes narrowed against the sun reflecting off the lake's shimmering surface. "What line of research brings you here in these troubled and troubling times?"

"My superiors are interested in how Earth perceives the growing unrest in the OutWorlds and the mysterious paramilitary strikes against cartels and misbehaving corporations."

"To what end?"

"The same as always, advancing the Foundation's goals. We're still only operating in the Rim and neighboring sectors. Our board of directors wants to expand across the entire Commonwealth."

He gave her a knowing nod.

"Then the curiosity you mentioned last night wasn't merely idle, nor did Senator Annear's office arrange for an invitation out of mere courtesy, *n'est-ce pas?*"

Steiger raised a hand.

"Guilty, Your Honor. Shall we peruse the menu?"

"Nice deflection." He chuckled. "By all means, let's see what seems tempting today."

In the end, they both chose *truite amandine*, a delicate freshwater fish with a butter-lemon sauce topped by roasted almond slices.

"Tell me," Bauchan said, pushing away his empty plate, "other than stalking official functions, how will you carry out your mission?"

"Mission? Your military leanings are showing again, Andreas. Surely you mean my research."

He held up his right hand, palm facing her.

"I swear I never served a single day in any military organization whatsoever, but people like you and I are mission-driven, no?"

Steiger gave him an amused look.

"You might say that about everyone with a vision of what their lives should be."

"Perhaps. And what's your vision?"

She let out an amused peal of laughter. "Now that would be telling. And we don't know each other well enough yet."

A sardonic smile lit up his face, and he inclined his head. "Once again, touché. At this point, you'll count coup so often I might never catch up."

"You will." Steiger took another sip of wine, her eyes never leaving his. "I think you're the sort who always wins in the end."

Bauchan raised his wine glass and winked at her.

"Tell you what. The defense budget hearings are being held in the *Salle du Conseil* beginning this afternoon. It has spectator seating — by invitation only for those not working in the Palace of the Stars — but I can escort you. Listening to the senators as they grill Grand Admiral Larsson and his staff might give you an idea of the general mood around here."

"And in return for this unexpected and delightful privilege?"

"You accept my invitation to dinner."

— Fourteen —

Callsign one-four-alpha, seven Special Forces operators under the command of Staff Sergeant Salford Lambrix, quickly found the game trail used by the previous night's watchers. Unlike the local wildlife, they'd left plenty of traces — broken twigs, crushed leaves, and dislodged stones. In Lambrix's professional estimation, they weren't particularly good at fieldcraft, which ruled out trained military personnel. That, or they simply didn't care, which indicated a sloppiness no one in Ghost Squadron would countenance.

The patrol, unarmored but wearing chameleon combat uniforms complete with tactical harness, helmets and carrying both carbines and packs, paralleled the game trail, careful to leave no clues of its passage until the woods thinned near the drop-off. Lambrix ordered a halt by raising his fist over his head and tapped his wingman, Corporal Leroy Taggart, on the shoulder. While the others watched and waited, Lambrix and Taggart found the spot where the drone caught the moonlight reflection and scanned it with their handheld battlefield sensors.

They installed the Special Forces version of game cameras, tiny spheres covered with a layer of chameleon paint, in well-hidden spots. The cameras were linked with the sensors and would alert them to any humans moving around.

Once Lambrix was satisfied, he moved one-four-alpha back into the woods and away from the game trail. They found a secluded dip in the ground and set up camp. Two Marines would monitor the sensors, two would stand guard over the hide, while the other four rested.

As per Major Delgado's orders, they carried food, water, and instrumentation power packs for forty-eight hours, though Lambrix knew he could tack another twelve onto that without breaking a sweat. He checked in with the operations center over an encrypted link, then settled back and waited. Either someone would show up, or they wouldn't. Even in the Special Forces, life was long stretches of boredom punctuated by bursts of high speed, low drag activity.

The hour of Grand Admiral Larsson's departure for Geneva came and went with nothing to report other than timid deer, a few hares, and plenty of birds, but none of the troopers complained. Sitting out in the fresh air, with the scent of pine needles tickling nostrils, on the world where their species evolved and to which it still had an atavistic sense of belonging, beat convoy escort, let alone ceremonial duties.

Those on sentry duty and on the sensors swapped places with those who'd been resting every two hours. But otherwise, nothing moved in their little hollow.

Finally, as the shadows lengthened, the cameras' simple sensors detected something the general size of a human being. One of the two on sensor duty scurried over to Lambrix and tapped him on the shoulder.

"Sarge, there's movement in the target area," the man whispered in a voice that didn't carry.

"Hot damn."

Lambrix took the proffered sensor and stared at its small screen. Three figures, adult humans, one female, two males, wearing camouflage clothes of the sort preferred by wild game hunters. One of them carried a long-range optical sensor, a piece of civilian gear available from most high-end electronics retailers. The others had simple binoculars hanging from straps around their necks. They could be perfectly innocent birdwatchers for all he knew.

He checked the time. Almost seventeen hundred hours, which meant the Grand Admiral's convoy would soon leave Geneva for Turenne Base, there being no social function that day, so the timing was a little too close for coincidence. A male voice came through his helmet's earpieces.

"Remember, they'll be taking a different route from last night's. Standard VIP protection protocols — never use the same itinerary twice in a row — so look sharp."

"I hope Team Alpha keeps that in mind," the woman said in a sour tone.

"Simply because you don't like Mueller doesn't mean he and his people aren't on the ball, Carrie."

Lambrix felt his eyebrows rise. Two observation posts, one tracking the Turenne Base to Geneva run and one the return trip? That sounded a bit more professional and lowered the likelihood of being spotted. He pointed at his assistant, Sergeant Osmin Sberna, and made the 'come here gesture.'

"Contact?" The latter asked, crouching beside Lambrix.

"Three tangos. Find their transport and tag it, then stay there and observe."

"Roger that." Sberna stood and gestured at his half of the patrol, twirling his right index finger, the signal to mount up.

Moments later, Lambrix, Corporal Taggart, and two lance corporals were the only ones left in the hide. The latter stood guard while the former concentrated on the feed from the two cameras. They watched the trio settle in, then the binocular-equipped pair swept the countryside near the city limits while the second man set up his long-range optics, ready to zero in on the convoy once his partners spotted it.

Lambrix opened the encrypted frequency with the operations center and gave Sergeant First Class Testo a brief report of events. No doubt, one of the escort drones would make a closer sweep to this area, its pickups looking straight at the watchers, but this time in daylight.

Almost half an hour passed before a voice said, "Contact. I spotted the convoy."

The woman rattled off directions using intersections and landmarks to orient her colleagues, proving she not only knew the area well but was a trained observer.

"Seen. Recording," the man with the long-range device said.

"Check." The one with the second set of binoculars added.

After what Lambrix figured was enough time for the run to Turenne Base, the first male voice reached his ears again.

"Done. Time to go home."

He waited while they packed, then opened a link with Sberna.

"Tangos extracting."

"Ack. I tagged their car. The tag is inactive at the moment in case they scan before leaving. I'll flip it on remotely once they move out."

"Good."

Lambrix switched to the company frequency.

"Zero, this is one-four-alpha. Tangos are extracting."

A few seconds later, Testo replied, "Pretty much as expected. Once they're clear, head for the pickup point. No need to spend the night if they're gone. We'll put you in again tomorrow afternoon."

"Acknowledged."

"Zero, out."

**

After ensuring Grand Admiral Larsson and the delegation were secure and would receive their meals in the VIP accommodation block's private dining room, Major Delgado headed for the officers' mess. Though he could eat with the aides, he needed a break from remaining constantly alert while fighting off boredom. Unfortunately, he couldn't dine with his sergeants. Here in the 1st Marine Regiment's home station, officers and non-commissioned officers lived separate lives.

The opening phase of the defense budget hearings had been incredibly painful, with various senators bloviating like so many demented heads of cattle. As far as Delgado could tell, they had accomplished nothing in those three and a half hours of empty posturing. It reminded him of a quip he'd read long ago, uttered by a pre-diaspora politician who characterized such speeches as an army of pompous phrases moving over the landscape in search of an idea.

His only entertainment had been discretely watching Miko and her target in the audience. Whoever that was, he clearly enjoyed her company, and seeing her behave in a subtly seductive manner seemed hysterically funny, considering what Delgado knew of her usual persona.

After filling a tray at the buffet, Delgado looked for an open table where he could eat in peace and quiet. Then, he spotted Claressa Mori, sitting by herself near the windows, and a yen for mischief overcame his usual discretion.

He walked up to Mori's table unnoticed and sat across from her.

"You look like you need a friend, Claressa. Hard day robbing dogs for General Bowen?"

Mori glared at him with eyes that, if they spat plasma, would kill him instantly. "What I need is my privacy, Major, sir."

"You need to loosen up, Captain," he replied in a pleasant tone, grinning. "A meal with an old comrade is what the psychiatrist ordered."

Delgado unfolded his napkin, picked up a fork, and speared a chunk of chicken in a creamy sauce. "Want to hear about my day?"

By her expression, he could see Mori parsing her courses of action. Stand and walk away in a huff from the handsome Special Forces major in front of her fellow 1st Marine Regiment officers, or make the best of it until she finished her meal?

"Let's eat, pretend to be civil and talk as little as possible, Major. Though lord knows how you finagled oak leaves before I did," she added in a sour mutter.

"Life choices, Claressa. And please call me Curtis. We're sharing a meal, not standing on the parade square behind our respective flag officers."

Her faint sneer told him she didn't think much of dropping the formalities under the circumstances.

"See, it's like this," he said after swallowing another mouthful. "When you screwed me out of my slot for OTS and crapped on my reputation, I doubled down instead of wallowing in self-pity. I passed the Special Forces selection process on the first try — with flying colors. While you attended OTS, I graduated from the Pathfinder School and the Special Forces assaulter course. Graduation from the latter came with a staff sergeant's rocker."

Another irritated glare.

"I'll bet when they asked which regiment you wanted, you picked the 1st because you knew you were never going back to the 22nd after what you did to me. And so, while you were here primping for parades hoping you'd be noticed, I was carrying out actual combat missions all over the Commonwealth," Delgado leaned over, whispering, "and beyond."

He winked and straightened again. After finishing the main course, he dabbed his lips with the napkin.

"Those missions earned me a slot on the Special Forces Troop Leader Course and an accelerated promotion to command sergeant. And in SOCOM, command sergeants with a future in the officer corps are directly commissioned as captains. And captains who show stellar potential become majors. That is why I earned my oak leaf wreaths before you, even if your commission predates mine by many years. Now that you know what I did since we last spoke, what about you? Are you on track to become a career captain, or is this stint as Bowen's aide your way of climbing up the greasy pole without exposing yourself to enemy fire?"

Mori leaned over and said, in a voice meant for his ears only, "Go fuck yourself, Major, sir."

She stood, picked up her tray, and walked away without looking back.

"Nice speaking with you, Claressa." Delgado sighed.

He'd probably hit a bullseye with his career captain remark, based on her uncharacteristic vulgarity, and that was pretty much the only payback he could toss at her. Not that he was looking for vengeance. His career had turned out more challenging and rewarding this way.

Chances were good he'd be the one facing life as a career captain if it hadn't been for her backstabbing ways and he owed her his thanks. The 22nd didn't see much action in the intervening years, and young, relatively junior sergeants who went through OTS needed to prove themselves as lieutenants if they wanted more. Garrison duty didn't give them much by way of opportunities.

No, the best route, better even than the Academy in many respects, was becoming an enlisted platoon or troop leader and taking a direct commission as captain to command a company. Do that young enough, and a general's stars weren't beyond reach.

Lieutenant Colonel Decker was a case in point. He'd been a command sergeant who became a chief warrant officer when he joined intelligence before taking his commission as a major. And rumors were he was next in line as CO of the 1st Special Forces Regiment when Colonel Ryent put up his first star.

If this mission weren't dry, Delgado would toast his career with a wee dram of scotch, the real stuff distilled on this world, at the northern tip of a small island. Instead, he helped himself to a second cup of coffee and strolled out onto the patio so he could enjoy the sights and scents of sunset.

Inevitably, the low Jura Mountains filling the northwestern horizon drew his eyes, and he wondered who the secret watchers worked for, what they intended, and of equal importance, where the observers called Team Alpha hid to spy on the Turenne Base to Geneva run.

Were they preparing a strike, and if so, when and how?

— Fifteen —

"Another perfect meal, Andreas. Keep taking me out like this, and my clothes will no longer fit." Miko Steiger smiled fondly at Bauchan as they strolled along the shores of the *Lac Léman*, as he called it, for the third evening in a row.

"I doubt that, my dear. You're fitter than any other woman I've met. How many hours per day do you spend in the hotel gym?"

"One hour before breakfast. How are you aware I frequent the hotel gym? Are you having me watched?"

Steiger already knew the answer. She'd spotted the *Sécurité Spéciale* agents almost at once the morning after the SecGen's reception.

"Yes."

"Should I be flattered or worried?"

"I'm sure you understand a man in my position can never be too careful. After all, I work for the most powerful individual in the Commonwealth."

"Next, you'll tell me your people on Cimmeria looked into my background."

"Yes, and my suspicions were correct. You are more than a mere researcher for the Deep Space Foundation."

"Am I now?" She kept her manner breezy, though her heart almost skipped a beat.

"And apparently you own a nice apartment in Howard's Landing. What street is it on now?" He snapped his fingers. "Bessemer Avenue."

"Bertrand Avenue, as you well know. Number 11, apartment 305."

"Right."

As traps went, that one was clumsy, and Steiger wondered what Bauchan intended. Or perhaps he thought it clever because he was a bureaucrat who never worked in the field.

"Why is one of the Deep Space Foundation's leading operatives on Earth, Britta? Isn't this a little far from your usual territory?"

"As I said, the board of directors wants to expand. Setting up an office here, at the heart of the Commonwealth, would help immensely. My job is evaluating the proposal in light of the current political and social atmosphere on this planet."

"As in, are there enough activists and agitators who would take the Foundation's coin in exchange for advancing its political aims?"

"More or less. We heard about the protests and riots on Earth." Miko gestured at the star-studded sky. "Out there, we use such unfocused forces and channel them in a way that promotes a closer union of the various human-settled star systems."

"You mean in a way that promotes the abolition of the sovereign star systems principle."

Miko stopped and turned toward him, laughing with delight.

"Your directness is very provocative, and perhaps even a little inviting." She reached out and touched his cheek with her fingertips. "Yes, the Foundation's goal is abolishing sovereign star systems to pave the way for a happier time when humanity will be synchronized and governed the same way, no matter where, thereby ending the chances for conflict permanently. But I'm not telling you anything new."

"Of course. We keep track of individuals and organizations whose goals align with those of the Commonwealth government. The Deep Space Foundation has certainly blossomed since the assassination of Louis Sorne and Antoine Hakkam."

They resumed walking, this time away from the waterfront as Bauchan guided her toward a residential sector.

"Just between us, Louis was something of a drag. He and Antoine didn't think big enough, though Louis was desperate for a seat at the big table, alongside the major zaibatsus. The assassin did those of us with more vision a big favor."

"You realize the killer was from the Armed Services."

"We suspect as much. The Fleet will not tolerate changes to the political status quo and sees us as the enemy." Steiger's mysterious smile wasn't because of her putative employer's status, however. She still found Commodore Talyn's subversion of a subversive organization deliciously ironic. "Tell me, one reads of the same political disorder here as on many OutWorlds, yet Geneva is almost boringly calm."

An amused chuckle.

"Do you really think we'd allow riots in Geneva? We monitor United Commonwealth Front street theater closely and confine it to designated areas where the participants can enjoy their revolutionary live-action role-playing without frightening the bourgeoisie and causing material damage."

She gave him a questioning glance.

"You mean the disturbances aren't a grassroots phenomenon?"

"Heavens, no. They're crowds of useful idiots we manipulate to push a political narrative, just like your Foundation has done for years. Did you ever hear of a man named Thomas Sowell?"

"No."

"He famously said, long ago, that activism is a way for useless people to feel important even if the consequences of their activism are counterproductive for those they claim to be helping and damaging to the fabric of society as a whole."

"Is it the same for the protesters on the OutWorlds?"

"Certainly. They riot in favor of more control from Earth. However, most don't know it — as I said, useful idiots — and those on Earth protest against the suppression of their OutWorld fellow travelers by sovereign star system governments. It's literally a page from the Deep Space Foundation's playbook."

Miko, aware by now they were no longer in the lively waterfront part of town, asked, "Where are we going?"

"I thought we might finish the evening with cognac at my residence while we explore the possibilities of helping each other."

"I'm honored a senior Commonwealth official thinks I might offer more than just my company."

"My dear, your company is reward enough for many things. You are, without a doubt, the most interesting woman I've ever met. I would very much enjoy us developing a long-term friendship, and the best of them are built on mutual backscratching, if I may use that word without implying a double entendre."

"Imply anything you want." She gave him a wink.

They turned onto a quiet street, lit only by soft glow globes hovering at regular intervals. The houses behind ivy-covered stone walls and wrought iron fences reeked of centuries-old wealth. Many facades could easily date back to a time before humanity exploded across the galaxy aboard the first faster than light starships. A person-sized door cut into a wider gate opened silently at their approach.

Bauchan ushered her through and into a miniature park of carefully tended lawns and shrubs bordering stone walk and driveways. Miko's practiced eye spotted enough hidden sensors to tell her this was a well-secured property.

"Nice. You must really be someone of consequence in the Secretary-General's office to live in such splendor, and with such a sophisticated surveillance network."

"Well spotted." He led her up a set of broad stairs to where a heavy oak door swung open. "Most of the senior officials in town enjoy this lifestyle, along with serious protection. It's both the reward and burden of helping the SecGen run a fractious Commonwealth spread across the expanse of countless light-years."

The mansion's foyer matched its facade and surroundings — marble floor, grandiose winding staircase, chandelier hanging from a high ceiling, mahogany furniture, and a subtle smattering of paintings, statues, and other art.

"You live alone?"

"Sadly, yes. But it's probably for the best. Most of the house is automated, with service and cleaning droids keeping it spotless, though I enjoy cooking. Perhaps I can prepare a meal for you in the coming days." He gestured toward an open ground level door. "The sitting room is through there."

At its threshold, the marble floor gave way to hardwood turned a deep amber with age. A massive fireplace dominated one end, flanked by bookcases, while another wall was almost entirely made up of French doors giving onto the rear of the house. Miko figured they were paned with transparent aluminum and not ordinary glass. Nothing less would do for the SecGen's spymaster.

More of the heavy mahogany furniture was scattered around the room, but Bauchan indicated a pair of facing sofas in front of the fireplace, separated by a low table.

"We'll be comfortable there. Settle in while I pour the cognac. Will the Renaud Louis Quatorze do?"

Steiger let out a low whistle at hearing the name. It was considered one of the finest ever distilled and sold for an eye-watering price.

"Your taste in fine drinks is impeccable."

"As is my taste in companions." He busied himself at the small bar in one corner, then crossed the room, a snifter in each hand. He offered her one and raised his. "To what I hope will be a beautiful friendship."

They took a sip, and she marveled at the richness of the amber liquid.

"Wonderful," she said after it burned a satisfying path down her throat.

"Isn't it? Please sit." Bauchan took the sofa across from her, and they studied each other in silence for a few moments. "Would you be miffed if I said you're both attractive and intriguing?"

"Of course not. Compliment me all night long if that strikes your fancy. I find that I often intimidate men."

"No doubt." He took another sip. "But not me. I must confess, we've been thinking about reaching out to the Deep Space Foundation for a while now. Your appearance at the SecGen's reception was rather fortuitous."

"In that case, here's to fate smiling on us." She raised her glass again and drank. "Who is this we?"

"Those of us charged with protecting the Commonwealth's current political order from domestic enemies."

"The Fleet being chief among them?" She arched a finely sculpted eyebrow.

"Now you're the provocative one, but yes. Under the leadership of Grand Admiral Larsson and his predecessors, it's become a force untethered by the traditional constraints of civilian control over the military."

Steiger briefly wondered how Bauchan would react if he found out he was flirting with the enemy.

"And not just any force, but one capable of ravaging entire star systems."

He nodded. "Indeed, though not every one of his admirals and generals would go along with a scheme that opposes efforts to strengthen the Commonwealth government."

"The ones assigned to the 1st Fleet and the 1st Marine Division, no doubt. I daresay their opposition would be rather irrelevant if the rest follow Larsson's lead. There aren't many with combat experience in those formations."

He smiled again. "You certainly know the Fleet better than I expected."

"By necessity. It opposes the Foundation's goals." A sip of cognac, then, "Why not target Larsson with protests? If you control the protesters, surely you can keep them away from Geneva's core."

"Too risky. An unplanned incident could trigger a constitutional crisis if Larsson ends up injured or dies. Or protester blood runs in the streets. As you're surely aware, the riots have taken a toll on local police forces and counter-protesters both here and in the OutWorlds. Those troopers protecting him are deadly, and they will not hesitate to kill if Larsson's life is threatened, no matter what the SecGen or other high officials say. The man in charge, a Major Curtis Delgado, will probably refuse orders from anyone but his superiors on Caledonia should something happen to Larsson. If we can compare the Fleet to the proverbial loose cannon, then its Special Forces are that cannon's ammunition, short-fused and ready to go off at the slightest provocation."

Don't I know it, Steiger thought, *and thank the Almighty. Otherwise, I'd be dead.*

"However, we are keeping our options open, should opportunity knock." He drained his glass. "Enough talk of business. We can continue this conversation tomorrow and see how the Deep Space Foundation might help us, and how we can help the Foundation."

"You keep talking of we and us. Will you eventually tell me who that is?"

"In good time, my dear. Shall I show you the rest of the house?"

"Certainly."

— Sixteen —

"Any news from Earth?" Decker tossed his beret on Talyn's desk and dropped into a chair across from her.

"As a matter of fact, yes."

Before she could go any further, a balding petty officer stuck his head into the open office doorway.

"Pardon the interruption, Commodore, but there's a Marine lieutenant out here who says you summoned her."

Decker gave Talyn a suspicious glance.

"Send her in, PO."

The moment he heard a set of feet stomping to attention behind him, he turned around.

"Lieutenant Saga Decker reporting to the commodore as ordered."

Zack jumped up, beaming with fatherly pride. There she stood, his only child, tall, handsome, with his piercing blue eyes and her mother's short blond hair. She wore a silver-trimmed black uniform with a lieutenant's twin pips on the collar, and the Intelligence Branch compass rose insignia on her sky blue beret.

"At ease, Lieutenant, and say hello to your father before he dies of apoplexy."

Decker pulled his daughter into a bear hug.

"I've missed you, my little girl."

"I've missed you too, dad, but since we now draw our clothes from the same quartermaster stores, I'm not your little girl anymore."

"You'll always be that to me, even if you're almost as tall as I am." He released her. "Done with Intelligence School?"

"That, and a stint at Camp X, so I could learn first-hand how we develop HUMINT."

"We? As in?"

"The Corps posted me to the Political Analysis Directorate upstairs. The summons to Commodore Talyn's office came in shortly after I reported to my director less than an hour ago."

Decker chuckled.

"Will wonders never cease. The Corps finally handed out an assignment based on real world qualifications."

"Officers with a doctorate in political history are rather uncommon," Talyn said. "Besides, I made sure the Intelligence Branch career manager understood posting Saga to a regiment on the frontier as assistant S-2 would not be in the interests of the service."

"Gotta love good old nepotism. Give Hera a hug and thank her. Assistant S-2s in a unit on garrison duty fetch coffee for the S-2 and not much else."

The two women embraced, then Talyn gestured at the chairs.

"Thank you, Hera," the younger Decker said once they were seated. "From what I heard about regimental duty for a junior intelligence officer, I'd probably have either gone mad or faced a disciplinary hearing. And since I'm my father's daughter, the latter would be more likely. We've seen where that lands us Deckers. Next thing you know, I'd be roaming the galaxy, assassinating evildoers, and overthrowing planetary governments."

"I won't lie," Zack said, grinning at her, "those were some of the best times of my entire career, and if I hadn't screwed up by the numbers, they wouldn't have happened."

"No doubt. The Camp X instructors mentioned your enthusiasm for the blackest of black ops. But since I don't plan on learning to jump out of perfectly good shuttles from low orbit, I'll work on being the analytical brains of the family."

"Wise choice," Talyn said, smirking at her partner. "The experience is overrated anyhow, and don't let your father try convincing you otherwise. Colonel Burnside, her new boss, will make sure she contributes more to our operations than you can imagine, Zack."

Decker raised his hands in surrender.

"No arguments from me. Even though Saga is a commissioned Marine Corps officer, I'm still a father who'd rather not see his only child go through what he endured." He turned to her. "Where are you living?"

"In the junior officers' accommodations block on base. A nice little suite that'll do fine."

"Don't worry, Zack. I'll keep an ersatz motherly eye on Saga and make sure she doesn't fall into evil company at the mess. Besides," Talyn winked at him, "Saga merely needs to mention her dad is a Special Forces lieutenant colonel, and just like that, no one will bother her."

"Well, at least we can spend time together on the weekends I visit Sanctum. And maybe you'll visit me at the fort now and then. My apartment has a nice, private little guest suite, and there are a few troopers who wouldn't mind buying you a drink at the Pegasus. The guys who were with us when we rescued you took a keen interest in your career progression."

"Absolutely. I'd love it."

"I'll bring her up with me the next time we spend a weekend in the backcountry instead of Sanctum's sophistication."

Saga looked from her father to Hera Talyn and back.

"Why do I think you're acting like a married couple? Did you tie the knot and forget to tell me?"

Zack shook his head.

"No. But many of our friends wish we'd finally make it official, complete with a massive blowout at the Pegasus after the ceremony."

"The grand old man of the Pathfinder community marrying the Fleet's senior serving NILO?" Talyn laughed with delight. "It wouldn't just be a blowout, honey. You'd be rebuilding the Pegasus from the ground up afterward."

"That's what I told Kal when he brought it up the last time. Didn't faze him in the slightest."

"Well," Saga's lips twitched with mischief, "you two are somewhat legendary in certain circles. Going through Intelligence School, let alone Camp X, as the daughter of Lieutenant Colonel Zachary Thomas Decker was — how shall I put this — interesting."

"That, I do not doubt. Just remember you should take any tall tales about Hera and me with a few asteroid-sized lumps of salt."

Saga gave her father an amused smile.

"Actually, the stories I heard were exceedingly believable. Are you in Sanctum long?"

"I've been here since last night. Hera and I are seeing the CNI this morning, then it's back to Fort Arnhem."

"Shame. I'd have sprung for supper."

Zack and Hera exchanged glances.

"Call Josh and tell him you're staying another night because of Saga," the latter said. "He'll tell Kal. Besides, there's nothing terribly urgent waiting for you."

"Fair enough. I'll do it. But that means tonight we eat in the mess, in uniform. I want everyone to see me with my only child and understand messing with her will not end well. This HQ is full of backstabbers and other assorted shitbirds who wouldn't think twice about screwing over a mere lieutenant."

Saga gave Talyn a beseeching look.

"Could you please tell my father I'm a grown woman who can take care of herself."

"As it happens, Zack has a point. You've never worked in a large headquarters before, so you're unaware of what goes on behind the scenes. It's probably best if folks saw you dine with a commodore and an infamous Special Forces officer, one big and mean enough to rip the arms off assorted staff idiots."

Saga contemplated both in silence, then shook her head.

"I suppose I need to remind myself I'm still on the learning curve's steep upslope."

"So are we all. Your father and I merely have a few decades of experience in dealing with the inevitable lowlifes who infiltrate every part of our beloved Fleet."

"And on that note, I should return to Colonel Burnside's office. We can pick up this conversation over drinks. And they'll be on me."

Decker winked at his daughter. "Can't refuse an offer like that. See you at five in the main lounge."

Saga stood and came to attention.

"With your permission, Commodore?"

"Dismissed, Lieutenant."

When they were alone, Talyn gave Zack a wry smile.

"She's a chip off the old blockhead."

"Thank the Almighty!"

"Thank good genes. Saga will make her father proud in the coming years, even if she doesn't become a Pathfinder."

Decker shook his head, smiling. "I'm already proud enough to burst. Anything else is pure gravy."

"I can tell."

They looked at each other with affection for a few silent moments.

"What's the news from Earth."

"Miko Steiger, believe it or not, connected with Andreas Bauchan, the director-general of the *Sécurité Spéciale* during the SecGen's welcome reception in the Palace of the Stars. It appears Bauchan took a shine to her tall, strong, and mysterious good looks."

"Evidently, Bauchan is a man of taste." Decker gave his partner a teasing wink.

"Are you really putting yourself in the same league as the head of our opposition?"

"*De gustibus non est disputandum.* I can't help it if this Bauchan's roving eye shares commonalities with mine. Does that mean she can slip him twenty centimeters of cold, hard steel instead of a warm tongue while we pull a Kowalski on the rest of his organization?"

"That's the question of the moment. Grand Admiral Larsson forbade us from acting while he was away, but as Sun Tzu famously said, what is essential in war is victory, not prolonged operations. A company from Ghost Squadron on Earth can considerably shorten our campaign against the opposition. I'm sure Major Delgado will be game for a hard strike the moment Larsson is safely back aboard *Terra* and on his way to the hyperlimit."

"What about extracting the Erinyes, if that's what we're contemplating?"

"*Iolanthe* is on her way to Earth. Or she will be once she queries the nearest subspace array for fresh orders. I diverted her moments after reading Steiger's report."

"I'm still amazed you can order Special Operations Command units around at will."

Talyn gave him a sweet smile.

"If it weren't for me, SOCOM wouldn't know what to do with itself. You and your buddies are what we call ammo, fired by what we squids call guns. Now be a dear and work with me around this new development when we brief the CNI."

"You'll suggest we disregard Larsson's orders and move up the timetable."

"That's what I love about you, Big Boy. You catch on real fast."

"How the hell did she end up so close to this Bauchan clown anyhow?"

"Nerys Annear's office got her an invitation at our behest."

A light went on in Decker's eyes.

"Ah. Friends in high places for once. Picturing Miko in that august assembly of hot air generators and fart catchers boggles the mind."

"Only because you've never seen her sophisticated side."

"I didn't know she had one. Were you hoping she'd catch Bauchan's eye?"

"The thought crossed my mind. According to our dossier on him, she's his type, and as you might remember, our Miko can be a seductress when she wants to."

"So long as she charms Bauchan into her parlor rather than ending in one of the *Sécurité Spéciale*'s dungeons."

"Miko is a survivor, just like we were in the day."

"Except we could count on each other while she's operating solo."

"Her choice, but she has a backup on tap." Talyn glanced at the time. "We'd better head for the CNI's office."

"Is Admiral Ulrich joining us?"

"No. He's too busy with his new responsibilities. For all intents and purposes, the Special Operations Division is now mine. The formal handover should occur by month's end."

"In that case, congratulations."

— Seventeen —

"Extraordinary." Admiral Kruczek leaned forward and placed his forearms on the desktop once Talyn finished relaying both Delgado and Steiger's reports. "I can't believe one of our agents is literally in bed with the director-general of the *Sécurité Spéciale*. Surely, he has her watched twenty-four hours a day. How did your warrant officer send her report?"

"Embedded in an encrypted message for her nominal superiors at the Deep Space Foundation. Bauchan's people will see nothing more than a dutiful field operative reporting in. Once they break through the Deep Space Foundation's encryption layer, they'll see nothing more than a factual outline of her interactions with Bauchan so far and a hope the Foundation might be tapped by the SecGen's office to become a bigger player in the Centralist cause. They'll have no reason to look for deeper layers, and if they do find one and try to decrypt it, the data will self-destruct."

"What is the intended endgame with Bauchan? I understand Warrant Officer Steiger meeting him and striking up a friendship was purely accidental, but by now, you must be plotting something so we can exploit the situation."

"That's what we should discuss, sir. We know we need to take the *Sécurité Spéciale* off the board eventually, and Colonel Decker has outlined several courses of action."

Kruczek nodded.

"Kowalski's Purge updated for the twenty-sixth century. Do you plan on using your agent as an assassin and decapitate the opposition?"

"That is one option. Of course, since Colonel Decker didn't know about Warrant Officer Steiger's success with Bauchan, it doesn't figure in any of his courses of action, but as a trigger event, it fits with every one of them."

The admiral tapped his fingers on the polished wood.

"There is just one problem with assassinating Bauchan."

She nodded.

"Retaliation. I know, sir. That's why I'm not making any firm recommendations at this point. Even if Steiger makes an untraceable kill, Bauchan's people will suspect us right away. Of course, they enjoy neither the reach nor the ability to target you, sir. At least not without us noticing. And since few people know about the *Sécurité Spéciale*'s existence to begin with, the political fallout won't be anywhere near as alarming as the one that came from Grand Admiral Kowalski's wiping out the Special Security Bureau."

"Perhaps, but retaliation remains a concern, and tit for tat killings often go out of control. If that happens, we will find ourselves in the hot civil war we're trying to avoid." He shook his head. "We certainly can't do anything while the Grand Admiral is on Earth."

"But we can once *Terra* crosses the hyperlimit and jumps out. One of our courses of action involves leaving Erinye Company behind, totally black, with the mission to seize and destroy the *Sécurité Spéciale*'s headquarters. At the same time, other Special Forces units take care of the sectoral nodes. I diverted *Iolanthe* to Earth so she could support and recover them, should you approve. I would see *Terra* transfer the Erinyes to *Iolanthe* at Earth's heliopause, far from prying eyes. Considering the amount of starship traffic in the Home System, another innocuous freighter won't attract attention. And since she's carrying Ghost Squadron's Keres Company, Major Delgado will have another hundred or so operators at his disposal."

"I'm sure Colonel Decker wishes he could join them along with the rest of his command." Kruczek gave the Marine an amused look. "Right?"

"You know it, sir," the Marine replied. "But since we don't know when the political endgame will happen, chances are good I might arrive too late, and if we move up the purge timetable, I'll be plenty busy here. Colonel Ryent appointed me as the action officer for the operation. Besides, Curtis Delgado can handle both companies. He'll be commanding Ghost Squadron in a few years."

"I've also taken the liberty of ordering the deployment of the 1ˢᵗ Special Forces Regiment's other squadrons. They will cover the *Sécurité Spéciale*'s sectoral and sub-sectoral nodes, sir," Talyn said, "and head out as Q-ships and other transports become available. If the operation isn't approved, it'll be a valuable training exercise, but should we receive the go-ahead, we can carry out simultaneous strikes."

"Always five steps ahead of the rest of us, aren't you, Commodore?" Kruczek tapped his desktop a few more times. "Let me discuss this with General Politis before we go any further."

It was the answer Talyn expected. General Thanh Politis, the Commandant of the Commonwealth Marine Corps, was also the Armed Services' deputy supreme commander. With Larsson away, he held full powers over humanity's star-spanning military and naval forces.

"Yes, sir."

"In the meantime, run me through your courses of action, Colonel."

Once Decker fell silent almost twenty minutes later, Kruczek nodded.

"Every single one is eminently workable with no throw-away course of action. I can tell you never attended staff college. Which is just as well. Theorists rarely beat pragmatists who have actual field experience. Now, let's discuss Major Delgado's report. What's this about observation teams tracking Grand Admiral Larsson's movements between the Palace of the Stars and Turenne Base?"

"We suspect they're *Sécurité Spéciale*. Delgado's people tagged the car of the team they found and traced it back into Geneva, but not to one of the *Sécurité Spéciale*'s known offices. They're still looking for the second team. So far, the observers are merely tracking and scanning the convoy. Whether it's for nefarious purposes at a future date, we don't know. But since they saw no protests, let alone riots in that part of Europe, they'd be hard-pressed to take direct action and blame it on rioters. Bauchan is equally aware of the retaliation problem. He knows his organization is the first we'd come gunning for if something happens to the Grand Admiral. Delgado has people watching the known observation post every time the Grand Admiral moves. If the tangos show up armed with long-range weapons, his Marines will take them out."

Kruczek grimaced.

"Except we don't know that they would launch an assassination attempt from that observation post."

"True. As an added precaution, Major Delgado is transporting the Grand Admiral in one of the combat cars borrowed from the 1st Marine Regiment. He's ensured the cars in the escort look alike and that the one carrying the Grand Admiral is never in the same order of march two trips in a row. At this point, Delgado's done what he could. And that's it, sir."

"Thanks, Commodore. Nice seeing you again, Colonel."

Talyn and Decker stood and came to attention. "With your permission?"

"Dismissed."

Once back in the hallway, Decker said, "They won't go for it, will they?"

She shook her head.

"Doubtful. If the CNI hasn't wrapped his head around the idea of a purge yet, it's a given no other four-star, not even the one running SOCOM, is ready for such a step."

"How can you tell he hasn't?"

"I see him just about once a day, and I've learned his tells. When he's on board with a plan, he doesn't hesitate for a second. He hesitated just now. And we're talking about the most ruthless four-star in the Fleet."

"Shame. Will you order *Iolanthe* and Keres Company back on their original mission to New Tasman?"

"Not yet. It can wait a few more days while our betters decide. Since you're here until tomorrow, you can work through the planning details with my staff for the rest of today."

"Your staff." He chuckled. "Aren't you just the cutest flag officer?"

"Careful, Marine. We who wear stars take our dignity seriously."

"I suppose someone has to." He gave her a sideways leer.

That evening, Decker was a proud father once more as he and Talyn enjoyed drinks and then dined with Saga in full view of everyone in the officers' mess.

He particularly cherished the curious looks his daughter got when onlookers realized she was socializing with a Navy commodore and a Special Forces lieutenant colonel. Many eventually figured out the latter was a blood relative of the lieutenant, because of the obvious resemblance.

And since the three of them were ostensibly on the secret squirrel side of the Fleet — Talyn was well known around Fleet HQ as one of Naval Intelligence's power brokers — they studiously ignored the trio. And that was Zack Decker's desired outcome.

Shortly after arriving at Fort Arnhem the next morning and settling in for another day of administrivia while his three companies were light-years away, Major Bayliss stuck his head through the office door.

"And? Did the brass give us the go-ahead?"

Decker pointed at a chair.

"No. The CNI will discuss it with the Commandant. But Hera figures our enthusiasm for taking out the assholes behind the political unrest on the OutWorlds isn't quite contagious enough just yet. She did, however, divert Wash and the Keres to Earth. Or more accurately, she diverted *Iolanthe* in case the powers that be decide our idea of leaving Curtis behind for a strike on *Sécurité Spéciale* headquarters is righteous."

"It pays to be prepared."

"Listen to this, Josh — Miko picked up a new boyfriend in Geneva. A chap by the name Andreas Bauchan." He waited while Bayliss ran the name through his capacious organic memory banks. When Bayliss' eyes widened,

Decker grinned. "Yep, the top *Sécurité Spéciale* rat in person."

"Knife, jugular, some assembly required."

"If Hera, or more precisely the CNI, allows Miko to assassinate Bauchan, it'll be a bit more subtle than that." Decker then told his second in command about Delgado and the suspected *Sécurité Spéciale* observation teams.

"They wouldn't dare."

"Why not? This is the most vulnerable Larsson will be until his term as Grand Admiral ends. Move him out of the way, then force Admiral Bavadra down our throats, and there you are — no more Fleet interference in dirty politics and even dirtier business dealings."

"The HQ commandos in Sanctum will never accept Bavadra."

"Do you see them mutinying *en masse?*"

Bayliss let out a long exhalation and shook his head.

"Not really. They'll run circles around her, though, and that'll disrupt the Fleet's strategic planning capability, which will screw us up just as badly in the end. Curtis and his Erinyes are the best in the business. If they can't keep Larsson safe, it means the Almighty has other plans for us."

"In a few weeks, Larsson will be back in his fine office while Curtis and the Erinyes will strain at the leash for a new mission. Meanwhile, we'll still be slow-marching the plan to purge this galaxy of the damned *Sécurité Spéciale.*"

"Now who's being pessimistic, Zack? Look at how much we achieved in the short time since Ghost Squadron became intelligence's direct action dagger. Give your partner a little more time. She'll work this one through the HQ maze as well. Less than two years ago, sending our people to terminate revolutionary wannabes on sovereign Commonwealth worlds was a wet dream. Now? It's just another day at the office. And that's because of Hera."

Decker gave his old friend a tired smile.

"Trust you to talk me down again."

"Since you're listening nowadays, it's worth my while. Want another piece of advice? With the Erinyes on Earth, the Keres headed for New Tasman, and the Moirae breaking heads on Merseaux, why don't you go fishing up north? Or hunting. Or watching nature. Whatever makes you forget the hustle and bustle of drawing up plans that'll never be executed."

Decker narrowed his eyes.

"Any particular reason you want me out of the way?"

"Maybe I'm tired of watching you pace around like an imprisoned sand devil. In today's Special Forces, lieutenant colonels don't charge across the galaxy, blowing things up. Their majors and captains do it for them. That's reality. Since Hera won't let you relinquish your rank, find a way of dealing with life as it is."

"Are you conducting an intervention?"

"No. But I've been commiserating with Sergeant Major Paavola and Jory Virk. Trust me when I say this. All of us want to be out on a mission. But that's not how things work when you run the premier black ops squadron. We have too many missions and too few troopers. It'll ease when the 2nd and 3rd Regiments come online. Just be thankful division isn't taxing us for personnel to round them out. We're untouchable precisely because of our operational tempo."

Decker let out a disconsolate grunt. "I know."

"Adapt and overcome. When you move into Kal Ryent's office, you'll be taking another step away from the pointy end. The time when colonels led their regiments into battle on horseback ended well before the first humans left Earth."

"How about colonels who led their regiments from the crew commander's hatch of a main battle tank?"

"Still pre-diaspora. If you want to re-enact a mad, mounted charge, I can arrange one out in the training area when our companies are back home and ready for mischief. Probably not on horseback, but I can borrow armored cars from the 42nd. One of my old buddies is CO of the support battalion."

"Buddies outside the Pathfinder tribe? How did that happen?"

"He was a jumper back in the day but smartened up and returned to the legs. Took his commission years before I did."

Decker made a dismissive gesture.

"Never mind the heroic charge. I'll just keep fantasizing about one last squadron-sized mission before the Corps kicks me upstairs."

— Eighteen —

"Got 'em." Sergeant First Class Metellus Testo pumped his fist in the air. Aided by the drones and the command post AI, he'd been searching for the Team Alpha observation post over the past four days, looking closely for the electronic signature of the enhanced optical sensor used by Team Bravo. He tapped the secure communicator on his worktable. "Niner, this is Zero."

"Niner here," Delgado replied a few seconds later from the combat car carrying Grand Admiral Larsson and his aides.

"Found the other observation team." Testo rattled off a set of coordinates. "That corresponds to a government-owned communications tower on the southern outskirts of Geneva, just off *Chemin de Praleta*. I'm sending a drone for a closer look."

"Which pretty much confirms we're dealing with *Sécurité Spéciale*. You need more than just a winning personality and a smile to climb up one of those towers without raising a ruckus."

For the first time in days, Delgado felt his boredom pushed aside by a hint of action, no matter how small. An Erinye Company patrol had been watching the Team Bravo observation post every afternoon since the first time. And like clockwork, the same three operatives appeared, set up, watched the convoy come back from the Palace of the Stars, then returned to the city. It was as dull as working a desk job.

"Send a squad from the ready Troop to that tower. I want visuals of the watchers and a car on their tail."

"Roger."

"Niner, out."

Testo glanced at the duty roster and picked up his communicator.

"One-four-alpha, this is Zero."

"One-four-alpha."

"You are go. Target coordinates follow."

Within minutes, Lambrix, Corporal Taggart, and two lance corporals climbed aboard an unmarked, armed, and armored skimmer Delgado had borrowed from the Turenne Base military police contingent and sped off. They wore civilian clothes, their sidearms hidden beneath loose jackets. Taggart and one of the lance corporals also carried battlefield sensors in ordinary waist pouches, the sort used by people across the Commonwealth to carry minor items as they went about their daily business.

The communications tower, which could see right into Turenne Base, was visible through the skimmer's front window for the entire trip. Taggart and his comrade subjected it to intense scans while the other lance corporal ensured they reached it in record time.

As they pulled onto *Chemin de Praleta*, the Marines saw three figures, one carrying the same model of optical sensor used by the other observers, leave the tower via a ground level door.

"Gotcha." Taggart recorded the operatives and their car for later analysis.

"Let's see if we can tail them without being noticed," Lambrix said to the driver. "You took the tactical driving course last year, right?"

"Yep, and aced it, Sarge. Tell you what. If I blow our cover, the drinks are on me when we're home."

They slowed to let the observers' vehicle exit the communication tower's compound. It turned toward downtown Geneva, and for the next fifteen minutes, the Marines slipped through traffic, never losing sight of their prey, never coming closer, until it turned off a side street and vanished down an underground parking garage ramp.

Sergeant Testo, who'd been following the chase from the operations center, said, "The same place as the other team. If they're from the *Sécurité Spéciale*, then we've found a second location, separate from HQ at the other end of town. Come on home, one-four-alpha."

**

Andreas Bauchan ushered Miko Steiger through a garden gate and into a small, intimate park-like area where dozens of tastefully dressed men and women mingled, champagne glasses in hand. The garden, tucked away in a corner of a government complex that occupied a fair chunk of Geneva on the lake's eastern shore, was abuzz with conversation underscored by soft laughter. They took glasses from a tray proffered by a passing waiter and toasted each other silently.

"So, what is this?" She gestured at the party.

"The regular Friday afternoon cabinet get-together. We celebrate the end of the workweek in style around here. Come, I'll introduce you to a few people."

"Does that mean you occupy a cabinet-level position?"

"Something like that."

He led her toward a stout, sixty-something, dark-complexioned woman whose robust features were framed by short, curly black hair. Inquisitive brown eyes watched them as they approached.

"Angelique, may I present Britta Trulson of Cimmeria. She represents the Deep Space Foundation. Britta, this is Angelique Onofre, Commonwealth Secretary for Public Safety."

Steiger bowed her head formally.

"Honored, Madame Secretary."

Onofre returned the bow, although more casually, as befits someone of her station when greeting a social inferior.

"Welcome to Earth, Britta — we stay informal during our Friday fetes, by the way. What brings you here?"

"The Foundation's board of directors wants to expand our reach beyond the Rim Sector and its immediate neighbors. They sent me to take the pulse of things in the Commonwealth capital and see if I can find interlocutors with whom we can negotiate partnerships."

"And you found Andreas. Well done."

Steiger gave Bauchan a quick, yet warm smile. "It was he who found me at the Secretary-General's reception for Grand Admiral Larsson."

Upon hearing Larsson's name, a faint but unmistakable frown briefly creased Onofre's broad forehead.

"Andreas does zero in on opportunities with remarkable precision. Considering recent events in the OutWorlds and even more so the doings in the *Salle du Conseil* this week, I daresay an important, if still regional not-for-profit who shares this administration's aspirations could definitely find interlocutors."

"Things aren't going well with the Grand Admiral?" Steiger asked, putting on the air of an innocent abroad.

"The hearings started off on a reasonably even keel, but Larsson is showing an increasing lack of deference toward the Senate committee and the cabinet members in attendance. It's as if he imagines himself an equal to us, who govern the Commonwealth, instead of remembering he's a servant of the state."

Based on Onofre's tone, Steiger deduced that the honorable senators and cabinet members weren't treating

Larsson with the respect due to a man who commanded the most powerful naval and military forces in the known galaxy. One who no doubt considered himself, with reason, equal to the Commonwealth's most senior officials, save for the Secretary-General himself.

She wasn't terribly surprised. Bauchan and the other officials she'd met over the previous days suffered from an overweening sense of self-importance. No wonder they didn't like sovereign star systems, especially the outer ones, telling Earth to stop interfering with planetary governance.

"I understand Larsson can be difficult. His minions certainly are. Their illegal and unwarranted interference with Deep Space Foundation initiatives is rather infuriating. A shame the Secretary-General can't simply dismiss him and appoint an admiral who'll obey orders from Earth."

Onofre shrugged.

"A Grand Admiral who takes orders from the Defense Secretary would quickly lose control of the Fleet's senior commanders if said orders go against the current Fleet ethos."

"And an admiral who enjoys the respect of his or her peers would ignore orders from Earth that go against said ethos. A truly vexing standoff, one with no reasonable solution under the current conditions."

Onofre gave Bauchan a quick glance.

"Your friend has a remarkably good grasp of the situation, Andreas. We could do worse than enter into discussions with her Foundation. Not-for-profit allies who'll spread the right message can only help us counter the increasing trend toward political disunity."

"That's what I'm thinking."

For a few heartbeats, Steiger couldn't quite believe she'd not only surpassed her mission parameters but that Commodore Talyn subverting the Deep Space Foundation as cover for her agents was taking her well beyond its intended use. She thanked the Almighty for Talyn's philosophy of letting operatives take the initiative and develop new avenues of attack in the covert war. Otherwise, Naval Intelligence would have missed one of the best chances ever of infiltrating the enemy's central command node. As a wise sage once said, victory was a matter of opportunities clearly seen and swiftly seized.

**

"Top, take a look at the starboard display."

Hak, traveling in the combat car outfitted as a command post, turned to where the corporal was pointing and frowned. The convoy was within sight of Turenne Base, and a welcome supper after seeing Grand Admiral Larsson to his quarters.

"Where did those clowns in black come from?"

Young men — Hak saw no female faces among the forty or so individuals milling about on a small commercial plaza — stared at the military vehicles, many of them making obscene gestures.

"Remind you of something?" The corporal asked.

"Yep. Add helmets, so-called improvised weapons, face masks, and protest signs, and we found ourselves an OutWorld revolutionary posse. So much for the local authorities keeping their homegrown radical pukes away from Geneva."

"Technically, this isn't Geneva anymore, Top."

Hak grunted. "True."

He flicked to the operations frequency.

"Zero, this is Niner-Alpha, over."

Testo's voice came on within seconds.

"Zero here."

"Are your eyes in the sky on that bunch of youths loitering by the supermarket one klick from the main gate?"

"Just picked them up with the escort drones. They weren't there when callsign one-three," Testo said, referring to C Troop, "proved the route five minutes ago."

"This is Niner," Delgado's voice cut in. "I want continuous surveillance on that group until they disperse. They remind me too much of the tangos we often neutralize."

"Could the opposition be stepping up activity, intending to provoke a reaction?" Hak asked. "Headline on the news nets — Grand Admiral Larsson's escort injure and kill peaceful protesters demonstrating against military brutality in the OutWorlds."

"Typical play for the *Sécurité Spéciale*'s useful idiots."

"Aye. We need to fiddle with the timings tomorrow, sir, the Senate be damned."

"It's Saturday. They don't work around here on weekends, which means we enjoy a break as well."

"Monday, then."

"I'll raise the issue. Niner, out."

Delgado, who'd been wearing his combat helmet so he could talk to the convoy without disturbing Larsson, raised the visor and glanced over his shoulder.

"Sir, there's a development you should know about."

When Delgado finished relaying the latest news, Larsson sat back and shook his head.

"Why do they insist on doing this sort of thing?"

"Provocation, sir. Street theater designed to elicit a violent response and discredit anyone wearing an Armed Services uniform."

"Question is," Commodore Lee said, "why on a Friday, right before two days without us leaving Turenne Base?"

"Perhaps they're hoping we send patrols over the weekend to find and neutralize them, sir."

"Will you?" Larsson asked.

"No, sir. But come Monday morning, I strongly recommend we leave an hour earlier than usual, and through one of the secondary gates, with a reduced convoy. I'll send a few cars out via the main gate at the normal time."

Larsson let out an exasperated exhalation.

"That we must use deception schemes on Earth, within sight of the Commonwealth capital, is highly offensive."

"People inside the Commonwealth government are instigating this, sir. They're calling the tune for now, and prudence says we dance accordingly." Delgado allowed himself a cruel smile. "Or I could send hit teams into town over the weekend. We took video records of the faces. It wouldn't be hard to find a few of them and use corrective measures to warn the rest. They're mostly bullies who run at the first sign of a determined push back."

"I'd rather you didn't, Major."

"Understood, sir. It was more of a facetious proposal. I will, however, send a few of my troopers out on liberty, in civvies, looking as seedy as possible. They'll determine where those would-be revolutionary live-action role players are congregating while we enjoy time off under Turenne Base's defensive dome."

— Nineteen —

"Are you sure we can't bust heads, sir?" Command Sergeant Painter asked once Delgado finished discussing the weekend's reconnaissance mission. "A dose of prevention beats combat cars running those useless pussies down because they don't understand we're not like the local police. We won't stop to let them throw Molotov cocktails at our air intakes."

"When I made the proposal, Grand Admiral Larsson said, and I quote, I'd rather you didn't, Major. When a five-star speaks like that, Marines who enjoy their careers in the Corps take heed."

"Roger that, sir. But bar fights are still okay? I mean, shit happens when the booze flows and those pencil-necked assholes think they're for real."

"No comments, Sergeant."

A lazy grin split Painter's face.

"Message received loud and clear."

"We'll let the AI run overnight to match faces with names and particulars from the available data banks and reconvene tomorrow after breakfast for assignments. I wish I could buy everyone a beer after this week, but it'll wait."

"Lift the no booze order when we're back in *Terra* and past the Home System's heliopause, and we'll call it even, Skipper," First Sergeant Hak said.

"Done. Night posts, everyone, and thank you for another day of loyal service in our magnificent Corps."

"Oo-rah, sir!"

The next day, after a morning spent quartering the area around Turenne Base with drones, looking for suspicious activity, the Marines of A and B Troops left via side gates in groups of two or three — fire team buddies used to watching each other's backs. They looked unremarkable in civilian clothing, and since it was a bright day, no one could see watchful eyes behind sunglasses.

Anyone who noticed them leave the base wouldn't immediately think Special Forces, and those who crossed their paths in one of the suburb clusters dotting the landscape south of Geneva wouldn't think Marine Corps, period.

After a quiet and solitary lunch, Delgado settled into the operations center with Hak and Testo, eyes on the drone video feeds, ears alert for signals from the Marines' personal communicators. As reconnaissance missions went, this one wasn't much different from those they'd carried out on other worlds in recent months, looking for revolutionary wannabes, useful idiots, and the undercover operatives manipulating them to spread violence in the name of human unity under a benevolent Earth.

But not unexpectedly, the afternoon tourists saw no one of interest, and none of the faces picked up by Hak's command combat car and the escort drones the day before. They did, however, find several likely spots where rioters might assemble far from prying eyes, yet close enough to the base. Those included a few youth hostels near Greater Geneva Transit Authority stations, convenient for quick getaways.

Late afternoon saw the Marines back at the base where they briefed their C and D Troop comrades on the lay of the land. Once the sun dropped over the Jura Mountains, Delgado released the evening shift, which, with luck, would spot known faces in some of the many bars and entertainment joints clustered around commercial plazas served by the GGTA.

Useful idiots would likely enjoy a Saturday night on the town, carousing just like anyone else. He didn't warn the Marines about sticking to non-alcoholic drinks. There was no need. Every trooper understood they were on an operational footing, not out for rest and recreation, let alone the version preferred among Special Forces operators — intercourse and intoxication.

Staff Sergeant Lambrix and his fire team wingman, Corporal Taggart, were among the few who left Turenne Base via the main gate. They headed for the plaza where the black-clad young men with the usual United

Commonwealth Front affiliate telltales were loitering the previous day.

It was still early for the greasy fleshpots dotting Geneva's less pristine southern suburbs, so they wandered idly through the square kilometer of industrial buildings, offices, and commercial storefronts Testo assigned them. It didn't take long before they spotted a handful of known faces loitering in front of a youth hostel, murmuring among themselves and eying passers-by with suspicion, as if they expected trouble. Which, since they were practiced and paid UCF troublemakers, wasn't surprising.

Like the veteran stalkers they were, Lambrix and Taggart made sure to never walk along the same street twice. Eventually, they were back on the plaza where loud music now came from one of the nightspots whose doors were wide open to the cool evening air. Others were also stirring to life as roof signs flickered on, while the stores lining one side went dark.

Flashing lights came through the opening, diffuse twins to those on the facade advertising inexpensive fun within. The two Marines looked at each other with matching grimaces of dismay. While the syncopated sounds and wailing voices might appeal to a particular segment, mostly those under thirty, it wasn't the sort they and most of their comrades considered good music. Lambrix privately called the style primitive tribal crap.

"How about we just take a pew over there?" Taggart suggested, nodding at a bench near the entrance of the

GGTA station across the plaza from the nightclub. "My eardrums aren't ready to party yet."

"Roger that."

As the night deepened, more people appeared on the plaza's fringes, mostly in groups intent on whiling away the time, and no one gave the slightly seedy-looking men with hard eyes a second glance.

"There." Taggart nodded at four black-clad young men entering the square from the direction of the youth hostel. "Our friends are coming out to play."

Lambrix compared their faces to the ones he'd memorized and made at least one definite match.

"Yep. Let's see which dive they'll grace with their presence."

"I hope it's not the one spewing what makes me think of Shrehari electronic music."

"With our luck?" Lambrix shrugged. They watched the men out of the corners of their eyes as they crossed the plaza and entered through the larger nightclub's open doors. "Time to earn our danger pay, buddy."

"I wonder whether the skipper will accept a letter of resignation before we're back home."

"Not a chance." Lambrix climbed to his feet, imitated by Taggart.

"Figures."

The music hit them like a physical presence when they crossed the threshold while the pulsating lights burned their retinas, or so it seemed to Lambrix. After a few seconds, he saw a long bar on one side of a shimmering dance floor crowded with young people of every description. It was surrounded by tables and chairs and overlooked by an equally crowded mezzanine accessible via spiral staircases in each corner. Their targets were making themselves a space at the copper-topped slab, crowding others away.

Whenever someone made to protest, the meaner looking of the four gave him or her the typical menacing sneer perfected by bullies everywhere. But Lambrix knew he'd back away the moment someone told him to piss off. Their sort weren't fighters. If intimidation didn't work, they'd find victims elsewhere.

"We just need an excuse," Taggart muttered as they wound their way through the crowded space. "A few swings and wham, before anyone knows it, those scum suckers are sitting on their asses wondering what happened."

"Maybe this is a place where fights break out when folks are drinking."

The Marines didn't need to bully their way to a place at the bar. A simple excuse me, followed by a smile sufficed. Lambrix came across as imposing, even though he wasn't the biggest man in D Troop. He wasn't even the biggest in one-four-alpha. Taggart held that honor, and his presence behind the pleasant looking, bearded man with the emotionless eyes helped.

"Human bar attendants," Taggart whispered in Lambrix's ear. "Classy."

"Probably cheaper than a bunch of service droids the club's patrons damage every Saturday evening because they're cretins who can't do anything other than consume and destroy — you know, Earthers. Besides, trashing a human being costs a lot more than doing it to a machine once it involves the cops."

One of the bar attendants, a middle-aged woman with short hair, a hard, narrow face, and a bland expression came up to them.

"What'll it be?" She asked in accented Anglic, shouting over the music, her practiced eye having determined they weren't locals who'd speak French.

"Ethanol-free ale, if you have it."

She cocked an amused eyebrow at him.

"A slab of a man like you doesn't drink?"

"When you like it too much, you face a choice, right? Ethanol-free or pay for a liver transplant."

"And your friend?"

"We're both watching our intake."

She nodded skeptically.

"You know who else watches their intake? Cops."

"Which is a good thing. You don't want some armed idiot getting an alcohol buzz. He might decide it's time for target shooting and cap your ass."

The woman let out a bark of laughter.

"Okay, funny man. Two virgin beers." She pointed at a screen embedded in the countertop. "Tap your card there."

Lambrix, who was carrying an anonymous cred chip like every other Erinye, did as she asked, paying for the drinks. Once each held a foaming plastic mug, the sergeant toasted his winger.

"Another night of fun minus the fun juice."

Movement by the door caught his eye. A half dozen youths, with at least two known faces he could remember among them. They stopped, looked around, then headed for the earlier arrivals, who promptly nudged more people out of the way while wearing unpleasant sneers. A few moments later, Sergeant Sberna and his fire team buddy, Lance Corporal Torres, entered as well.

"Seen," Taggart said without prompting. "Could be we hit the node."

Lambrix's eyes met those of his second in command. In the space of a fraction of a second, they acknowledged each other and communicated their mutual understanding. They would operate independently unless the shit hit the fan.

Sberna and Torres found an abandoned table near the bar's far end and sat on the curved bench lining the painted concrete wall. The six they'd been trailing merged with the other four, driving even more of the regular partygoers away. And yet no one objected, be it patrons or the staff. Was it a desire to avoid trouble with obvious wannabe thugs, or were the agitators already well enough known to command respect? And if the latter, how long had they been stalking Turenne Base?

A young woman, long-haired, wearing fashionably minimalistic clothes, tried to make her way to the bar beside the thugs. The one Lambrix identified as the leader reached out and wrapped his right hand around her left arm, just above the elbow.

She protested and tried to shake off the hand, which only caused the black-clad thug to tighten his grip as a cruel smile twisted his thin, bloodless lips. The bar attendant hurried over, only to be met by menacing leers from several of the other so-called revolutionaries.

"If you'll pardon me." Taggart put his drink down and plowed through the crowd like a main battle tank on a combat run. He reached over a pair of goons and tapped the leader on the shoulder with fingers the size of sausages.

"How about you let the lady go?" Taggart's voice boomed over the loud music and frenzied conversations.

They turned toward him, astonished at the sudden appearance of a big, muscular, mean-looking man who not only showed no fear but was seemingly in the mood for a fight.

"You gonna get hurt, man," the closest of them said in a growl mean to frighten, but merely sounded ridiculous.

Taggart ignored him and tapped the leader on the shoulder again, this time with his entire hand.

"Let the lady go. I won't ask again."

When the man didn't immediately obey, Taggart grabbed his left ear and twisted, gently at first, then with greater strength until he released the woman. She quickly slipped away without ordering. Humiliation welled up in the man's eyes.

"You'll pay for this."

"Sure. Let's go outside and see who pays." Taggart nodded at the door.

A cruel smile replaced the earlier air of embarrassment.

"Your funeral, *arschloch*."

Taggart didn't need to check over his shoulder. He knew Lambrix was right behind him while Sberna and Torres were already on their feet, ready for action. Four Special Forces operators against ten skinny bullies in black, whose only ability was scaring ordinary citizens by acting like savages, wasn't even a close contest.

Once the first of them walked into Taggart's fist, the rest would look for the nearest escape route. This was a reconnaissance mission, sure. But the major said nothing about them not doing a little recce by fire.

He turned on his heels and headed for the door, Lambrix hard on his heels. The leader made a gesture, and, after downing their drinks, they followed suit, unaware of Sberna and Torres moving out.

—Twenty—

The plaza played host to half a dozen competing sound streams, the different musical styles erupting from nightclubs, and turning the atmosphere into a thick soup of dissonance. Victim of the assault, Lambrix understood why the good *burghers* of Geneva banished these sorts of establishments to the industrial and commercial peripheries, far enough from respectable suburbs, let alone the historical city center. It ensured the ears of the bourgeoisie didn't suffer.

Taggart stopped in the middle of the plaza and turned to face the thugs, who now wore masks over their lower faces. They were pulling objects from their pockets and pouches — lengths of chain, batons, knives — the standard UCF tools, as they tried forming a circle around their prey. But Taggart kept moving like a trained fighter, denying his opponents the chance to box him in, while distracting them, so they didn't notice three more large, hard-faced men approaching from behind.

Lambrix, Sberna, and Torres spread out in turn, each choosing a primary target from among the UCF goons. At Lambrix's signal, they closed the distance, placed a hand on their respective victim's shoulder, spun him around, and punched him in the face. The first three collapsed like sacks of soggy rice, dropping their improvised weapons. Before the rest realized they were being taken from behind, the Marines were already choosing three more and laid them out in a matter of seconds.

"Back." Lambrix barked out the order in his best parade ground voice.

He, Sberna, and Torres disengaged while Taggart circled the UCF cluster to join his mates. With six of their comrades out of action, the remaining four suddenly understood the odds were now one to one when they preferred ten or more to one.

They ran, leaving their comrades lying on the cold cobblestones.

"When the going gets tough, the UCF pussies haul ass," Torres said, voice dripping with contempt.

"Think the skipper will mind?"

Lambrix winked at his second in command.

"Recce by fire, Osmin, it's a time-honored tradition. Besides, this bit of calisthenics gives me an idea I'll run by him."

He walked over to the UCF leader, still flat on his back, and nudged him with a booted foot.

"Wakey, wakey, dipshit."

When the man's eyes fluttered open, Lambrix leaned over.

"Tell your friends the counter-revolutionary hunters' league is in town, and we have no bag limit." He straightened his back and let out a mocking laugh. "No bag limits on bagless wonders. This much fun has to be illegal around here."

"Only if you get caught, and I see no cops looking for action," Sberna replied.

"Because they're not interested in busting UCF heads. Or were told to back off if things got a little out of hand. The local, meaning Earth, authorities brought these lovely lads here so they could rattle the big man's cage. Won't happen. Let's go home."

After meandering through avenues and side streets, looking for tails, the four Marines re-entered Turenne Base via one of the lesser-known gates and reported to the Erinye Company operations center. There, they found Delgado playing cards with Hak, Testo, and Bazhukov.

"One-four-alpha reporting in, sir, or at least half of it." Lambrix gave his superiors a quick summary of their evening and the ease with which they neutralized the wannabe thugs.

"Does anything strike you as unusual, Sergeant?" Delgado asked once Lambrix fell silent.

"It was too easy, sir. They had no situational awareness and no clue about threat assessment. They didn't peg Leroy Taggart as a deadly opponent, nor did they sense us coming up behind them. Sure, if Leroy had been alone, he'd have taken a few hits before sending the survivors running. But then, if Leroy were alone, he'd have used another tactic than just lead them out in the open where the rest of us could strike. Tell you what, sir, the ones we took out in the Rim Sector were a lot tougher. This bunch? They're playing tough guys. But I saw no follow-through."

The major nodded.

"Yep. One-four-bravo came in ten minutes before you and reported much the same. A face-off with youths who acted like typical UCF players. They ran when fists started flying a kilometer or so northeast of your position, near the next GGTA station."

"Methinks the opposition wants an incident involving the Grand Admiral, not tear Geneva's suburbs apart, sir," Sergeant Testo said. "Harmless youth exercising their right to protest against rampant militarism murdered by evil Marines. The budget negotiations must not be going well for the government."

"My thoughts exactly. The UCF affiliates out in the Rim aim at destabilizing local and planetary governments, something that won't be tolerated here, not if the *Sécurité Spéciale* is the UCF's trained backbone. Counter-revolutionary hunters' league, eh?" Delgado gave Lambrix a quick grin. "Why not? I'll discuss it with Sergeant Saxer tomorrow and see if putting D Troop out on the streets Monday morning as anti-UCF protesters will collapse this farce."

"Will you discuss it with Commodore Lee or the Grand Admiral?" Hak asked once Lambrix and his Marines left the operations center.

"No. This comes under the heading of night and fog."

"Roger that, Skipper. So long as no one gets seriously hurt."

"That's the difference between the opposition and us. We know precisely how much force is needed to stop a problem, as D Troop proved tonight. There'll be a few sore heads and bleeding noses, but that's it. They know how to *be* the problem."

"Problems with bruised egos, I hope."

**

Precise as the legendary Swiss watches of a bygone era, Bauchan's chief of staff stuck his head through the former's open office door precisely fifteen minutes after Bauchan settled in to read the overnighters. He and the *Sécurité Spéciale*'s top leadership occupied offices in the Palace of the Stars, like any other upper echelon Commonwealth government functionaries.

After all, the *Sécurité Spéciale* didn't really exist. Bauchan and his people were merely the SecGen's security and intelligence advisers. Those handling the agency's day-to-day work occupied an ordinary office complex just north of town, which seemed innocuous to the untrained eye. It was, however, the most heavily protected compound other than Turenne Base in the entire capital district.

"Good morning, sir."

"And a good morning to you too, Edouard. Come in." Bauchan nodded at the chair facing his desk. "What's this about a counter-revolutionary hunters' league knocking UCF heads over the weekend?"

"No idea, sir. Came right out of the blue. We received a few separate reports from our people in the southern suburbs describing brief, fierce fistfights outside nightclubs that sent the UCF protesters assembling near Turenne Base back to their hostels at hyperspeed."

Bauchan tapped an extended index finger on his chin, eyes looking up at the high ceiling.

"Could the Marines of Larsson's escort be playing silly buggers?"

"A distinct possibility, sir. But we can't tell with the public surveillance sensors offline in the area." Edouard Metivier didn't add, 'at our request' since Bauchan was the one who'd implemented the policy of asking local law enforcement to ignore UCF activities. "Still, our foot soldiers will protest outside Turenne Base as planned this morning."

"A protest for the news nets, no more, I fear. Not if these so-called counter-revolutionary hunters are Special Forces operators. The Grand Admiral's convoy will take a wholly different exit from the one we've seen him use over the last week. Perhaps even different vehicles. The man in charge of his security—"

"Major Curtis Delgado, 1st Special Forces Regiment," Edouard helpfully offered.

"This Major Delgado seems adaptable. But then, they'd hardly appoint anyone other than the best as Larsson's minder."

Before Edouard could reply, his communicator buzzed. He glanced at Bauchan, who made a go-ahead gesture.

"Metivier."

"Geneva Operations Room, sir, you asked we keep you informed of developments around the spontaneous anti-militarism protest outside Turenne Base."

"Yes."

"As the protesters were assembling, an opposing group of between twenty and thirty started a running street fight that dispersed them. They didn't reach Turenne Base, nor did they block traffic on the avenue outside its perimeter."

Bauchan and Metivier exchanged knowing looks.

"Thank you. What about the Grand Admiral's convoy?"

"It left via the front gate a few minutes ago and is headed for downtown Geneva unimpeded."

"Thank you. Metivier, out."

"Give this Delgado props. He was a step or two ahead of us. There won't be a lurid video of Marines clearing away protesters on his watch. Not if he can deploy his counter so fast and effectively."

"Shall we try again, sir?"

Bauchan thought for a moment, then shook his head.

"There's no point. Our tame UCF boys won't face trained street fighters again, at least not without stiffening, and we don't want the sort of riots we've been inflicting on other places. It might turn the narrative against our aims."

"Agreed, though it leaves us with few options, other than direct action, and we can't risk something that might make the captain of Larsson's space control ship in orbit decide Earth is in a state of insurrection."

Bauchan let out a soft snort.

"I'd be more worried about Delgado and his company of trained killers. They wouldn't take an assassination attempt kindly, and Fleet Special Forces aren't known for respecting a minor annoyance such as the law when dealing with what they consider threats to the Commonwealth. Who do you think has been slaughtering our UCF affiliates, *Sécurité Spéciale* stiffeners included, out there? Oh, we found no evidence so far, but Naval Intelligence isn't shy about dropping hints in the hopes we'll stop. Tell you what, I'll wager this Delgado is an old hand at disrupting, if not destroying our foot soldiers."

"Then what do we aim for, sir?"

"At this point, Brüggemann won't thank me for causing more than a ripple of disturbance. If we can come up with another way of discrediting Larsson before the budget hearings end, good. Otherwise, we must admit the enemy outplayed us this time around."

"Outplayed us how?" A husky, feminine voice asked from the open door.

"Britta." Bauchan stood. "Please come in. Edouard and I were just discussing our latest setback in the campaign to make Grand Admiral Larsson come across as a militarist fool."

Metivier gave his boss a sharp look, which the latter ignored. Bauchan had a type, and Britta Trulson was it, down to the last detail, hatred for those promoting the concept of sovereign star systems included. That she enjoyed free access to Bauchan's office didn't sit well with the agency's chief of staff. But he was familiar with his superior's appetites. Once Trulson left Earth and returned home, Bauchan would turn his attentions elsewhere and forget her. It wasn't as if he spoke out of turn. Otherwise, his tenure as chief of the SecGen's private security and intelligence service would have ended long ago.

"Larsson is no one's fool, my dear." Steiger took the other chair facing Bauchan's desk. "But he's not reckless either, nor is he a militarist in the strictest sense of the word. That doesn't make him any less dangerous for those of us who prefer a closer union of human star systems. If your intention is discrediting him at the very heart of the Commonwealth, then I would advise against doing so."

"Oh?" Metivier gave her a look that mixed skepticism with a touch of condescension.

"One of the many things that will come from a closer partnership between the Commonwealth government and the Deep Space Foundation is a better understanding of the socio-political atmosphere in the outer star systems. Most people in this fair city don't understand that OutWorld citizens and colonists have a vastly different outlook on almost everything. Political maneuvers and propaganda that might work in the older, core star systems will produce diametrically opposed results, the sort that will accrue to the Fleet's advantage, not ours. Trying to discredit Grand Admiral Larsson will inevitably backfire beyond Earth and the Commonwealth's core and make things worse for those who believe in greater unity."

When she saw the skepticism on Metivier's face, Steiger chuckled.

"I'm surprised at how provincial you folks here in Geneva can be. You automatically assume everyone in our little chunk of the galaxy thinks as you do, has the same likes and dislikes, and sees the Commonwealth's future in the same light. Nothing could be further from the truth. If it weren't for the existence of non-human, spacefaring species who can threaten our worlds, the Commonwealth would be split into dozens of independent star systems or star system clusters by now."

"She has a point, Edouard. While I was willing to see if Larsson's escort might make a serious misstep when confronted by UCF activists, I'm not prepared to go any further. Let's call it a learning experience and a reminder our opposition is more cunning than we think. Call off the dogs and send them home."

— Twenty-One —

"Ran like rabbits, they did." Sergeant Lambrix chuckled as he climbed out of the unmarked skimmer that brought him and his troopers back to Turenne Base after they dispersed the rather weak-kneed rioters.

"Nicely done. We saw every moment from the drones," Hak replied. "Niner has a new job for D Troop, so off to the operations center with you. Faruq's already there."

"Isn't the skipper riding Larsson's call sign?"

"He is. Metellus will give the briefing."

"Anything that saves us from babysitting a bunch of star-spangled brass hats should be good."

"This one is. Word came from home while you were hunting black-clad cretins."

Lambrix was the last of D Troop's three section leaders to arrive. Command Sergeant Faruq Saxer, leaning against Testo's worktable, pointed at an empty chair.

"Now that everyone's here, good show this morning, folks. A lot of noise, a little blood, and plenty of fear, just the way we like it. Whatever the opposition intended with those UCF wannabes, it failed spectacularly. With the rest of the company in Geneva already and the skipper not wanting to sit on the mission, we avoid playing bodyguards for another day." He glanced at Testo. "The floor's yours."

"We received orders from home via subspace while you were disrupting dumbasses."

An aerial view appeared on the primary display.

"This is the northern part of Geneva." He pointed at the image. "That's *Lac Léman*, and that's the Palace of the Stars."

He touched his controls, and the image shifted away from both lake and city in a northerly direction. Then, it zoomed in on a group of buildings nestled at the heart of a park-like setting, just outside a small agglomeration labeled Cessy.

"This is the *Sécurité Spéciale*'s headquarters. SOCOM, or more likely, our favorite Naval Intelligence commodore, designated it Objective Smiley. The top leadership usually works out of the Palace of the Stars, so we can assume it's an operational HQ rather than an administrative one. Our job is doing a thorough recce of the place as if we were planning a strike like the one on Mission Colony a few weeks ago. Go in, seize the computer core, destroy what we can and extract."

Saxer grunted. "I guess the commodore wants to stop pussyfooting around with those bastards."

"Probably. We know they're behind the UCF crap. But this recce mission doesn't mean a strike is on. Call it using our presence here to prepare for various contingencies and not speculate any further. Now, this is probably the most closely guarded site in the area. Perhaps even on the planet, so waltzing in disguised as cleaners won't work, nor will drone overflights, which means observation posts and drive-by scans, that sort of thing. Our essential elements of information are as follows. How many work there? What security protocols are in place? Is it defended by a sensor network and automated weapon stations? Does it operate twenty-four seven, and if so, are there reduced staffing times? Others, meaning Naval Intelligence operatives, will look for more about the interior. How, I couldn't say. But Warrant Officer Steiger is inside enemy lines, posing as a sympathizer."

"And living the high life, no doubt."

"Since she's pals with the *Sécurité Spéciale* boss, that's a given."

Lambrix let out a low whistle.

"Well done, Miko. She can inflict more damage on the *Sécurité Spéciale* with a stiletto than Erinye Company in full battle armor supported by a wing of dropships."

"If the goal is taking out the top leadership, sure. But I'm thinking Naval Intelligence wants information on the agency's operations so we can end them for good across the Commonwealth in one fell swoop. Which means going in to rip out the computer core."

A nod. "Seen."

"Don't worry about a possible strike. I doubt we'll be involved since we didn't come here with our own tactical transport. I'll now entertain questions. After that, you're free to draw up recce plans for the skipper's approval once he's back from downtown. And yes, that means he expects a full briefing after supper tonight, with operations beginning tomorrow, because our time on Earth is running out."

**

Once the convoy was moving, headed back to Turenne Base, Larsson reached out and tapped Delgado on the shoulder.

"Major."

"Sir." He turned the crew commander's seat around to face the aft personnel compartment.

"I understand there was a bit of trouble near the base this morning, shortly before we left."

"The local branch of the United Commonwealth Front intent on mischief, I believe, sir. Apparently, counter-protesters showed up and disrupted whatever the UCF boys were planning."

Larsson gave him a suspicious look.

"You wouldn't be involved with that, now would you?"

Larsson's eyes searched Delgado's for an answer. The Grand Admiral must have seen one because he sat back.

"Never mind, Major. So long as no one was hurt."

"Other than a few egos, you mean, sir?"

Delgado turned back to his console.

"Those can be the most painful bruises, apt to leave lasting grudges in their wake."

"Yes, sir. But they can be educational as well. Learning you shouldn't stick your hand into a fire the hard way not only hurts but is something no one ever forgets."

Larsson let out a dry chuckle.

"I can see I'm in the presence of a Special Forces philosopher. Well done, Major. Let's leave the counter-hooliganism to the local police from now on, shall we?"

"Understood, sir. There shouldn't be any more incidents. Last Friday's show on the plaza, along with this morning's events, was a probe to see how we would react. They now realize there won't be any Marines in combat cars running over so-called peaceful protesters."

"And those Marines aren't above a little undercover disruption as well."

"We do a lot of our best work that way, sir. It saves lives in the long run."

A soft snort.

"Based on what Commodore Talyn reports, I believe you, Major."

Delgado couldn't figure out how he should answer and chose to stay silent, busying himself with the convoy's dispositions as it raced through downtown Geneva on its way south. What the locals thought of the twice-daily military procession, he had no idea and didn't much care. The sooner this was over, the better.

**

"Impregnable?" Sergeant First Class Lambrix studied the *Sécurité Spéciale* HQ, built atop the former Large Hadron Collider's Point Five, using powerful optical sensors. He and Sergeant Sberna sat in an observation post at the top of Mont Mourex. "Or a walk in the park?"

Sberna, whose eyes were glued to a second unit, let out a grunt.

"The outside perimeter? Probably not a big deal. You don't want to make it in your face obvious an agency that doesn't exist operates behind those walls. But that thing sits on a section of what used to be an underground particle physics research facility before the diaspora, remember? If they repurposed it as a secure facility, the computer core, along with the most sensitive sections, will be underground."

"Yeah. A walk in the park, this won't be for whoever they tap."

"On the other hand, no one will expect a commando strike on Earth, so there's one advantage." Sberna fell silent for a few minutes, then let out a sad grunt as he glanced away from the optics to give his eyes a rest. "Join the black ops mob, they said. You'll see nonstop action, they said. Seems to me like the only thing we've been doing for weeks is babysitting the brass and running observation posts. I'm thinking I should see what's happening in the private sector these days."

"Grass ain't any greener on the other side, buddy. Most merc outfits do nothing more than rent-a-cop jobs. And those who find excitement often end up on the wrong end of our guns, like the buffoons stiffening those idiotic revolutionaries. But hey, could be we'll get lucky and be the ones walking through that park. We brought our combat gear."

"Won't happen. No way anyone punches through the defenses without using massive firepower, which we *didn't* bring." Sberna held out his hand. "Twenty creds say this observation op isn't leading anywhere either."

"Done and done." Lambrix shook his second in command's hand, then turned his eyes back on Point Five. "Truth be told, I probably won't mind if you win."

**

"There's no two ways about it, Skipper." Sergeant First Class Testo lit up the primary display with results culled from the first three days of observation. "We won't enter on the surface by tiptoeing through the defensive perimeter. Any breach will be noisy, visible, and messy."

Testo gestured at the display.

"Red dots indicate known remote weapon stations; blue dots, known sensors; green, suspected RWS and purple, suspected sensors. One entry point heavily guarded with a chicane to slow attackers. Perimeter berm can't be climbed. Attackers must either breach or jump, and that's where the RWS come in. Whoever set up the security there knew what they were doing. Which leaves entering through the old Large Hadron Collider tunnel, and that, in turn, means finding a vulnerable spot at another surface point. There are a fair number scattered around the perimeter."

The image of Point Five vanished, replaced by a schematic.

"This is the site before the particle physics research ended. I couldn't dig up anything more recent, but I put in an ask with Commodore Talyn's office. Hopefully, they'll find something. Still, there are eight main points, a few of them with several surface access possibilities. The problem is, we don't know what's underneath. The surface buildings look innocuous enough. Maybe Miko can find out for us."

"Which will take time since we can't speak with her directly." Delgado shrugged. "I'll prepare a message for the commodore once we're done here. In the meantime, let's put observation teams on each of those sites in the morning and develop a situational picture. It might prove useful later."

"Roger that, Skipper."

**

"Nothing doing," Testo reported the next evening when Delgado returned from Geneva. "The other sites are heavily protected, just like Point Five. Whatever they're up to below ground, it isn't particle physics research. You can bet your firstborn's immortal soul on that. Breaching any of the sites will be noisy. Then there's the matter of what a theoretical raider would find at the bottom of an access shaft."

He called up images of one point after another and described the critical features picked up by C and D Troop's reconnaissance patrols.

"Okay. So be it." Delgado tapped the tabletop with both hands once Testo finished speaking. "Wrap everything up in a neat package and send it home. Stand down the patrols and observation posts. The Grand Admiral is done. We leave the day after tomorrow, meaning tomorrow we escort him and the delegation through the planned celebratory events, including a formal dinner at the Palace of the Stars. Then we pack, load, see him through a farewell parade, and bugger off."

"Not before time. Though it's a shame we won't finish the job of finding out what's hiding under Geneva's outskirts."

"Miko will eventually come through, but by then, it'll be someone else's problem."

— Twenty-Two —

As the last of the ruffles and flourishes faded away, Grand Admiral Larsson lowered his hand and stepped off the dais. The Marines of the 1st Regiment held the 'present arms' position as he headed for his shuttle, flanked by Major Delgado and First Sergeant Hak, along with Erinye Company's Alpha and Bravo Troops. Commodore Lee, Lieutenant Colonel Hisk, and the rest of the delegation followed behind them.

Once Larsson set foot on the aft ramp of the shuttle bearing the Grand Admiral's flag, a blue rectangle with five stars arranged in a circle, the parade commander gave the shoulder-arms. Above Turenne Base, a squadron from the flagship circled lazily, waiting to escort the supreme commander's party.

Delgado felt a small measure of relief when the ramp closed, cutting them off from Earth's enervating atmosphere. He made his way to the flight deck and, after silently asking the pilot if he could take one of the jump seats, he strapped in, eyes on the Jura Mountains filling most of the front window.

"Fun and games, Major?" The pilot, a Navy petty officer, asked.

"Games aplenty. Fun, not so much. We kick ass for a living, and there's not much around here we're allowed to cut loose on."

"I hear you, sir."

The sound of thrusters spooling up reached Delgado's ears, and he settled back to prepare for takeoff. As far as he was concerned, if Erinye Company never saw Earth again, that would suit him and his troopers fine. Scientists could speak of atavistic memories and longings for the world that birthed humanity, but Delgado felt no affection for the place. He was an OutWorlder, born in a star system where humans breathed freely and shaped their own destinies instead of owing their existence to a benevolent government.

The shuttle lifted smoothly and rose into the early afternoon air, accompanied by its four consorts, carrying the delegation and the rest of Erinye Company. At five thousand meters, the flagship's combat squadron closed in on the VIP flight, alert to any threats. Soon, they entered a cloud layer, and Geneva vanished from sight.

After an uneventful trip, the shuttles landed one by one on *Terra*'s cavernous hangar deck, and when the space doors were closed, a side party marched through the main airlock, followed by the ship's captain and his coxswain. They halted at the foot of Larsson's shuttle, and as soon as the ramp dropped, the ship's bosun and five of her mates raised their calls to their lips. The captain ordered the side party to present arms and raised his right hand in salute. Larsson returned the compliment as he strode down the ramp with what seemed like renewed energy.

"Welcome back, sir."

"Glad to *be* back. You may break out of orbit as soon as Traffic Control grants us clearance."

"Yes, sir."

For form's sake, if nothing else, a pair of Marines from Charlie Troop escorted Larsson back to his quarters while the rest of the Erinyes headed for the ship's Marine barracks and a well-earned rest.

"Glad that's over," Hak muttered as they left the hangar deck. "Never were so many this bored by such a high-profile mission."

Delgado chuckled.

"A successful close protection job should be boring, Top. The aim is deterring assassins, not setting up killer ambushes for shits and giggles, which means adrenaline junkies such as us don't fit the personality profile. But no fears. I'm sure we'll be bashing heads and taking names soon enough."

"Preferably without the need to bring dress and mess uniforms. There's nothing worse than dressing for an evening of fine dining and watching everyone else enjoy the meal while we're drinking water and sneaking in the odd stale sandwich."

"I'll suggest the colonel hold a regimental mess dinner the next time most of us are home."

Hak scoffed.

"Those don't qualify as fine dining, sir. Rubber chicken, followed by stupid drunken games, might be fun for the youngsters. At my age, I prefer more refined entertainment, especially if I'm wearing my most expensive, least comfortable clothes. Plus, we can't head into town from Fort Arnhem wearing full fig afterward and enjoy the rest of the evening in the finest bars. Carrick doesn't have fine bars; it has rustic pubs and assorted dives."

"That's the price of serving in the most elite military unit ever fielded by humanity. If you'd rather transfer to a line regiment stationed near a major city with the nicest bars and restaurants imaginable, let me know."

Delgado winked at his first sergeant, then opened the door to his cabin along with the front closure of his dress uniform tunic.

"Don't forget you've allowed everyone two drinks now that we're back aboard."

"Nice try, Top. I said once we pass the heliopause."

"How about we meet in the middle, Skipper — when this tub goes FTL at the hyperlimit?"

"Since I won't hear the end of this unless I agree, let's raise a drink together after we jump."

"That's why you're our revered leader, sir. Always ready to see reason when his first sergeant helpfully points out the errors of his company commander's ways."

Hak's cabin door closed behind him before Delgado could reply. He merely allowed himself a smile as he stripped off his formal uniform and carefully packed it away. Slipping back into battledress, this time without a sidearm on his hip, felt good. Mission accomplished, and without either causing or suffering casualties.

Now, the only thing that remained was writing up the full report for Colonel Decker and Commodore Talyn's eyes. Then it would be nothing more than a nice cruise with little by way of responsibilities beyond ensuring the Erinyes didn't go soft from lack of daily physical training. Not that Special Forces operators let themselves go. Most suffered from a distinct aversion to inactivity, and two or three hours a day in a starship's gym helped keep idleness-caused unease at bay.

No sooner did he settle on his bunk with a tablet to draft the report that his communicator chimed.

"Delgado."

"Signals, sir. We received an encrypted message from SOCOM which concerns you. We're to meet with the Q-ship *Iolanthe* at the heliopause and transfer you over. SOCOM didn't say why."

"Thanks."

"That was it, sir. Signals, out."

Delgado dropped his tablet, joined his hands behind his head, and sat back. A new mission already? The operational tempo was really going into overdrive. But no one would complain. He dialed up the first sergeant, the troop leaders, and his HQ noncoms on the company net.

"Folks, we're not sailing home in *Terra*, so don't get too comfortable. She's meeting our new ride, *Iolanthe*, at the heliopause. Where we go from there is anyone's guess. *Iolanthe* will have our orders, and as usual, they'll be the sort we can't discuss with the regular Navy. Figure on shifting ship in twelve to fifteen hours from now, depending on how skilled both navigators are."

"If it's the same one as before in *Iolanthe*, she can drop her out of hyperspace within a few meters of the intended coordinates," Command Sergeant Painter said.

Faruq Saxer let out a bark of laughter.

"Still sweet on her, Rolf?"

"You know how much astrogation turns me on, buddy."

"Okay, folks. We share a drink in the Marine mess right after *Terra* goes FTL, then it's off to our quarters and a snooze so that we're bright-eyed and ready to shift ship in the morning."

Delgado called Commodore Lee next and told her of their impending departure on a new mission.

"SOCOM never sleeps. I understand that, and so does the Grand Admiral. He'll want a few words with you before Erinye Company leaves. It can either be tonight or just before your departure."

"How about tomorrow, sir? I promised my folks a libation later, and I can't well duck out on them."

"Done. I'll set time aside when we emerge at the heliopause."

**

"Ah, Major."

Larsson looked up from his desk. He wore the same shipboard uniform as *Terra*'s crew, no doubt equally thrilled to hang up his formal tunic for a while.

"Please come in and sit."

Delgado stopped at the regulation three paces, saluted, and after Larsson returned the compliment, he stood at ease before taking one of the chairs.

"As your commanding officer, albeit temporarily for a few weeks, it behooves me to comment on your performance, even if it is only via a letter for your actual CO."

The Marine nodded once.

"Yes, sir."

"Since you're leaving us prematurely, I wanted to tell you what this letter will say, so there are no surprises. I find you an intelligent, capable, and highly adaptable officer who, moreover, knows precisely how much and what he should share with his commanding officer, a rare talent, in my experience. Most officers either speak too little or too much. I shall recommend the Commandant of the Marine Corps make your acting appointment substantive. Since the link between rank and position in Special Forces units isn't as rigid as elsewhere in the Armed Services, I'm sure you'll stay in command of Erinye Company as a major until your superiors need you elsewhere."

Delgado bowed his head. "Thank you, sir."

"There is no need for thanks. You're a credit to your regiment and the Corps. I wish more officers possessed your mixture of daring and judgment. Sadly, I know too many colonels, captains, admirals, and generals who can't achieve the right balance. I suppose those are the failings of a largely peacetime military force. And those who do aren't on the fast career track." Larsson exhaled. "In any case, please pass my personal thanks along to Erinye Company. I did not, at any moment during our trip, feel exposed."

"Will do, sir."

Larsson stood, imitated by Delgado. The former stuck out his hand.

"I hope you'll meet with success after success, Major, and perhaps one day you'll wear stars on your collar as one of the Special Forces community's leading lights."

They shook.

"Thank you, sir."

"Dismissed."

Delgado saluted again, then turned on his heels and left Grand Admiral Larsson's day cabin. An hour later, wearing combat armor with tactical harness and weapons, and carrying his belongings in a pair of duffel bags, he entered the hangar where Erinye Company was forming up by troops, ready for departure.

He walked to where the rest of his company HQ waited and dropped his bags on the deck, watching while the troop leaders, closely monitored by First Sergeant Hak, organized their Marines for loading. Shifting from one starship to another was routine, but Hak didn't like cutting corners.

Especially not when they would do so aboard the flagship's shuttles.

Delgado spotted movement at the main airlock and stiffened as he saw Commodore Lee, wearing her gold braid aide-de-camp aiguillettes, come through. Grand Admiral Fredrik Larsson followed on her heels.

"Erinye Company, atten-SHUN."

The words erupted from Delgado's throat as if by reflex. All movement ceased instantly. He raised his hand in salute.

"Sir."

"At ease, everyone." Larsson's surprisingly powerful voice reached every corner of the hangar deck. "I wanted to see you off in person. Considering our closeness over the last few weeks, it's the least I can do for those who were ready to step between me and incoming fire. I will personally convey my appreciation for your professionalism to the Commandant, the Commander SOCOM, and your regimental CO. You did the Marine Corps proud on Earth, whether in or out of uniform."

He paused to let the last sentence sink in and was rewarded with a few amused smiles.

"Although I'm your supreme commander, I don't know what new mission awaits you, but I do know you'll score another resounding success, and that's why I won't wish you good luck, but good hunting."

Delgado stepped forward and shouted, "Erinye Company!"

"OO-Rah!"

— Twenty-Three —

The Q-ship *Iolanthe*, second of that name and smaller than her illustrious Shrehari War era forebear, hung a few kilometers off *Terra*'s starboard side. The transfer, from Fleet flagship to unmarked Special Operations unit, was a short hop aboard the former's shuttles. Within a few minutes of leaving *Terra*, they nosed through the force field keeping *Iolanthe*'s hangar deck pressurized while the space doors were open.

Erinye Company's Marines tromped down open aft ramps and formed up in three ranks by the main airlock while the shuttles lifted off and left the hangar. Once the space doors were closed, the airlock opened, letting a lanky man with a familiar face through. Delgado lifted his helmet visor and grinned.

"Wash! Fancy meeting you here at Sol's heliopause, a short jump from Earth itself. What gives?"

"Hey, Major, sir." Captain Washburn Tesser, officer commanding Keres Company, mimed a salute, but since he wore civilian clothes, it was more like a friendly wave.

"We were minding our own business, headed for another head-bashing mission when SOCOM sent *Iolanthe* here."

"Just to give us a more stylish ride?"

Tesser shook his head.

"No. But HQ hasn't told me yet what they want, other than give that reprobate Delgado and his bums a lift, then loiter by Sol's heliopause until we receive fresh orders."

"Loiter? Sounds like either the grown-ups are still dithering or someone's moving assets into place elsewhere."

"That's what we figure." Tesser gestured toward the airlock. "Let's see you settled in, then I'll introduce you to Captain Haralda. You'll like her. She's the proverbial Q-ship pirate skipper. New to the job. So she has the enthusiasm of someone looking for action."

"There's nothing else on my agenda." Delgado glanced at Hak, who gave him thumbs-up.

Tesser led them to the ship's Marine barracks, a familiar route since *Iolanthe* was built along the same lines as the others of her type. Frigate-sized, with a patrol frigate's ordnance hidden behind camouflage plates, she could accommodate a full Special Forces squadron and a small drop ship air wing. Once there, he pointed at the embarked Marine unit commanding officer's cabin.

"I figure Colonel Decker wouldn't mind if you took that one instead of a company commander's broom closet, seeing as how you now hold the powers of life and death over half of Ghost Squadron."

"You're under my command?"

Tesser grinned. "Yes, sir, Major, sir. You're the senior mission officer on whatever comes next. Sir."

"Alright, cut it out with the chocolate soldier talk, Wash. I swallowed enough of that crap on Earth."

"I know. That's why it amuses me."

Tesser watched Delgado strip off his tin suit and nodded with approval. "You escaped the flagship in civvies. Nicely done. Captain Haralda is a stickler for pirate-chic when we're on a mission, the more roguish, the better."

"Sorry. I didn't pick up an eyepatch, frilly shirts, and leather pants while we were enjoying the delights of Geneva. But I'll let my beard go wild." Delgado finished stowing his gear, weapons included. "Alright, let's meet this paragon of undercover shenanigans."

Tesser led him up from the barracks to the command deck, at the Q-ship's armored heart, where the bridge and the combat information center bookended the conference room and adjoining captain's day cabin. When they entered the latter after announcing themselves, an energetic woman in a merchant captain's uniform sprang to her feet and came around her desk.

Short, dark hair framed a strong face dominated by an aquiline nose and deep-set green eyes. Silver earrings dangled from her lobes while more rings than regulations allowed adorned her long, slender fingers. She was as tall as Delgado, but not quite as broad or muscular under the dark blue tunic. However, her toothy, welcoming smile matched the Marine's usual friendly grin.

"You must be Major Delgado. Wash speaks well of you."

"Don't believe everything he says, sir. Or pretty much anything when it comes to his friends."

They shook hands.

"How was Earth?" She gestured at the chairs in front of her desk.

"Rather boring. On the other hand, running close protection duty on what we generally consider the safest planet in the Commonwealth has its challenges, such as keeping everyone alert while escorting the Grand Admiral."

"Understandable. I'm sure Wash told you we don't yet know what we're doing here, except hanging around and waiting for orders, and that you're the senior mission officer."

"Yes, sir. Though I could venture a few theories."

"Care to share them?"

"While on Earth, we received instructions to reconnoiter the headquarters of a secretive security and intelligence agency reporting directly to the Secretary-General of the Commonwealth. We think that agency is behind the unrest on the OutWorlds and the attempts to destabilize sovereign star system governments."

Tesser's eyebrows shot up.

"*Sécurité Spéciale*? You think the brass is contemplating a Kathryn Kowalski gambit?"

"Why else order us to spend days staring at the unremarkable aboveground waystations of what was once the premier underground particle physics laboratory of the pre-diaspora era. That tunnel system connects right back to Geneva. And if our information is correct, after the laboratory was closed for good, they put in a branch ending at the Palace of the Stars, one which passes beneath the Geneva Spaceport."

"If?" Haralda cocked a questioning eyebrow.

"Whatever the government is doing with the old sites and tunnels, they've kept it a secret from just about everyone, including the Fleet. My guess is right after Grand Admiral Kowalski did her thing last century, the Secretary-General of the day built himself and his government a little bunker complex that'll shrug off rods from God. And he made sure we didn't find out. Not that we cared much about doings on Earth after Kowalski moved Fleet HQ to Caledonia and set up the Constabulary on Wyvern."

Haralda nodded. "Until now."

"Naval Intelligence has an agent on the inside. She's the one who reported the *Sécurité Spéciale*'s headquarters were supposedly connected to the Palace of the Stars and the Geneva spaceport via the old Large Hadron Collider tunnel. Which, in turn, makes the idea of it also serving as a bolthole rather obvious."

Tesser gave Delgado a curious look.

"Is that agent anyone we know?"

"Remember your previous mission?"

A light went on in Tesser's eyes.

"Wow. Definitely the right person."

When he saw the question in Haralda's eyes, he grimaced.

"Sorry, Captain. Need to know only. We work with officers from Naval Intelligence's Special Operations

Division a lot. They're often our eyes and ears on the ground before we arrive, meaning their job is the most dangerous in the entire Fleet and their survival rate one of the worst outside actual combat."

"Understood. Let's hope our agent on the inside doesn't become one of those statistics."

Delgado nodded.

"That would be a shame."

"In any case, welcome aboard *Iolanthe*. As senior mission commander, you have a standing invitation to enter the bridge and the CIC."

"Thank you, sir."

After returning to barracks where they couldn't be overheard by the ship's crew, Tesser asked, "Miko is the agent, right?"

"Buddy, she's in thick with the head *Sécurité Spéciale* bastard himself, a man by the name of Andreas Bauchan. It wouldn't surprise me if he's wrapped around her little finger."

"In that case, I pity the fool. It won't end well for him."

Delgado grinned at his friend.

"If I didn't know better, I'd think you have a soft spot for the redoubtable Warrant Officer Steiger."

"You didn't watch her infiltrate the revolutionary trash on Ariel easy as can be. That is one scary woman."

"Which is why Commodore Talyn hired her on the spot. Birds of a feather."

"You really think we'll pull a Kowalski?"

Delgado nodded.

"Yep. It's just a matter of time. Cut off the snake's head, and we'll be spending less time chasing its various bits around the Commonwealth."

"And then what do we do with ourselves?"

"Wipe out the cartels and the zaibatsus who play footsie with them. *Sécurité Spéciale*-backed revolutionary trash is a distraction we can't afford."

**

"We just received word Erinye Company is aboard *Iolanthe*," Talyn said when Decker accepted the secure link from Fleet HQ. "They'll be stuck loitering for a while until the remaining assets are in position, and the Grand Admiral gives us the go-ahead."

"Which he won't do until he's here, and you've briefed him on the dispositions."

"General Politis will make sure it's one of the top items on his agenda upon arrival."

"Too bad he didn't pull the trigger himself. It's not like the *Sécurité Spéciale*'s elimination will go down in history with as much of a bang as the old SSB's. No one outside intelligence circles knows the buggers even exist, which means only the SecGen and his closest minions will realize they're gone."

"It'll be more than that, but none are the sort who'll scream from the rooftops and feed the news nets breathless tales of Fleet betrayal." She shrugged. "The decision is still momentous enough for a five-star's final sign-off, so I'm not complaining. Just be happy he'll strongly recommend immediate approval."

Decker exhaled loudly.

"You've become almost too reasonable since your promotion. Fine. I won't complain either, but let me tell you, Fort Arnhem feels damn empty these days. Just a bunch of field grade officers looking for meaningful work while every single company in the regiment is out there, either heading for a target or loitering near one. It's to the point where we plan on jumping with the School every second day, so we don't go crazy. And speaking of crazy, having all four of the regiment's squadrons out at the same time isn't sitting that well with Kal. He worries we might not be able to react if something else hits the fan."

"This could be our best chance, Zack."

"I know that, but it would still feel better if the 2nd Special Forces Regiment was operational."

"Ideal situations only exist in staff college scenarios."

"Thank the Almighty they never sent me. I'd have gone insane after the first week."

"And yet, you're doing a good chunk of the curriculum through distance learning."

"Sure, but at least I'm not sitting in a classroom with dunderheads who never heard a shot fired in anger and argue over the proper role of airborne troops in interstellar operations."

Talyn chuckled. "You'll be meeting a lot more of those dunderheads once you step away from field command."

"Or I could resign my commission and set up my own mercenary corporation. Then you could hire it for operations so black even SOCOM won't touch them."

"Sorry, darling. That's why we created Ghost Squadron. I'd rather not rely on grubby soldiers of fortune for my most sensitive missions."

"Spoilsport. Come to the fort tonight. We can go jumping together."

"The only jumping I still do is on you, Big Boy. My wings retired a while back, remember?"

He gave her a leer.

"Works for me. Come relieve my boredom with your wild antics."

"No time, sorry. But I'll make up for it when you're in Sanctum this weekend. Enjoy your jump. If you're getting really bored, raid the armory for plastic explosives and rearrange the training area. Make it a competition with Kal and the others." She blew him a kiss.

"Love you too, honey."

His display faded to black. Blowing things up usually broke him out of a funk. He tapped his communicator.

A few seconds later, a voice said, "Ryent."

"What would you say to a demolition challenge between the School and us underemployed field grade regimental officers? Hera suggested the training area could use a bit of remodeling."

"The old, when bored, blow things up principle? Sure. Why don't you call them and see if they want to play?"

— Twenty-Four —

"**I**s it just me, or does the city feel a lot more serene now that Larsson and his people are gone?"

Miko Steiger and Andreas Bauchan were strolling through one of the many parks surrounding the Commonwealth Government Precinct. The sky was a beautiful blue, dotted here and there by white clouds, and the air seemed unusually pure as if it had been entirely scrubbed overnight.

"It's not just you. Every five years, we go through this with a different Grand Admiral. Different, but cast from the same mold as Grand Admiral Kowalski. And in two years, it'll be the Chief Constable of the Commonwealth Constabulary. His sort shows more deference, but they mimic their Fleet counterparts in many ways."

"You were here for Larsson's predecessor?"

Bauchan nodded.

"Yes. And holding the same office. It was just as irritating back then."

Steiger wrapped her arm around his.

"They'll never change unless someone shocks the entire rotten system."

"Which is a bit difficult, considering Larsson and his ilk run the most powerful interstellar military force in the known galaxy, and it will only continue growing in size and strength. The legislation Kathryn Kowalski forced down the government's throat sees to that."

"Can't the government just tell Larsson his budget is frozen?"

He shook his head and gave her a sad smile.

"The OutWorld senators would raise a ruckus capable of threatening the unity of the Commonwealth. Ironic, isn't it? The government must increase funding in lockstep with expansion, increase in threats, and inflation, to ensure political cohesion. Meanwhile, the recipient of said funding resists attempts at repealing the sovereign star systems principle in favor of a tighter union."

Steiger cocked a sardonic eyebrow at him.

"So, in essence, the Commonwealth's constitutional arrangements are a suicide pact."

Bauchan chuckled.

"Perhaps not quite that dramatic, but yes. We face a standoff, which will only worsen with time, as more colonies achieve independence and find themselves de facto members of the OutWorld faction. Oh, the government is holding them back for as long as possible, but then colonial wars break out, and we send the Fleet, which, predictably, quells the rebellion and leaves an independence-minded regime in charge. Not federalizing colonies earlier was a big mistake. But accepting Kowalski's demand that planetary armed forces be forbidden to leave their home worlds was an even bigger one."

"I hear rumors the Fleet actually aids rebels, if they're of the right sort, so they can precipitate independence and thereby add another two OutWorld representatives in the Senate."

"Yes. It happened before colonies were federalized, and that was why the Commonwealth government took control of those deemed the most vulnerable, although we didn't publicize it in quite that way. I expect the few remaining colonies still run by sovereign star systems will come under Earth's direct rule in the next decade."

"Any fears the Fleet will try something more direct in the Home Systems?"

"They likely did so already. We think Special Forces are responsible for terminating Elize and Allard Hogue on Arcadia. You may be aware of their demise. Elize was Senator Graciela Hogue's grandmother, and Allard was her cousin. The Hogue family basically owned Arcadia before someone destroyed the family."

"The names are familiar."

Steiger, who'd been involved in the mission that ended the Hogues, kept a grave expression on her face, though their deaths had rejoiced her at the time.

"There were other unexplained incidents, such as the destruction of Amali's island on Pacifica some time before Elize and Allard Hogue's deaths. You know who the Amalis were?"

"Industrialists, I believe. They held a controlling interest in ComCorp, right?"

A nod.

"Yes. You're well informed. I like that in an ally. Many people favorable to the Centralist cause died in the conflagration. Half of the island itself simply vanished. We suspect the attackers used a tightly controlled sub-nuclear military explosive, one which mimics an antimatter device in many respects."

"Surely you don't mean MHX-19?"

"Oh, yes." Bauchan stopped and looked Steiger in the eye. "Just how extensive is the Deep Space Foundation's intelligence network? Not one person in a million knows about MHX-19."

"More developed than ComCorp's, if not as widely spread, since we're only operating in one part of the Commonwealth for now."

Steiger was well aware Talyn and Decker carried out the attack, their last act as field agents before returning to uniformed duty, and understood the operation would remain a deeply buried secret until the end of times. But she wanted Bauchan hungry for a new asset, one with tendrils in places his people couldn't access, and Talyn wouldn't object at her using insider knowledge to reel him in.

"That's the impression you gave me over the last few weeks. You mentioning MHX-19 confirms it."

She let a coy smile play on her lips.

"I can also tell you which Fleet ammunition depots hold the stuff."

He returned her smile measure for measure.

"We already know. Speaking of ComCorp, are you working with them, or perhaps through them? Their network is rather good."

"Are you?" Steiger arched an eyebrow.

"That would be telling."

"We keep an interested eye on their doings, just like everyone else. Our goals aren't well enough aligned for cooperation. The Foundation desires closer unity among human worlds, while ComCorp seeks profits without regard to the socio-political situation."

Steiger's lies had become so smooth, she sometimes wondered about the danger of believing them herself, of becoming Britta Trulson and forgetting the Fleet Intelligence Branch warrant officer on an undercover assignment.

"But back to my earlier question. Aren't you afraid the military will eventually strike at the very heart of a government it holds in contempt, based on what I saw of Larsson's attitude and that of his people?"

They resumed their stroll after Bauchan made a dismissive shrug.

"Earth isn't Arcadia or any of the other Home Systems, let alone an OutWorld. The likes of Larsson's escort, those dangerous Special Forces operators, can't do a damn thing that would hurt the Commonwealth government, even if they attacked in strength."

"There aren't many combat veterans in the 1st Marine Division or the 1st Fleet for that matter. Besides, an MHX-19 strike at the heart of Geneva while the Senate is in session would decapitate the Commonwealth government. If they used it before to kill so many notables on Pacifica, what's keeping them from doing so here?"

Bauchan didn't immediately reply. As his silence stretched on, Steiger briefly wondered whether she'd betrayed herself. Then, he stopped again, jaw muscles working as if he were parsing his thoughts.

"Given enough warning, the government can survive even the most savage attack, and by enough, I mean ten minutes or so, more than sufficient once we spot an inbound threat. An impenetrable aerospace defense dome covers Geneva, and thanks to a five centuries-old particle physics experiment, we can count on the most hardened bunker ever designed."

She turned her head and cocked an eyebrow at him.

"You've piqued my curiosity, darling."

**

"Please tell me you're visiting Fort Arnhem," Decker said by way of greeting when Talyn's image appeared on his office display via the secure link. He gave her a wistful look.

"Sorry, no. And you won't like what I'm about to say either."

"Oh?" He settled back in his chair, eyebrows raised.

"The Kowalski Purge Redux is off. Or at least most of it is."

"Grand Admiral Larsson demurred?"

"I nixed the operation."

Decker sat up. "What do you mean?"

"Miko's backup mission on Earth has become the main effort, thanks to her relationship with Andreas Bauchan. Besides, the *Sécurité Spéciale* is a tougher nut than we originally thought, based on Delgado's report and what Miko relayed. Breaching will leave a mark on the countryside, something we can't yet afford. That leaves old LHC tunnels, and we don't know what they're used for nowadays. Miko will eventually find out, but it could take a few more weeks."

"We're replacing a regimental strike with a honey pot? Walk me through this."

"Remember how skeptical you were when I proposed we infiltrate and subvert the Deep Space Foundation, essentially turning it into a mercenary intelligence service under our control after you shot Louis Sorne and Antoine Hakkam?"

"Sure."

"It finally paid off in a big way. I sent Miko to Earth under an assumed identity as a Deep Space Foundation researcher looking for friendly ears in the Commonwealth government. She played it so well that Bauchan offered a strategic alliance between the Foundation and the *Sécurité Spéciale*."

"Aha. I see. You'll infiltrate Bauchan's bunch as well and destroy them from the inside."

"Something like that. It's more elegant than brute force and doesn't present the risk of precipitating a constitutional crisis ahead of time."

"And you can never resist the temptation to subvert the enemy."

She gave him a sweet smile.

"I'm all about subtlety. But there's still a bit of brute force involved. The Foundation operates mainly in the Rim and adjacent sectors, though we've been looking at ways of expanding its reach, and that's where the *Sécurité Spéciale* is the weakest because of your outstanding work. I'd like to destroy what's left so Bauchan will have no choice but rely on the Foundation as his eyes and ears in that part of the Commonwealth."

Decker nodded as a grin split his square face.

"Then, you'll feed him bullshit every day and twice on Sundays."

"We intelligence specialists prefer the term disinformation, but essentially, yes. My new plan is collapsing the *Sécurité Spéciale* from within by making it ineffective and unreliable. That'll advance our cause much more effectively than an actual decapitation. At first, we'll feed Miko verifiable information, the sort one can reasonably expect from the Deep Space Foundation's in-house covert network, to prove her bona fides. Once Bauchan decides he wants more, we'll give him ambiguous intelligence, the sort that might be deemed wrong because of misinterpretation, if ever he runs an in-depth check. Then, should everything go well, the disinformation campaign can begin."

"Twisted, but I like it. Make the *Sécurité Spéciale* trust Miko, then send them chasing their own tails until they vanish into a black hole."

"Confusion to the enemy — my favorite toast and game."

"So, what's your plan for destroying the *Sécurité Spéciale*'s assets in those sectors? You plan on taking out the nodes as per Kowalski Redux?"

"No. Bauchan isn't an idiot. Losing his people in one fell swoop right after his newest paramour talks him into an alliance between the Deep Space Foundation and the *Sécurité Spéciale* would raise suspicions. We'll approach this in a piecemeal manner and make it look like one or more of the cartels have declared war. It'll take time, but then, we're in it for the long haul. While the politicians and their minions can only think in terms of election cycles, our plan covers the next few decades, and that's our strength."

Decker chuckled.

"I'm supposed to be the philosophical one, yet that sounded suspiciously like a deep thought. But I agree with the sentiment. Those with a longer time preference will always laugh last. Back to the immediate plan, honey. Unless you're still figuring it out."

"*Iolanthe* with Keres Company will return to her original mission of taking out the Galindez Cartel on New Tasman along with an additional secondary task of terminating the

Sécurité Spéciale agents working with Galindez. On her way there, she'll meet with one of the disposable ships at a point equidistant from both New Tasman and Cascadia and transfer Erinye Company over. Delgado will then receive orders to make the Cascadia *Sécurité Spéciale* node vanish."

"Night and fog."

Talyn nodded.

"Precisely. It'll blind Bauchan on a strategic frontier colony and cut off his outlying assets from their sectoral locus. That's step one. Step two will depend on how he reacts. With any luck, he'll decide another cartel has designs on taking over the Cascadian Sector and pushing the Galindez organisation out. He'll be desperate for intelligence until the remote units bypass the vanished node and speak with Earth directly."

"Enter Miko Steiger, or whatever she calls herself right now, and the Deep Space Foundation, which you essentially own. I guess there's no chance you can get me aboard that disposable."

"No. Your face is too well known by the opposition. Curtis, not so much. Sorry, but in terms of undercover operations, you're benched for good."

"So long as I'm not benched permanently in all respects."

"Your day of glory will come."

— Twenty-Five —

"This is getting even more mysterious than usual," Captain Haralda said when Delgado and Tesser entered her day cabin, summoned shortly after *Iolanthe* received a subspace message from HQ. She waved at the chairs in front of her desk.

"We're resuming our trip to New Tasman, where your mission is still on." She nodded at Tesser. "While you, Major, will board the Merchant Vessel *Kobe Maru* when we meet it in a few days. What happens with you afterward, the orders don't say."

"Dang." Tesser glanced at his friend. "No purge. Sorry, old buddy. I know you were gunning for the head bastard."

Delgado shrugged.

"Easy come easy go. If they're shipping us off in what sounds like a disposable, my consolation prize should be rather good."

"Disposable?" A puzzled frown creased Haralda's forehead.

"Right — you joined SOCOM recently and wouldn't know about the secret Navy it runs. From time to time, we capture civilian starships engaged in illegal activities and use them for our hairier missions, the sort where we can't risk a valuable Q-ship like this one or can't afford the slightest hint we're Fleet. They receive a quick upgrade to improve survivability, better weapons, and naval grade communications gear. The disposables are about as black as black ops get. Their crews are volunteers with Q-ship time."

"Why volunteers?"

"Because, if necessary, the ships can and will be abandoned, scuttled, or otherwise rendered inoperable. Considering how much you spacers love your rides, working disposables takes a different mindset. For one thing, the crews aren't much larger than they would be under civilian ownership. And for another, many of them can't outrun something they can't outshoot, so the chances of taking casualties are much higher than in a ship like *Iolanthe*. Fortunately, SOCOM has lost no one since the disposable program began, but it's just a matter of time."

When he saw a gleam in Haralda's eyes, Delgado chuckled.

"Sorry, Captain. You're not eligible. The disposables are a two-and-a-half ringer's command, and you wear three full ones. But don't worry, nowadays, a tour of command in a Q-ship will give you the most excitement the Navy can offer short of running something like *Kobe Maru*."

Delgado turned to Tesser.

"And while we're on that subject, we'll leave our uniforms and military gear with you, Wash. Can't take that stuff with us aboard a disposable. I just hope it's bringing untraceable gear because I'm not carrying any."

"No worries. We'll pack your dunnage in containers and stow them with the squadron stores when we're home."

Erinye Company's commanding officer gave Haralda a quick grin.

"The joys of shifting from fully legit to totally black on the same deployment. Sometimes we don't know whether we'll ever see our expensive mess uniforms again, let alone personal gear that saved our lives more than once."

"Seems like I have a lot to learn about special ops."

"Like the rest of us when we first signed up, sight unseen."

"Isn't that the truth," Tesser drawled. "And you can't leave once they swear you in. We're kind of like the cartels that way."

"Except we're the anti-cartels," Delgado responded. "And anti-every other evil that humanity can conjure."

Haralda looked from one to the other.

"So long as we remember that staring into the abyss long enough will result in it staring back at us."

The two Marines gave each other a droll glance. Then Delgado said, "I see the captain knows her Nietzsche."

"And more," she growled, but no one would mistake the pleased smile on her lips for anything else.

Later, when they were returning to barracks, Delgado asked, "Speaking of someone who stared into her own deadly abyss, what's Aleksa up to these days? Rumors say she's working with your lot this time around."

"Already on New Tasman as part of our advance party, wondering why we haven't shown up yet. The Constabulary takes care of law and order there. She'll be our inside source, deflection, and native guide, so to speak."

"Lucky you. With her there and Miko on Earth, my advance party, wherever that is, will be from the spook division, extra secret."

"With a dash of extra secret sauce."

Delgado gave his friend a strange look.

"Has anyone ever mentioned you seem a tad bizarre at times?"

"Only those who don't appreciate my particular brand of humor."

"If that's what you call it, then count me among those who consider you a little touched in the head," he replied, patting Tesser on the shoulder.

**

"Erinye Company is really going down in the world," Delgado said in a voice pitched for Tesser's ears only when *Kobe Maru*'s image appeared on the CIC's primary display. "From flagship of the Fleet to Q-ship, to disposable. And a ratty looking one at that."

"Forget about a private cabin and the amenities, buddy," Tesser replied in the same tone.

The freighter, a sloop-sized ship capable of entering standard atmospheres and landing on standard gee planets, was covered with black streaks, patches, dents, and dings. Even the two hyperdrive nacelles framing an inelegant, rectangular hull bore evidence of a hard life.

Either *Kobe Maru* had been worn out before entering service with SOCOM, or the shipwrights at that well-hidden yard on a minor colony gave it the tired appearance common among tramps roaming the frontiers. Delgado sincerely hoped the latter was true. He didn't relish operating from a starship that was on its last legs.

"They're calling us, sir," the communications watchkeeper said, raising his hand. "Right frequency, right identification code."

Haralda glanced over her shoulder.

"Put them on."

Kobe Maru's image dissolved. Its place was taken by that of a man sitting in a command chair. Black-haired, with lean features, sharp brown eyes, and high cheekbones, he wore a spacer's dark blue tunic with no adornments, not even a shoulder strap displaying merchant rank insignia.

"Lieutenant Commander Dien Bahn, *Kobe Maru*."

"Commander Anneke Haralda, Q-ship *Iolanthe*."

A faint smile briefly crossed Bahn's lips.

"I heard rumors the Navy commissioned a successor to Admiral Dunmoore's famous raider but could never find evidence."

"The original's bell is on my bridge, and although I wasn't there, I know Admiral Dunmoore was present at her christening, though she declined the honor of being *Iolanthe*'s sponsor on the grounds of her extremely advanced age. Thea Holt, the granddaughter of the original's second commanding officer, stepped in at Dunmoore's recommendation."

"I wish you joy of her, Captain." Bahn's gaze turned on Delgado, sitting alongside Tesser at unoccupied stations behind the command chair. "I gather you're my newest passenger, Major?"

"Indeed. Curtis Delgado with one-hundred fifteen Marines. Please tell me you're carrying our combat gear."

"Armor, weapons, electronics, ammo, explosives, spare clothing, and shuttles. Everything is sterile and untraceable. It'll be tight quarters, though."

"So long as the environmental systems can handle us, we've seen worse."

Bahn's faint smile returned.

"She may seem like junkyard garbage, but her systems are almost brand new beneath the veneer of grime and repair patches. Her previous owners didn't stint on maintenance."

"Good to know."

"How do you want to handle this, Captain Haralda? Should I send my shuttles over, or will you send yours?"

"Since your hangar deck is probably a quarter the size of ours, it's best if you come to fetch Major Delgado and his unit."

"If they're packed and ready, I can launch within the next few minutes."

Delgado chuckled.

"Oh, we're ready, and we carry little by way of luggage. Most of what we brought on our earlier deployment is returning home with *Iolanthe* since almost none of it can be considered sufficiently sterile if things go sideways. That's why I asked whether you carried our gear."

"Good. I prefer passengers who travel light. Stand by."

Forty-five minutes later, after landing on *Kobe Maru*'s hangar deck, Delgado and his troopers stepped off shuttles that weren't much to look at from the outside, but surprisingly clean and well maintained inside. The hangar was no different, though considerably smaller than the one they'd just left, where heavily armed dropships were parked alongside more innocuous looking small craft. Evidently, *Kobe Maru* didn't carry combat shuttles because he only saw a few more of the same model that transported them from *Iolanthe*.

Lieutenant Commander Bahn came through the main airlock, now that the space doors were closed, trailed by a compact, olive-skinned man whose bald dome shone under the compartment's harsh lighting. He, too, wore a merchant spacer's uniform without rank insignia.

"Welcome aboard, Major." He gestured at his colleague. "This is Lieutenant Ivor Mucha, my first officer."

Mucha nodded politely, dark, hooded eyes studying the Marine.

"Thank you, Captain, and this is First Sergeant Emery Hak, my top kick and second in command."

Hak briefly came to attention.

"Sir."

"You're the only commissioned officer in your company?"

"The ratio of officers to non-commissioned officers in the Special Forces is a little more lopsided than in the rest of the Corps. And many, if not most, of us who hold a commission came up through the ranks. Products of the Armed Services Academy are usually more interested in a career that leads to flag rank." Delgado grinned. "And Special Forces isn't one of them, in large part because they classify our service records beyond what a promotion board can see. Strip the top-secret stuff, and what's left won't pull you over the promotion cut-off line."

Bahn let out a grim chuckle.

"It's not much different in SOCOM's naval branch, Major."

"Please call me Curtis. Since we'll be living cheek by jowl for a few weeks and we're both O-4s..." Delgado let his voice trail off after using the universal rank identifier for Marine Corps and Army majors, Navy lieutenant commanders, and Constabulary superintendents.

"Dien." He gestured at his first officer. "Ivor can work with your top kick and see that Erinye Company settles in. I'd like to be on my way as soon as possible."

"Where are we headed?"

"Cascadia. Your sealed orders are in my day cabin, which also doubles as my night cabin. We can drop your bag off in your quarters on the way there. We have a few passenger berths for your senior people, but most of your Marines will bunk in cargo holds converted to barracks by loading personnel modules with room for ten disguised as shipping containers. One of the holds has messing modules, complete with galley, dining facilities, and a few amenities."

"That'll be just fine, so long as you allow us the use of this hangar deck, and perhaps a few corridors so we can set up a parkour course. Staying in shape is a must."

"Ivor and your top kick can discuss that as well."

As expected, Delgado's cabin was little more than a broom closet with a private head, and he briefly wondered whether bunking with the troopers would be better, but that might insult his host.

Once in Bahn's quarters, *Kobe Maru*'s captain gestured at a chair facing a small desk tucked into one corner. "Grab a seat while I call up your orders."

As Delgado complied, the public address system came to life.

"Now hear this. Transition to hyperspace in one minute. That is all."

"You don't mess around."

"The chances of being spotted in the same area as *Iolanthe* may be vanishingly small, but they're not nil. Especially if one of us picked up a tail."

"And you're suitably paranoid."

"In this business, looking over your shoulder helps you live longer, right?"

"Right."

He handed the Marine a tablet. "There you go. It's waiting for your authorization code."

At that moment, a klaxon sounded three times.

"Now hear this. Brace for transition in ten seconds. That is all."

Delgado felt his stomach clench instinctively at the oncoming, though mercifully brief burst of nausea. His wasn't as bad as some, but it remained one of his least favorite experiences, alongside finding himself under effective enemy artillery fire. The universe turned into a multicolored pretzel as his stomach tried to make a run for it. But the moment passed just as quickly as it came on.

After taking a few breaths, he concentrated on the tablet and entered his personal code. The encryption layer dissolved almost at once, and he breathed a sigh of relief. Fumble the code three times, and the orders self-destruct, which would entail asking HQ for a new set, not something an acting major who'd like his rank made substantive could afford.

He went through the text once, then let out a low whistle. It wasn't the Kowalski Purge Redux he'd expected while loitering at Earth's hyperlimit, but his mission on Cascadia seemed like the start of something similar.

"Interesting orders?" Bahn asked.

Delgado gave him a lazy grin.

"Aren't they always in our strange little SOCOM universe?"

— Twenty-Six —

"Ah! Britta, my dear." Bauchan rose from behind his desk and came around it to hug Steiger. "How is your new office?"

"Excellent." She gave him a chaste kiss on the lips, though her squeeze promised more later. "Thank you so much for arranging things."

"If we want the Deep Space Foundation as a major player in this city, it surely needs proper accommodations, something with prestige as well as security."

They took comfortable chairs facing each other over a low coffee table. "Will you be hiring locals?"

She shook her head.

"Considering our plans, no. I can't adequately vet candidates on my own. The risk is too great. However, colleagues from Cimmeria will join me in due course."

"Perhaps I can help with the vetting. One or two staff members familiar with Geneva and the inner workings of the Commonwealth government will be incredibly useful."

Steiger knew Bauchan's real aim was planting *Sécurité Spéciale* agents, but since he'd not yet told her about the organization's existence, she couldn't very well refuse. Besides, his people watching her every move wouldn't matter. Steiger was now, for all intents and purposes, Britta Trulson, Deep Space Foundation intelligence operative, who took her orders from head office on Cimmeria.

She graced Bauchan with a radiant smile.

"I'd really appreciate that, Andreas. And in return, I would like to offer you a little something. It came via the subspace packet from my superiors this morning, ably funneled to my new office."

He tilted his head like a curious bird.

"Oh?"

"Call it an engagement present from the Foundation to the Secretary-General's Senior Security Adviser. A good luck charm for a successful and mutually profitable union. My superiors were most insistent."

"How kind of them. I should like to meet those superiors one day."

The look Steiger gave Bauchan hid her amusement at the idea of Commodore Hera Talyn in the same room as him. Only one would come out alive, and it wasn't the man sitting across from her. He'd die without even knowing what just hit him. Or Talyn would watch Bauchan's soul merge with the Infinite Void while sipping a gin and tonic and telling him exactly who she was.

That way, he would suffer eternal torment at knowing he'd lost the war between the *Sécurité Spéciale* and Naval

Intelligence. Probably the latter, she figured. Commodore Talyn struck her as an exquisite cruelty artist. Steiger understood what Zack Decker saw in her. Or didn't see, as the case might be.

"I'm sure they'd be delighted."

"And their gift?"

"The colonial government on Marengo, heavily infiltrated by Fleet and OutWorld faction supporters, will soon issue a unilateral declaration of independence. They'll claim it's the only way they can stop the endless guerrilla war. Of course, we know the guerrillas are funded by interests whose aim is keeping the government weak and pliable, but they're losing to the Fleet's counterinsurgency forces. And losing badly, hence the upcoming UDI."

Bauchan nodded, his face betraying no emotions whatsoever. Her offering matched precisely what his analysts told him a few days ago. But he'd not yet decided whether to let the matter become a political problem or look for a solution that might give the guerrillas renewed strength.

A colony issuing a UDI didn't affect the Commonwealth's political balance, since only star systems who attained independence constitutionally could send a pair of senators to Earth. But the situation might become messy.

Marengo had been in a state of unrest for years, despite the Marine units stationed there at the colonial government's request. Whenever they doused one brush fire, Bauchan ensured they faced three more. Yet it couldn't last, as history proved many times over.

Garonne, one of Marengo's neighboring star systems, issued its own UDI several years earlier after a successful revolt against the Celeste-imposed colonial administration. Yet the provisional regime ruling the star system was still battling the Commonwealth government through the courts to get formal recognition. The only reason for its continued existence was the support of sovereign star systems in that sector who would never countenance the restoration of colonial rule, not even from Earth.

"A cogent appraisal of the situation, my dear. Thank you. I accept the offering with gratitude."

Steiger inclined her head.

"As you can see, we don't lack for insight and operatives."

"What's the Foundation's estimation on when the Marengo government will make its move?"

"Four to six weeks, no more."

Bauchan contemplated her in silence for a few moments.

"That is our estimate as well. Nicely done."

"The Deep Space Foundation is more than just a charitable organization dedicated to human unity across the stars. You can expect more of the same going forward."

"Let your superiors know we appreciate the generous offer of cooperation and will reciprocate in the same spirit."

Steiger wondered whether Bauchan would feed her the same sort of horse manure Talyn intended for him. Lies for lies. Things could get interesting.

"Certainly. And where are you taking me tonight?"

"I thought I'd cook you a memorable meal myself. There's something about staying home to enjoy a little cognac under the stars after a repast fit for Secretaries-General."

**

"Warrant Officer Steiger has established herself as the Deep Space Foundation liaison in Geneva, whose role is sharing intelligence with Andreas Bauchan. He still hasn't revealed the *Sécurité Spéciale*'s existence, so she's playing it with a light touch. However, I believe we can now shape the Commonwealth government's perception of events in the outer sectors."

"And make the *Sécurité Spéciale* self-destruct, or at least destroy its credibility while weakening the Centralists by taking away reliable eyes and ears on the OutWorlds." Larsson inclined his head by way of congratulations. "Well done, Commodore. I like that solution much better than imitating my distant predecessor, even though I would have endorsed General Politis' decision to go ahead. I'm sure it'll work better and at a lower cost."

"Thank you, sir. We'll push the process along with targeted attacks against *Sécurité Spéciale*'s assets so Bauchan relies more and more on Steiger and the Deep Space Foundation."

"Isn't there a risk he might uncover your scheme if too many assets vanish in sectors where the Foundation is active?"

Talyn nodded.

"Absolutely, sir. I assume Bauchan is as paranoid as I am and will notice small anomalies. But since we've already been taking out their assets involved with the cartels, the UCF, and allied movements, I'm betting he'll think it's more of the same. Besides, I'm spreading the direct actions out across that entire quadrant, so it doesn't appear a particular sector is being targeted. The first strikes will be on Cascadia, to remove the sectoral node, and New Tasman to eliminate a joint Galindez Cartel-*Sécurité Spéciale* operation aimed at expanding Galindez control on that part of the frontier. Though in reality, the *Sécurité Spéciale* is using the cartel as unwitting foot soldiers for its own aims."

"Is New Tasman under threat?"

She shook her head.

"Not directly. Since it's a federal colony, Bauchan's people will make sure the local government remains untouched. Besides, the governor is a friend of the SecGen's. And my contact on Wyvern tells me that the 19th Constabulary Regiment reported several unsuccessful attempts by criminal elements at corrupting its members, something the Cascadian Sector's PCB unit confirmed. The New Tasman Regiment, on the other hand, could be vulnerable. It wouldn't be the first time the cartels or the *Sécurité Spéciale* subvert Army personnel. But the company from Ghost Squadron headed for New Tasman won't interact with either regiment. They're going in fully sterile. Same for the company headed to Cascadia."

Larsson gave her a thoughtful look.

"Direct action on a sector capital is a tad riskier, no?"

"It wouldn't be the first time, sir. A company from the 1st Special Forces helped us terminate the Coalition-funded terrorists on Cimmeria."

"That's right. The Constabulary cooperated with you at the time, didn't it?"

"Not during the cleanup phase. The senior officer working with us was uncomfortable about black ops back then."

"Are you saying that's no longer the case?"

"She's accepted certain things are necessary if we're to avoid another messy civil war. Better yet, she joined the Political Anti-Corruption Unit on Wyvern recently and can do even more for us now."

"Your contact who said the 19th wasn't corrupted." Larsson's flat tone made it a statement.

"Yes, sir." Talyn let a faint smile play on her lips. "The unit headed for Cascadia is Major Delgado's Erinye Company. They used their time on Earth to acquaint themselves with operations on more advanced worlds."

Larsson let out a bark of laughter.

"Of course. Let me guess, if you'd gone ahead with Operation Kowalski Redux, his mission would have been a strike on *Sécurité Spéciale* HQ in Geneva?"

"Indeed, sir. Why waste weeks of reconnaissance? Another company from Ghost Squadron was ready to back him up — the one now heading for New Tasman. In any case, a company from the 1st Special Forces Regiment's B

Squadron is now headed for Marengo to help the colonial administration when it issues a unilateral declaration of independence and severs ties with Celeste. That UDI will fulfill the prophecy Warrant Officer Steiger passed on to Andreas Bauchan as the Deep Space Foundation's proof of goodwill."

Larsson sat back and studied Talyn.

"I don't know whether I should be alarmed at your machinations or pleased with them, Commodore. Your mind certainly works in strange ways."

"That's why Admiral Ulrich recruited me back in the day, sir."

"What's Colonel Decker doing with himself while his squadron is scattered across the Commonwealth?"

"He's understudying the regiment's CO in preparation for his upcoming promotion, sir. Brigadier General Martinson will receive his second star and stand up the Marine Corps Special Forces Division in a few weeks when the 2nd Special Forces Regiment formally joins the order of battle. The 1st Regiment's CO, Colonel Kal Ryent, who is also the designated assistant divisional commander, will spend increasingly more time in Sanctum helping Martinson and preparing for his new role. But Zack is champing at the bit, sir. He'd rather be out there with his troopers."

The Grand Admiral chuckled.

"I can imagine. Tell Colonel Decker I said direct action strikes are for the young in body, and not those who are merely young at heart."

**

"What did he mean by merely young at heart?" Decker frowned at Talyn's image on his bedroom's primary display. "I can hunt with my Marines and not break a sweat. Heck, I'm racking up more jumps than they are these days."

"Only because of boredom. Yes, I'll concede you're in excellent shape for a man your age — I of all people should know." She blew him a kiss. "But you're old enough to have a daughter with a Ph.D. serving as an Intelligence Branch officer, Zack. Your days of sneak and stab warfare are over, especially now that you're preparing for command of the regiment. But cheer up. The COs of line regiments and those of most detached regular battle groups don't see action nowadays either."

"Remind me again why I'm not still a chief warrant officer playing the man of a thousand faces out there with Miko and the others?"

"Because you and Miko teaming up would cause trouble Naval Intelligence can't afford."

"Oh, ye of little faith. My roving days are long gone."

A sweet smile tugged at Talyn's lips.

"No question, darling. Focus on the regiment. Over the coming years, your remaining squadrons will replicate Ghost Squadron's missions. Eroding the *Sécurité Spéciale*'s capabilities and replacing its intelligence sources with our own *dezinformatsiya* is now one of the most vital early phases of our updated long-range plan. We can't do that without your people. The 2ⁿᵈ Special Forces Regiment will be fully occupied fighting the various revolutionary movements sponsored by Centralist interests, ditto the 3ʳᵈ in a year or so. Things will get a lot worse before getting better, Zack. The more we push back, the harder they'll try destabilizing entire sectors. It may not seem so yet, but this is turning into an existential battle for the soul of humanity."

He cocked a skeptical eyebrow.

"Existential? A tad dramatic, no?"

"As they said in the olden days, keep your powder dry."

"Hah! Two historical references in the space of five minutes. Are you finally catching up with my interest in pre-diaspora history?"

"Do I have a choice, considering history repeats itself if we don't learn from it?"

"Wise beyond your already advanced years, my dear Commodore."

"Careful, Marine."

"Or what?"

— Twenty-Seven —

Iolanthe made New Tasman orbit in record time, faster than the navigation plot provided by HQ on Caledonia should have allowed. Commander Anneke Haralda wasn't the sort who questioned fate and simply turned control of the mission over to Washburn Tesser, whose first request was an encrypted link over a rarely used communications band and a seat at a commo console.

"Universal Exports Ship *Liparus* to Deep Space Foundation Branch Office Hobart. Code Rosebud, over."

Tesser sat back, knowing it might be a while before Warrant Officer Kine could reply. Her receiver would store his message until she accessed it.

"Branch Office here," an androgynous voice replied almost a full minute later. "Code Rosebud acknowledged. Stand by for cargo handling instructions."

Kine's reply matched the response to the challenge word for word. Since she was conditioned, no interrogator could extract the precise wording. Unless said interrogator possessed Commodore Talyn's skills. And only a handful of humans in the entire Commonwealth did. But there was still one last check.

"How is Sam?"

The reply came almost instantly.

"Still dead."

Tesser, eyes on the planet filling the CIC's primary display, nodded once.

"We're good, Captain."

"What happened?" Aleksa Kine, for it was her behind the voice, asked. "You're a tad behind schedule."

"Head office temporarily diverted us, but the delivery is still as per purchase order. How's the place these days?"

"Damp, with a touch of extra moisture. And chilly. We haven't seen the sun for a few weeks. The sales of Vitamin D supplements are soaring."

"Figures. Crappy weather just as we're arriving."

Kine let out a bark of laughter.

"There's no such thing as good weather half of the year in these parts, thanks to the joys of unrestrained ocean currents swirling around a solitary Pangaea-like continent. Although I understand there are fewer clouds during what passes for winter. They say if you want sun, head for the central desert, but bring plenty of water."

"Pass. We won't be here long enough for tourism. What about the arrangements?"

"I rented a warehouse at the far end of the Hobart Spaceport on behalf of the Deep Space Foundation. It has enough room for the shuttles, along with everything else." An image appeared on the display showing a large, nondescript building with a high roof and tall doors no different from others around it. "Ground Control will vector you directly to the private apron."

"Any danger of a customs inspection?"

"No. The Foundation pays well for discretion and anonymity."

In other words, Naval Intelligence bought off the locals, Tesser thought as he exchanged a glance with First Sergeant Gade. The abyss was already staring back.

As if Kine could read Tesser's thoughts, she added, "Like everyone else around here. It makes for a level playing field. No one wants to work a corrupt system with one hand tied behind the back, us included."

Haralda glanced at him.

"Does that sort of thinking turn Nietzsche's abyss into a roadside ditch?"

"Probably," Tesser replied, ignoring Kine's suppressed guffaw. "When's the best time to land, Branch Office?"

"Between midnight and oh-five-hundred, when every other smuggler, organized criminal, and shady operator is moving about, on account of the Traffic Control and spaceport night shifts taking gratuities for not noticing irregular activity while law-abiding citizens are sound asleep."

A smile briefly lit up Tesser's face when he saw Haralda's sour expression.

"Welcome to the ugly underside of the Commonwealth, Captain. You'll find this stuff on most of the outer colonies. The amount of money passing through places like New

Tasman because of illegal activities is staggering. A lot of that money ends up in the pockets of the highest and mightiest on Earth and the Home Worlds, so the incentives for fighting petty corruption among public officials are low."

"Doesn't the Constabulary Regiment do anything about it?"

A peal of delighted laughter came through the CIC speakers.

"It's spread thin, and Constabulary investigators won't go after aerospace traffic controllers pocketing an extra five hundred creds a month without someone lodging a complaint. They're busy with more urgent cases, such as murder, human trafficking, and the like. Besides, those best placed to lodge such a complaint are mostly on the take themselves. Generally speaking, money flows uphill. Mind you, if someone high in the colonial administration's food chain steps out of line, the Constabulary's Professional Compliance Bureau will take an interest."

When Haralda shook her head in disbelief, Tesser shrugged.

"Like I said, it isn't pretty, Captain. But no one cares except those who fall victim to organized criminals, and that's the unfortunate part. Unless something totally outrageous happens on an outer world, most humans won't even think about contacting their senators and demanding action. That's the biggest tragedy of federalizing sovereign star system colonies — they become a problem for a distant, impersonal Earth."

"A result of the law of unintended consequences, something our betters on Earth can't understand," Kine said.

Haralda scoffed.

"Politicians are rather good at ignoring second and third-order effects if they even know what those are."

"It's just after sixteen hundred there, right?" Tesser asked, wanting to move away from philosophical matters and focus on the mission.

"Yes."

"If we launch shuttles in eight hours, that will put us on Traffic Control sensors at the start of the night shift. I can see that the people and cargo are ready by then." He glanced at Haralda. "Captain?"

She nodded.

"No problems. I'll start an eight-hour timer right now."

"Branch Office?"

"We'll be waiting."

**

Shortly before midnight, Hobart time, Keres Company's Marines assembled on the hangar deck, looking like nothing so much as disreputable muscle for hire. Each carried a pair of scuffed, mismatched duffel bags containing weapons, armor, and other carefully sanitized combat gear, the sort mercenaries used, only better under the skin.

The aft ramps of five civilian-pattern shuttles were down, ready to receive the troopers. Though not nearly as well-armed as the dropships lining the hangar's opposite side, they still packed a wicked punch thanks to weapon systems retracted behind camouflage plates. In effect, the shuttles were *Iolanthe*'s spiritual children, miniature, sublight Q-ships.

After going through the roll call ritual, Tesser raised his right hand above his head, index finger extended, and made a circling motion.

"Mount up."

When the last of his Marines were aboard, Tesser jogged up the command shuttle's aft ramp and made his way to the flight deck. There, he took a jump seat behind the pilot who glanced at him over his shoulder.

"Ready for launch, sir?"

"Let her rip."

Moments later, a red light strobed as the hangar deck space doors retracted, leaving a shimmering force field in their wake.

"Rosebud Flight, this is Control."

"Rosebud."

"You're cleared for departure. Hobart Spaceport is expecting five shuttles from MV *Liparus*. Call the tower when you pass through ten thousand meters."

"Roger that, Control. Lifting now." The pilot paused for a few seconds. "Rosebud Flight, light on the skids in order of march."

The other four shuttle pilots responded one after the other, then the command ship rose, pivoted toward the starboard space doors, and slowly nosed its way out into space. From orbit, New Tasman's night side seemed utterly devoid of life, the lights of its major settlements smothered by thick clouds along the sole mega-continent's coasts. The occasional flash of lightning caught Tesser's eye as he searched for signs of Hobart, which he knew was halfway between the equator and the north pole on the eastern shore.

He absently heard the pilot speak with Traffic Control as they neared the cloud blanket and knew they were passing through ten thousand meters after a leisurely spiral descent. As much as Tesser enjoyed pedal to the metal missions, he didn't mind the slower pace. It made for a pleasant change, though the adrenaline would pump during the actual strike and subsequent extraction.

With a suddenness that roused him from his idle contemplation, they plunged into an otherworldly place. The clouds cut off his view of the stars above, and for the first time, he saw their position lights glowing on either beam, another sign they weren't going in hot. Otherwise, the shuttles would be utterly dark.

Passing through not only took a long time but felt unaccountably rough because of the turbulence. Just as Tesser wondered whether they'd emerge nap of the earth, their shuttle broke through the ceiling. Hobart, in all its nightly glory, lay less than a kilometer beneath them.

"It's bloody pouring rain outside," the pilot said in a tone of faint disgust. "Did we arrive during the monsoon, perchance?"

"I'm afraid the rain is a quasi-permanent feature during the warm months. But since we're not here as tourists, who cares? Besides, foul weather almost always favors the attacker in our business."

The pilot nodded. "True. But better you than me."

Tesser clapped him on the shoulder. "We're landing in a dry space, so no worries."

"Good. You know how the Navy works. Nothing is too good for us."

"And nothing you will get."

The man chuckled. It was an ancient joke that somehow never lost its edge. He turned his attention back to the primary display as they followed Traffic Control's instructions and approached Hobart Spaceport on the desired vector. Other small craft crisscrossed the sky, their position lights moving stars against the low cloud canopy.

As they dropped beneath three hundred meters, the shuttle's forward momentum bled away until the downward view showed them directly above an apron running along dozens of identical warehouses on the spaceport's outer edge. A tiny figure stood in the light spilling through the open doors of the one whose coordinates marked it as their target.

The five shuttles came down vertically in a single line facing the doors, shedding what was left of their momentum until they hovered a bare meter above the cracked and blackened concrete. Tesser touched the gunner's display and was rewarded with a close-in view of a woman's lean, angular face framed by black hair —

Warrant Officer Aleksa Kine, the Commonwealth Constabulary liaison officer assigned to Ghost Squadron.

"That's our advance party," Tesser said. "We're good."

A pair of hazel eyes framing an aquiline nose studied the shuttles impassively for a few seconds before she backed into the hangar, making 'come on' motions with her raised hands.

One by one, the craft entered and settled on marked spots after pivoting one-hundred and eighty degrees, so their noses faced the exit. Once the last shuttle cleared the doors, they slid shut, sealing them off from the rain and from curious eyes. Tesser released his seat restraints and stood.

"We can offload now."

"Right-o."

As Tesser left the flight deck, he heard the aft ramp latches releasing it. Once in the passenger compartment, he picked up his bags, imitated by First Sergeant Gade and the company HQ noncoms, and walked out into what, for official purposes, was the Deep Space Foundation's Hobart Branch Office warehouse, where Kine waited, arms crossed.

"Hello, Aleksa," he said, smiling as he came within earshot. "Everything's nominal, I hope."

She returned the smile.

"If it weren't, did you think I'd have let you land?"

"Of course not."

An inner door opened, and a stocky, thickset man with dark hair and a full beard came through. He wore what Tesser thought of as backcountry chic.

"Who's that?"

"A friend of ours," Kine replied, using a phrase borrowed from organized crime, one which identified the newcomer as a member of the Fleet intelligence and Special Forces community. If he was a local contact, she would have called him 'a friend of mine.'

"Wash, meet Khurshid. Khurshid, Wash."

The two men shook hands while giving each other the once-over. As per field protocol, Kine didn't use last names or ranks, let alone affiliation. Khurshid might not even be his first name, and for all the agent knew, Wash might be an alias as well.

"Pleasure." The former's voice was as deep and resonant as his grip was powerful. Khurshid's steady gaze told Tesser this was one of Commodore Talyn's agents, no mistake.

"Likewise."

"Khurshid's been on New Tasman for a few months and dug up most of what we know."

"Call me the closest thing to a native guide you'll get. And you'll need one, trust me."

— Twenty-Eight —

Keres Company's operations noncom, Sergeant First Class Boyd Brantingham, BB to his friends, let out a soft grunt as he studied the Galindez Cartel's compound north of Hobart through unpowered optical sensors. He, Washburn Tesser, Aleksa Kine, and Khurshid were tucked away in a hide overlooking the narrow valley owned by the cartel.

"I can't help but think death from above would be the cleanest way on this one, Skipper. A dropship strike, or simply rods from God and done. But yeah," BB, a compact, swarthy thirty-six-year-old with dark hair, beetling brows, and a boxer's flattened nose, raised a hand before Tesser could object, "I know. Our orders are finessing this one, so the cartel and the opposition go on the outs. And that means leaving traces of the attack."

Tesser gave his operations sergeant a knowing look.

"Under any other circumstances, I'd agree with you. Aleksa, are you sure the Galindez buggers aren't into human trafficking through this place?"

Kine nodded.

"Positive. This is the cartel's HQ, where their *presidente* holds court. They wouldn't risk attracting undue attention by using it as a way station. After the New Oberon business, every cartel knows human trafficking will attract the attention of forces who can dismantle their operations with no hope of reconstruction. The only humans in there are cartel members and, occasionally, visiting *Sécurité Spéciale* operatives."

Khurshid, who'd been silent up to now, let out a soft grunt.

"Friends or handlers? The latest UCF riots in Hobart included an unusual number of known cartel soldiers among the so-called peaceful protesters. The Almighty only knows how often that's replicated on other worlds where Galindez is active."

"Point taken. That just makes it more pressing we separate the two while eliminating the opposition's influence on colonial affairs in this star system."

"I'm done, Skipper." BB tucked his tablet in a jacket pocket and stowed the optical sensor. "I wouldn't mind a view from the opposite direction, but absent practicable roads, this, along with the aerials from *Iolanthe* will have to do."

"Then it's time we checked out the *Sécurité Spéciale* compound."

They made their way back through the damp, temperate rain forest, which covered most of the continent's coasts between the equator and the poles, careful to avoid startling the local wildlife. Since most native species rarely, if ever, met humans, they shrank into the shadows, both cautious and curious, and watched them leave.

The beat-up ground car was where they'd left it, and after Khurshid scanned both the vehicle and the surrounding forest, they climbed aboard and headed back to Hobart on a rough logging road. It was one of many crisscrossing the mountains and valleys inland from the capital and its elongated, bottle-shaped harbor.

"Cracking that one won't be simple," BB said once they were back on the main coastal highway overlooking a stormy sea beneath low gray clouds which promised another deluge before nightfall.

Khurshid snorted with amusement.

"The only easy day was yesterday."

His use of the old Marine Corps saying proved what Tesser already suspected. The taciturn agent came from his service, but not the 1st Special Forces Regiment. Otherwise, he'd remember seeing Khurshid's face around Fort Arnhem at some point.

"Oo-rah, brother."

The agent glanced over his shoulder and gave Tesser a knowing grin.

"Oo-rah, indeed. I was with the 251st Pathfinders in case you're curious. When it was deactivated, Colonel Ryent suggested I become a spook instead of spending the rest of my career behind a desk analyzing what others collected in the field. The rest, as they say, is history."

"You were the 251st's intelligence noncom?"

"For five utterly fascinating years. Your colonel took us places most Marines can only dream of back when he was a major."

"I figured you were one of us. You moved too smoothly through the forest this morning for a squid, or — present company excepted — a cop. Which means we all went through the same school at an unnamed Fort."

"Guilty as charged."

"Why did you let on, just now?"

"Secrecy is nice and well, but we're not only on the same side, we also wear the same colors. I figure we'll be trusting each other a lot more before this is over."

"Voice of experience?"

Khurshid nodded.

"Sure, working as a spook has its moments, but it's been a long time since I served with my own, let alone visited the Pegasus."

Tesser heard the longing in the agent's voice, a heartfelt feeling born of years living among people Khurshid trusted with his life. He understood the sentiment. Once you fought side-by-side with those who shared your values and ethos, anything else paled by comparison.

"The regiment can always use more liaison officers, or even field analysts if ever you want a change from searching underwear drawers for vital intelligence."

"Are you offering me a job?"

"I'm telling you there are options for Marines with experience working the blackest of black operations. But let's finish this one first. I assume you two plan on extracting with us?"

Kine nodded. "Yes."

"Then, we can discuss matters back aboard our ship in due course."

The rest of the trip back into Hobart and around the harbor passed in silence. Khurshid took them up a promontory overlooking the city and its surroundings and stopped at the top just as the heavens dumped a fresh deluge on the already waterlogged colony. Instead of inviting the others to brave the rain, he moved the car around until it sat broadside to a low wall at the edge of the observation platform.

"We don't melt," Tesser said in a droll tone.

"I know, but any idiot can be uncomfortable. Reference the communications tower on the heights across the bay, the one with four navigation lights flashing."

"Seen."

"Make the tower's base twelve o'clock. Halfway down the slope, at four o'clock, there's a low-rise apartment building with white walls and a green living roof."

"Seen."

"Four fingers from the building's three o'clock edge, a lone, flat-roofed house at the center of an enclosed property."

"The one with what looks like a driveway looping back on itself, similar to a question mark."

"Yes. That's the *Sécurité Spéciale*'s New Tasman station."

"At first glance, it seems like a much easier target than the cartel compound, Skipper," BB said, examining the site through his optical sensor.

Kine grimaced.

"You'd think so. I don't know whether they developed a heightened sense of paranoia working with the cartel or whether the first station chief posted here was nervous in the service, but that place is a small fortress with all the fixings. They've installed a sensor perimeter, remote weapon stations, hardened fence, gate, windows and doors, the works. And they're in a genteel neighborhood where senior functionaries rub elbows with local nabobs — ComCorp subsidiary executives, for the main part — organized crime capos, and other notables. A troop of mercenaries in that area would stick out like a Void Sister in a brothel at any hour of the day. Every property in the surroundings is equipped with security systems, making a sneak and strike more challenging. Whoever decided on setting up there was thinking ahead."

"I don't like the idea of our opposition smartening up," Tesser said with a grimace. "It makes things messier. Inevitable, though, I suppose. Even a sand devil eventually turns away from pain, and we've been giving the *Sécurité Spéciale* and its foot soldiers more than they can handle."

BB let out a low growl. "We'll find a way, never you mind, Skipper."

"And to find that way, we need surveillance on both sites for a few days, so start thinking about the roster."

"Drones?"

Tesser glanced at Kine. "What does their air defense look like?"

"No idea, but there's enough air traffic around Hobart that one more unmanned craft making a single pass won't raise the alarm. A drone hovering over a site, that's different."

"I wasn't thinking of a hover, not even with our stealthy machines. Let's do a drone pass once a day at random times, BB."

"Roger that, Skipper. One recce roster on its way."

Khurshid glanced over this shoulder again.

"Need more time here?"

Tesser shook his head.

"No. Let's head back to the barn for a hot tea and a bit of brainstorming once everyone studies the visuals we took."

After an evening meal of rations taken while the deluge outside continued unabated and lots of tea and coffee, Keres Company's senior non-commissioned officers sat in a semi-circle on scavenged folding chairs. They studied the target images projected on the hangar's smoothest, if not quite cleanest wall.

"Since we can't stomp and whomp on this one," Tesser said, "death from above isn't a practical course of action. The optimal outcome is leaving the infrastructure intact, albeit minus computer cores, and the two-legged vermin dead with nothing to show who did the deed except for the death cards. Hopefully, the latter will start a cartel war with the opposition stuck in the middle, taking fire from both ends. So, the trick is infiltrating the sites, doing the job, and exfiltrating with no one the wiser until the damage is discovered well after we're in interstellar space."

Khurshid raised his hand.

"One thing Aleksa and I observed since our arrival was, for lack of a better term, supply convoys from the spaceport to the Galindez Cartel's *hacienda*. Not regular, but a few times a month. Perhaps you noticed the place out in the hills doesn't offer much space for a tarmac, and with officials on the take, it's easier to use the port facilities. That's a potential entry vector. The cargo skimmers we've seen have cabs with polarized windows — crew can see out, no one can see in — and large, enclosed boxes, possibly shielded against casual sensor checks. Plenty of room for your company."

Tesser nodded.

"It's a good way into the compound. Thanks. How about the *Sécurité Spéciale* station?"

Khurshid shrugged.

"We saw nothing that might give us a hint."

"Well then, let's brainstorm. There's not much else on our agenda for tonight, and since it's pissing rain, a stroll in the double moonlight is out."

— Twenty-Nine —

Though the quarters were tighter than what Delgado and his company enjoyed during their cruise in the Fleet flagship and multiple Q-ship missions, the trip passed in reasonable comfort. Delgado was both pleased and impressed with the containerized accommodations and amenities. With a few minutes of warning, the Marines could shut themselves in and give a customs inspector the impression *Kobe Maru* carried nothing but cargo. Even military-grade sensors couldn't pierce the masking field that showed various industrial goods when it was activated.

The Fleet engineering wizards on the unnamed colony that built and refurbished equipment for SOCOM's growing list of missions had outdone themselves. But no one intercepted *Kobe Maru* during her fast passage to Cascadia. Once Traffic Control assigned her a parking orbit around the sector capital, she became just another small tramp freighter that spent her life plying the outer shipping routes.

After one full orbit to make sure no one was paying *Kobe Maru* any undue interest, Delgado used the ship's encrypted communications facilities to send the as yet unknown advance party a message informing it of their arrival. A few hours passed before he received a reply, but it contained the expected code words and the extra layer of encryption with added proof the missive came from a Naval Intelligence operative. The chances of a cartel or the *Sécurité Spéciale* spoofing it were almost nil. Not entirely, but almost. The ultimate confirmation would come when Delgado met his contact in person. But would it be someone he knew?

"What now?" Lieutenant Commander Bahn asked after Delgado declared the response genuine.

"I arrange for a meeting with the advance party, head down in one of your shuttles, and conduct my preliminary reconnaissance."

"Alone?"

"My designated wingman, Sergeant Kuzek, will go with me. At this stage, it's best if we don't go around in large groups that might attract attention. First Sergeant Hak will be in charge while I'm gone, and if anything happens to me, he takes command."

"Got it. I'll make sure there's a shuttle standing by."

At that moment, the communications petty officer raised her hand.

"Major, another message from the same node for us."

"Pass it to my console," Delgado said from where he sat at the back of the bridge.

"Done."

He ran the decryption protocol and smiled.

"I'm invited to a meeting with my contact in a Gibsons pub called the Flying Unicorn, at thirteen-hundred hours tomorrow."

Bahn frowned. "Gibsons? Not the capital?"

Delgado, who'd called up a map of Cascadia's main continent, shrugged after finding Gibsons.

"We go where our advance party says. If they say a minor coastal town with a small spaceport instead of Squamish itself, then so be it."

"Fair enough. I'll see that you land thirty minutes before the appointed time. Just one question."

"Sure."

"You smiled as you read the message. Why?"

"Ever seen the ancient and venerable symbol of airborne troops — Pegasus, the winged horse?"

"Could be."

"The choice of a place called the Flying Unicorn can't be random. My advance party is either one of us or has worked with our sort. And that suits me fine."

The next day, Delgado and Kuzek, wearing ordinary civilian clothes and carrying only small-bore sidearms, stepped off the shuttle and into the chilly, damp, coastal air. Gray clouds scudding from east to west threatened rain, while squalls ruffled the waters separating the mainland from a chain of islands protecting this part of the coast from the worst storms. The tang of salt tickled their nostrils, along with a faint aroma of dead fish and rotting seaweed.

They walked to the small, mostly deserted terminal, flashing their undercover credentials at the automated entry control point, and were allowed through without problems.

Gibsons was a small agglomeration strung along a narrow stretch of reasonably flat ground between the sea and the mountains. Its spaceport was more of an afterthought, a tiny strip on the southern outskirts, where a narrow highway skirted the coast on its way to the capital, Squamish, two hours by ground vehicle, substantially less by aircar.

Delgado spied a cluster of commercial buildings crowding the road leading into town, one of them proudly displaying a sign with a winged, four-legged beast which bore no resemblance whatsoever to the mythical unicorn, or its more prosaic cousin, a horse. But from a distance, it might pass for a caricature of the venerated Pegasus if the observer was near-sighted and almost blind drunk.

He and Sergeant Kuzek walked past its front door and bay windows, studying the surroundings, alert for anything that might trigger their Special Forces operator's instincts. They went as far as the next crossroads, then turned back, satisfied no one paid them attention, and entered the Winged Unicorn.

The pub, a bright, airy place overlooking Horseshoe Bay, was mostly empty at the tail end of the noon meal hour on a weekday. A long, wooden counter, overseen by an elderly man, dominated one wall, while panoramic windows filled another. He nodded pleasantly at Delgado and Kuzek as they headed for a corner table, far from the few remaining customers.

At the stroke of thirteen-hundred hours, the door opened to admit a man and a woman. Delgado nearly choked on his own saliva as he recognized the latter. Kuzek gave his commanding officer a curious look, then watched the pair approach them. They slid into chairs facing the Marines.

"Long time no see, Curtis," the woman said in a melodious alto, smiling. Tall, with shoulder-length black hair, intelligent brown eyes, and a bodybuilder's physique, she appeared to be in her mid-forties.

"Ari." He nodded, studying Major Ariane Redmon, an erstwhile squadron commander in the 1st Special Forces Regiment.

"Surprise, surprise. You're probably wondering why I'm here when word around the old homestead was that I'd been benched indefinitely."

"Yep." Delgado glanced at Sergeant Kuzek. "Carl, meet Ariane, Ari, to her friends. She's one of us, though her time with the firm was before you came aboard."

Kuzek gave Redmon a friendly nod.

"Pleasure."

The latter gestured at her companion, a lean, fit, dark-complexioned man with a forgettable face framed by short dark hair.

"This is Destry. He's one of our close friends from head office." Meaning he was with Naval Intelligence's Special Operations Division, working for Commodore Talyn. "And I'm doing odd jobs for head office as well these days.

The big boss forgave my sins, made sure I couldn't talk out of turn again, and transferred me after a stint at school."

Delgado interpreted it as meaning Commodore Talyn had restored Redmon's security clearance, seen she was conditioned against interrogation and sent to Camp X for training as an undercover operative. He privately approved.

Redmon had been a reliable and well respected Special Forces officer who'd fallen in with the wrong crowd, a mistake that cost her almost everything before Colonel Decker brought her back from the dead. Atoning for the past by working one of the most dangerous jobs in the Service was an excellent path to redemption.

"Good to see you back in action."

"I hear you've become a mover and shaker."

"Scurrilous rumors, nothing more."

She snorted.

"Right. Just make sure you don't succumb to flattery on your way up, buddy. Otherwise, you might make unexpected detours before finding the way home."

"No danger of that. I'm quite happy to stay where I am until the Corps retires my sorry old ass. So, what's the lay of the land? Why are we meeting in this ratty little burg instead of Squamish?"

"How about a quick sandwich, and then we talk outdoors?" Redmon suggested.

"Sure."

They ordered, paid, and ate in watchful silence. Safe conversation topics for undercover operatives in public were somewhat limited. Twenty minutes later, the foursome walked along Gibsons' empty shoreline, Kuzek and Destry keeping watch while Redmon briefed Delgado.

"There's a slight problem in Squamish. One head office didn't foresee. A few weeks of tracking the Cascadian Sector station chief and her minions revealed heretofore unknown connections with the Cascadia Police Service. For example, the station chief, Flavia DeBrito, regularly meets with the Police Service's Chief Commissioner, Rupert Larow. Since she and her folks ostensibly work for the Commonwealth High Commission, I'm sure DeBrito is advertising herself as a senior intelligence and security adviser."

Delgado cocked a questioning eyebrow at Redmon.

"When you say they meet regularly, is it to share a meal or share a bed?"

She gave him an amused look.

"Yes."

"Ugh. That complicates matters."

"I know. Worse yet, from what we gleaned, the opposition feeds intel to the Police Service and vice versa."

"Which means the bastards could subvert the Cascadia Police Service from within."

Redmon nodded.

"No question about it. Which makes removing the sector station even more imperative."

"In proper Ghost Squadron style without leaving traces? Sounds like a tall order if the opposition is sheltering behind local law enforcement. It won't do our cause a damn bit of good if cops become collateral damage."

"I know. But when we reported back, the response was do your best before the CPS comes under enemy control. So here we are."

"Please tell me the opposition doesn't work out of the Commonwealth High Commission's offices downtown, next to the Cascadia Government Precinct."

"As a matter of fact, they own an anonymous station house on the southern outskirts, an operations center of sorts which runs night and day. The staff lives in the general area, except for DeBrito."

"At least that's something." They walked on in silence for a few minutes while Delgado digested the new developments. Finally, he asked, "Why meet us here?"

"Our strikes against the UCF and its allies in the outer sectors have made DeBrito nervous. She arranged for greater CPS scrutiny of incoming traffic through Larow. Except the police aren't resourced to cover every little landing strip. Besides, Cascadia immigration and customs protocols could be described as lax, and that's being generous. I figured no one was paying Gibsons any attention considering the larger, better-equipped spaceports both south and inland of Squamish, places with direct ground connections to the capital. Why waste one of them on a recce landing? Too many visits by shuttles from the same ship to the same strip will attract someone's attention."

"Understood. Since you've been on the ground for a while, what do you propose?"

Redmon stopped and stared out at Horseshoe Bay.

"Head office owns an old commercial facility in the rundown part of Squamish. It can accommodate a hundred people or so and should make an excellent base of operations. And it's close to the colony's original spaceport, now used for cargo only. That strip is a favorite for customs and excise evaders because bribes still work wonders around here."

"I see. Organized crime basically runs it, right? Our ship can land just so you know."

"She's not the usual, then?" Redmon asked, referring to SOCOM's Q-ships.

"No. A refurbished pirate sloop. *Kobe Maru* is registered to a legitimate shipping company, one of the many shell corporations home office uses. And she's not only sterile but disposable if ever we need to ditch her."

Redmon nodded.

"Convenient."

"Can you put Carl and me up for a day or two while we run reconnaissance with you?"

"Sure. We can put up as many as you like."

"Then let's go back to the landing strip so we can recover the bags we brought just in case and send the shuttle back upstairs."

— Thirty —

"What do we think?" Delgado asked as he dropped into a sagging easy chair in what passed for the safe house's living room. He, Sergeant Kuzek, Major Redmon, and Destry, who was clearly a naval officer, judging by his manners, had spent the rest of the day reconnoitering the *Sécurité Spéciale*'s Cascadia station as well as the agents' residences.

The safe house, a rundown building near the inland cargo spaceport, was in an area that dated back to the first landing, centuries earlier. Delgado figured their temporary abode could easily be among the first structures built, considering its general condition. The shuttered storefront, the blanked out windows, and the grimy facade spoke of an unloved place abandoned long ago. In reality, it belonged to Naval Intelligence, bought a few years earlier, and retrofitted with everything Commodore Talyn's operatives could wish for.

Delgado nodded at Sergeant Kuzek, the most junior in rank.

"You first, Carl."

"If we must make it in and out without creating a ruckus, then the best way is putting a gun to the station chief's head and turning her into our native guide while we round up the rest of them. Empty the station of people and computer cores, then back to the ship with our prisoners and home. Leave the families behind, of course. HQ can decide what we do with the spies. If any resist during the operation..."

Kuzek ran an extended index finger across his throat.

"Thanks."

The Erinye Company commander glanced at Redmon and Destry, in turn, until the former pointed at her colleague.

"He's the next junior."

"Go ahead."

"I figure Carl's idea is the best course of action. If we can carry it off without calling a Cascadia Police Service or National Guard counter-terrorism team on our heads, or worse, a rapid reaction unit from the 7th Marine Division. It wouldn't be the first time a star system government went straight to the Fleet when a threat assessment scared them shitless, or their own folks can't saddle up fast enough. They know Marine Corps RRUs are at much shorter notice to move than anyone else. But if we can seize the off-duty *Sécurité Spéciale* personnel simultaneously, then penetrate their compound using captured credentials, we should be good. They're paranoid, like all spies, but here in a star system capital where nothing ever happens, and the local cops are friendly, they'll be complacent. Perhaps even sloppy if we're lucky." Destry glanced at Redmon.

"I'm with Carl and Destry," she said. "Use the human factor rather than strike directly at the infrastructure."

Delgado nodded. Redmon knew as much as he did about black ops.

"I came to the same conclusion. But let's not risk tunnel vision. We'll watch the people and the station for a few days, maybe a week or more, to establish patterns and identify vulnerabilities. Other potential courses of action might crop up during that time. The question is, do I bring my people down via shuttle, or land *Kobe Maru* at the cargo spaceport. If the recce takes time, local authorities might wonder about a tramp freighter with pockets deep enough for more than a few days of docking fees."

"Do you need the entire company for surveillance?" Destry asked.

"No, but if I bring everyone down, I can make sure our marks don't see the same faces two days in a row. Besides, I'd rather my people protect this place, even if the friendly neighborhood crime fraternity takes us under its wing. Also, if we see an immediate opportunity, having my resources at hand will mean we can seize it."

Redmon nodded.

"I agree with Curtis. Here's what I suggest. Use shuttles instead of landing your ship. Save it for the extraction. The cargo spaceport will do fine for small craft. We'll rent enclosed transport skimmers and ferry them here, perhaps in two waves twelve to twenty-four hours apart. Two shuttles in two flights will be less noticeable than one flight of four. And like I said, this place has the infrastructure we need to house your people and keep a low profile. As a bonus, because of shady actors using this neighborhood, the CPS doesn't come sniffing unless there's a chance of making an arrest."

Delgado cocked an eyebrow.

"The same organized criminals controlling the cargo spaceport?"

"Yes. Proximity to it makes this area valuable real estate for folks who see nothing, hear nothing, and say nothing." Redmon chuckled. "Where would we black ops people be without enterprising scofflaws who unwittingly cover our tracks?"

"More obvious than a Void Sister in a nudist parade?" Kuzek suggested, an uncharacteristic smile lighting up his normally stoic features.

"They will disrobe in a good cause," Redmon replied. "Or so I hear. But back to the main subject. Bringing your company here won't be an issue if we follow the same patterns as the folks with whom we share this part of town."

Delgado gave her thumbs-up.

"Then let's do it."

"What's your bribe money allowance?"

"How much do you need?"

Redmon cited a large sum, but Delgado merely shrugged.

"Done. Expensive, though."

"This is the big city, and that means big city prices for everything, including payoffs."

"Isn't corruption grand. When can we call the shuttles?"

"Give Destry and me a day or so."

"Comms?"

She pointed downward.

"In the basement. This level looks as it should if squatters or a small-time crime outfit lived here. They divided the warehouse at the back into two sections. One with cargo doors opening onto the back alley — it looks exactly like an abandoned space — and the other, behind an inner wall. It can serve as barracks and garage for vehicles we don't want found during a casual inspection. The real safe house, with an armory, communications gear, interrogation room, and more, is in the basement. The staircases are behind well-hidden airlock-grade doors. You'd literally need to demolish this structure if you wanted to get past them." Redmon stood. "I'll show you around while Destry arranges transportation for your people. He'll also make sure the local version of the neighborhood watch sees and hears nothing for the next two or three weeks."

The man nodded and sprang to his feet.

"On my way."

Redmon gestured at the door leading to the warehouse section.

"If you'll follow me."

Once back in the living room after an exhaustive tour of the facility, Delgado said, "Impressive. It'll feel a little tight with over a hundred troopers and their gear, but I can't fault the amenities or the camouflage. How does this place stay secure between visitors?"

"No idea, but the neighborhood watch, run by one of Squamish's most powerful mobsters, is pretty effective at keeping trouble away from this area, and once bought, he stays so provided the protection payments keep rolling in. That way, everyone can keep making illicit profits. And yes, Destry and I met with him. He believes we're Deep Space Foundation operatives here to earn our employer extra, untraceable profits. Since the Foundation was doing unholy things under Sorne and Hakkam, he considers us dirty enough for comfort."

Delgado chuckled.

"Honor among thieves?"

"It's about business. As far as the local mob is concerned, we're just another outfit doing our thing, and taking care we don't step on anyone's toes."

Destry returned shortly after that.

"Done. Two enclosed cargo haulers will wait for us outside an hour after we say go, and we can use them as long as we want. The friendly folks who keep us safe from the police and unauthorized outsiders are waiting for our financial contribution."

"How much?"

Destry named the price, drawing a disconsolate grunt from Delgado.

"Ouch. My folks will bring enough unmarked cred chips."

**

Thirty-six hours later, as Squamish slept under the blanket of night, Delgado and Redmon climbed aboard one hauler while Destry and Kuzek took the other. Unmarked, save for registration tags, they looked like the sort of rundown skimmers a transport business barely hanging on might use, though Delgado couldn't fault their mechanical condition.

After a short drive along darkened streets, they entered the cargo spaceport via one of the side gates, admitted by the automated security station on the strength of Redmon and Destry's false credentials. They parked at the edge of the apron right on schedule, rear compartments toward the tarmac. Moments later, Delgado's communicator came to life.

"Cascadia branch office, this is *Kobe Maru* Shuttle One with the first delivery. We're on final, passing through one thousand."

"Branch office here — you're cleared to land. Home in on my signal. Two trucks at the edge of the apron, past the last hanger on the north side."

A few seconds later, "I have you on visual."

Delgado nodded at Redmon and climbed out of the cab to stand under the nearest light globe, so the shuttle pilots could see his face, imitated by Kuzek. He searched the sky for position lights outlining boxy shuttles and spotted them almost at once. Their rate of descent seemed annoyingly slow, and it soon became evident Traffic Control wouldn't let them land directly on the apron. Instead, the lights vanished from view for a while, then reappeared as both shuttlecrafts, now hovering half a dozen meters over the tarmac, rounded the hangar on his left. They pivoted one-hundred and eighty degrees, so their aft ramps would face the waiting trucks.

Once the whine of the thrusters faded away, Delgado and Kuzek stepped forward and waited for the ramps to drop. Once the first Marines came into view, they pointed at the waiting trucks and watched in silence as the backpack and duffel bag toting men, several of whom carried larger containers between them, quickly switched modes of transportation.

The last one off was Sergeant First Class Metellus Testo, who said, in a low voice as he passed Delgado, "Emery sends his best and wishes he were here."

"He's coming with the rest tomorrow night."

"And they're afraid they might miss the action."

"Just the recce will take more than a day."

"Tell it to Emery, not me, Skipper."

Then the operations noncom vanished into C Troop's truck, whose doors closed behind him. Delgado gave Kuzek thumbs-up, and they too climbed aboard while the shuttles, ramps up, thrusters spooling, prepared for departure.

Once back at the safe house, Redmon and Destry drove the trucks directly into the garage to unload away from prying eyes and parked beside ground cars bought used earlier that day from vendors who don't ask questions or remember customers.

Staff Sergeant Salford Lambrix and the rest of one-four-alpha were among the first to disembark and study their surroundings as they formed up by troops behind the haulers.

"Nice." Corporal Taggart nodded his head. "If you like post-industrial decor from early colonial days."

"Okay, people."

Delgado's voice rang out. Almost at once, everyone present fell silent and turned eyes on him.

"Welcome to our latest base of operations, an anonymous commercial structure shuttered long ago and repurposed. Our barracks are through the doors behind you in what was once the inner half of a warehouse space. For now, settle in. Ops will take care of the sentry roster. The entire building is a secure perimeter, and the standard rules of engagement for secure perimeters in unsecured territory apply. Our mission for the coming days will be surveillance — mobile observation posts to establish the various targets' routines and habits. Once we know what we face, I'll decide how we take them out. One last thing. A few of you might remember Ariane." He nodded at Redmon. "She and Destry are our advance team and work for head office, so avoid any attempts at auld lang syne. Questions?"

When no one raised a hand, Delgado said, "Dismissed."

"Holy crap," Lambrix muttered just loud enough for Saxer's ears as they filed through the inner doors. "Who'd have figured she would end up playing spook. Heck of a career change from door kicker."

"After what happened?" Saxer shrugged. "Can't say I blame her for going to the really dark side. She didn't have many prospects, from what I heard."

"Prospects for what?" Taggart asked in a whisper. "I smell a story."

"It happened before your time. You can ask around once we're back home, but like the skipper said, no reminiscing right now."

"Roger that."

"Don't worry. Major Redmon was damn good back then, and I'm sure she's just as good at her new job. Otherwise, the head office wouldn't assign her to work with us. We get only the best."

— Thirty-One —

"So, when do I finally see the secret tunnels beneath Geneva?" Miko Steiger ran feathery light fingertips over Andreas Bauchan's bare chest as she studied his profile, head propped up by her other hand. "You've been teasing me for weeks."

"And you're teasing me right now." He turned his head and smiled at her.

"That?" She brushed his chest again. "That's not teasing. This is."

Steiger reached under the sheet, and his smile widened.

"Clearly, you aim to make me a shadow of myself before this night is over."

"But a delighted shadow, one whose every appetite is sated." Steiger leaned over and kissed him.

"Succubus," he said once she released him. "How about tomorrow morning?"

"Oh?" Steiger's face took on a disappointed air. "I was hoping for at least once more tonight."

"The emergency government headquarters, or EGH, as we call the secret tunnels."

"I'd love to. And just for that…" She draped herself over him.

"You're insatiable."

"And you love it."

"Yes, I do." He pulled her head down for a kiss, ending their conversation.

The next day, just after ten, an elegantly dressed Miko Steiger breezed through the security gate at the Palace of the Stars' main entrance, thanks to her permanent visitor pass. She'd left a visibly pleased Bauchan shortly after midnight and returned home for a long, hot shower and a few peaceful hours by herself.

Breaking away from Britta Trulson at least once a day had become an absolute necessity, so she didn't lose touch with her true self, not least because she enjoyed the role too much for comfort. Brushing elbows with the most powerful in the Commonwealth, sleeping with the Secretary-General's chief of intelligence and security, and planning a bright, if fictitious future while undermining Bauchan was a heady mix. Especially for someone who came to the world of espionage after years as an Army noncom and then as a mercenary for hire.

Bauchan's admiring eyes spoke to her well before he opened his mouth.

"Britta, my dear. You look lovely. And so fresh, even after a late night."

He stood and embraced her, a gesture she returned with as much passion as was proper in a formal office near that of the man who governed humanity across the stars.

"Some late nights leave my soul refreshed, darling."

"And mine." He stepped back and examined her, noting the flat-heeled boots, loose trousers, and hip-length jacket. "I see you're sensibly dressed for a stroll. Good. The EGH has transport pod tubes, but they're generally switched off between periodic tests. Most of the complex isn't crewed during normal times, except for a few nodes that are accessed from the surface outside of emergency conditions. We won't be visiting those, of course. National security."

"Understood. I'm honored you trust me enough for even a quick peek at one of Geneva's closest-kept secrets."

Bauchan made a deprecating hand gesture.

"Considering how much you've trusted me with the Deep Space Foundation's secrets, it's the least I can do in return. We are rapidly becoming the closest of allies. Come."

He led her to the ground level, across the main hall, and into one of the smaller side buildings marked off-limits for visitors. There, they passed through three doors, which were clearly armored beneath imitation wood veneer, Bauchan waving his credentials each time to release mechanical locks.

Then, down several more flights of stairs and through armored doors until they stood in a high-ceilinged tunnel whose white walls glimmered dully under endless strings of glow globes. Steiger felt unaccountably small for a few heartbeats.

Bauchan indicated nearby rectangular protrusions covering huge tubes running along both walls. Each of the two sported four closed double doors.

"This is the pod transport Palace station. The tubes connect this terminus with every station along the former Large Hadron Collider complex. The deepest station, one-hundred seventy-five meters below ground level, is where the Secretary-General, the cabinet, and senior government officials have their emergency offices. Other stations, shallower, are for various departments. Theoretically, the Commonwealth government can function almost normally from here, although I hope we never test that theory."

"Agreed."

Steiger allowed herself a small, albeit feigned shiver.

"We're in luck." He led her toward a four-place open-top skimmer, the sort used to move around large complexes, such as spaceport passenger terminals, warehouses, and the like. "Instead of walking, we can ride, and perhaps cover the entire twenty-seven-kilometer circuit."

"I'd like that."

"This section," he said, as the skimmer silently whisked them into the tunnel, "runs beneath the Geneva Spaceport and isn't part of the original twenty-first-century complex. It was dug approximately fifty years ago, when the Secretary-General of the day decided the government needed a secret emergency headquarters, one the military wouldn't know about. As far as anyone stumbling across it is concerned, top-secret particle physics research has resumed after a long dormancy, and the new complex is merely an updated version of the original LHC."

"Ingenious."

"Isn't it?" He gave her a side glance. "One of the unintended consequences stemming from Grand Admiral Kowalski's reforms."

"Just out of idle curiosity, why hasn't anyone worked on reversing those reforms?"

Bauchan's lips twitched with amusement.

"Who says someone isn't? Unfortunately, the OutWorlds are generally satisfied by the current arrangements and the Fleet's freedom from grubby politics, so getting the requisite majority to repeal Kowalski's constitutional amendment is a momentous task. That's where a move away from the sovereign star systems principle and greater centralization of government will help."

"Of course."

The tunnel ended at a three-way intersection with enough doors and platforms in both directions to indicate this was a station, and Bauchan brought them to a full stop.

"This is the original LHC loop, and the sub-complex originally called Point Eight. Travel twenty-seven kilometers in either direction, and you'll end up right back here. Left or right?"

"Right."

As the skimmer turned in the desired direction, Bauchan asked, "Why?"

"Why right?"

"Yes."

Steiger realized she might have made a mistake — the distance to the *Sécurité Spéciale* headquarters, at Point Five, was shorter on the right than the left, meaning Bauchan would always turn in that direction whenever he visited his underlings via the tunnels.

She shrugged.

"Search me. It could be because I'm right-handed and will instinctively prefer that side. Is there something special about this direction?"

"No. I'm just my usual self, studying human nature. You still intrigue me, and likely always will. There are depths I've yet to plumb." He gave her a mischievous glance. "And I don't mean that in the carnal sense."

"Then you might miss out, I'm afraid." She patted his knee. "But thanks for the compliment."

"In that case, perhaps I won't exclude the carnal sense. There's no point in limiting oneself."

They rode along in silence, and Steiger quickly realized Bauchan was pointedly not identifying the functions that would be carried out at each station if the government moved to its emergency offices. However, she kept count of the points they passed and identified Point Five, beneath the *Sécurité Spéciale*'s headquarters. Steiger didn't dare bring any recording devices, even though Naval Intelligence equipped her with virtually undetectable specimens, just in case they'd underestimated the *Sécurité Spéciale*. She would rely on her quasi-photographic memory and rebuild the scene later instead.

Not giving Point Five more obvious attention than the others proved difficult. She was the first Naval Intelligence officer to see this space. Her recollection of it could prove vital at a later date, when and if the Fleet decided to eliminate Bauchan's organization. Then Point Five's station vanished around the curve behind them, and she felt herself mentally relax. A leisurely hour later, much of it spent in aimless persiflage, they were back at the branch leading into Geneva.

"Feeling underwhelmed?" He asked as their little skimmer left the loop.

"A bit. The engineering is impressive, but part of me hungers for what lies hidden behind the pod transport stations. And yes, I understand simply traveling the tunnel is a privilege few outsiders will ever enjoy, and for that, I'm eternally in your debt, darling." She gave Bauchan a radiant smile that promised new and inventive ways of repaying him.

Once back in the Palace of the Stars, Bauchan excused himself, citing a meeting with the SecGen at eleven-thirty, but was pleased when she accepted his invitation to dine at his residence once more. He watched her cross the main lobby, then headed upstairs to his office. Moments after he took a seat behind his desk, Edouard Metivier gave the door jamb a perfunctory knock and entered.

"Was it wise taking Madame Trulson through the EGH complex, sir?"

He shrugged.

"She didn't see anything that isn't common knowledge around here and knows nothing of the functions carried out at the various stations. It was a small courtesy that will, without a doubt, pay dividends. Besides, I'm thinking we should make the Deep Space Foundation an integral part of our organization, though it would continue operating under the not-for-profit cover. No one would suspect a charity of collecting intelligence for the government."

Metivier didn't hide his skepticism.

"With due respect, sir, don't you think you're moving a little too fast?"

"One must beat the iron while it's hot, Edouard. The Deep Space Foundation is an asset we cannot let slip from our grasp. Under its mantle, we can operate in the OutWorlds undisturbed by Naval Intelligence."

"I wonder, sir. We're certain Naval Intelligence assassinated Louis Sorne and the Foundation's former chair, Antoine Hakkam. They might still keep tabs on its activities."

Bauchan rubbed his chin as he gazed at Metivier with a thoughtful expression.

"Perhaps. But Intelligence hasn't targeted Foundation assets since the change in leadership, while it's been relentless toward us."

"As far as we know, sir. We are working mostly on Madame Trulson's say so."

"With corroboration from our own field offices."

Metivier saw the first signs of irritation beneath his superior's usually impassive facade, but he persisted.

"The absence of evidence is not evidence of absence."

"Don't worry, Edouard. We shall take every precaution. Now, if you'll excuse me, the SecGen awaits." Bauchan stood and picked up a thin tablet.

"Will you discuss your plans concerning the Deep Space Foundation with him?" Metivier stepped aside to allow Bauchan through the doorway.

"No. The less Monsieur Brüggemann is aware of our dealings, the better. He is a politician, and like others of his sort, he will use state secrets as bargaining chips if he considers it necessary. Subverting the Foundation so it becomes ours is of such importance that we can't afford mistakes. Only the most trusted among us will ever know."

Metivier inclined his head.

"Understood, sir."

As he watched the head of the *Sécurité Spéciale* take the executive corridor to the Secretary-General's office, Metivier couldn't help wondering why he felt uneasy while his superior didn't. On the other hand, Andreas Bauchan, for all his qualities, also suffered from a few blind spots, as his blossoming relationship with the mysterious Britta Trulson proved. He not only had an eye for her type, which made him less cautious than Metivier wished but sometimes underestimated their increasingly ruthless opponents within the Fleet's intelligence and security apparatus, at a growing cost in lost lives.

— Thirty-Two —

"A thought struck me earlier today." Decker settled back in his office chair after Talyn finished updating him on the latest developments in Sanctum and contemplated her image on the primary display.

"Should I be worried? Your thoughts involve high explosives more frequently than they should."

"Not this time, though we enjoyed our session on the demolition range, chipping the rust off our skill at making things go boom. You'd have enjoyed it."

"Doubtful. But please go ahead and share your newest brain wave."

"You know how we can't quite wrap our minds around whether the three Special Forces regiments should be Tier One, leaving the Fleet Pathfinder Squadrons as our sole Tier Two units. Or whether the 3rd Regiment should be Tier Two because we can't ramp up Tier One operators fast enough. Or whether each regiment should field a Tier One squadron backed up by three Tier Two squadrons."

"A little beyond my bailiwick, but sure."

"I realized the Corps has a half dozen battalions of finely honed Marines we often use for hardcore missions to back up regular line units. That's when we're not using them as cannon fodder."

"The Marine Light Infantry Regiment."

Decker nodded.

"Precisely. Assign them to the Special Forces Division as Tier Two units and make the three regiments Tier One."

"You'll face serious opposition if you bring that up with Jimmy Martinson and Kal Ryent."

He let out a derisive snort.

"Are you saying they're elitist snobs?"

"You folks who wear the winged dagger are overly fond of your own mystique and consider the rest of the Fleet lesser beings. I can only imagine how the average Special Forces member feels about a regiment of reformed military convicts."

"Ah, but you forget Ari Redmon and I are alumni of MLI basic training and once wore its cap badge. That makes two senior Special Forces officers who know how disciplined and combat-capable those battalions are. Besides, not every MLI member is an ex-convict. A fair number transfer over in search of redemption or adventure. It's very much our updated version of the foreign legions fielded by pre-diaspora Earth armies, and most were deemed elite fighting forces in their day. I'd certainly place more trust in an MLI battalion to back up my squadron on a tricky mission than one from a regular line regiment."

Talyn nodded thoughtfully.

"True. Though you'd be part of a small minority."

"Only because most never worked with the MLI. Ask those who did, like the Marines who fought on Marengo when Ari and I were there. They'll tell you there's no better disciplined, trained, and combat-ready light infantry in the galaxy. So why not use them more constructively than we do now?"

"Why are you discussing this with me rather than Jimmy or Kal?"

"Because you can make SOCOM do it over the objections of General Habad and his staff if necessary. Jimmy, bless his soul, doesn't have the same magic pull, even if he is the general's personal pick as divisional commander. If you disagree with me about recruiting the MLI battalions into SOCOM, then it's pointless that I even try convincing my immediate superiors."

"Tell you what. Talk to Jimmy and Kal. See what their reactions are, and we'll go from there. If neither is in favor, I won't override them by speaking directly with General Habad. I can't afford to antagonize SOCOM. If both are in favor, Jimmy can make the proposal to Habad directly, and I'll drop a word in his ear as well."

"Understood and thank you. I'll snag Kal when he gets back from Sanctum tonight. He can decide whether Jimmy should hear me out."

She blew him a kiss.

"There you go being reasonable again."

"It proves an old space dog can still learn new tricks."

**

"Oh, boy." Colonel (Brigadier General designate) Kal Ryent chuckled after Decker explained his idea of how SOCOM could quickly and easily increase its Tier Two capabilities. "Now I know what you do when you're otherwise underemployed — come up with wild ideas no one else is brave enough to touch."

"Yeah, but this one makes sense, admit it. Those are crack light troopers, Kal. Anyone who survives MLI basic has more than repaid their debt and can be relied upon in the worst situations. I should know. Been there, done that. So has Ari Redmon. And if we look closely enough, we'll find a few familiar faces in the ranks, people we can pull back into Special Forces and use in building up the 3rd Regiment's strength." Decker paused for a moment as a fresh idea surfaced. "Then, we can specialize the regiments. For example, task the 1st with the blackest of black ops—"

"And make it the Ghost Regiment?" An amused smile played on Ryent's lips. "Why not? If Operation Kowalski Redux had gone ahead, B, C, and D Squadrons would have joined yours in crossing over to the dark side."

"That's what I'm thinking. Turn the entire 1st into the Fleet's covert direction action arm and let 2nd and 3rd Regiments handle the usual Tier One missions, with the MLI as follow-on forces. Do you think Jimmy will buy that?"

"Oh? We're already talking about convincing Jimmy when you don't know what I think?"

Decker grinned at his commanding officer.

"I've known you for how many years now, Kal? You're playing hard to get, but you like the idea. And so will Jimmy. Consider it this way — enlisting the MLI will give the division four regiments, and we can permanently pair two MLI battalions with each SF regiment, so they train and work with each other. Come on, future deputy divisional commander, I can see the enthusiasm in your eyes. Besides, we would finally give the MLI a good home. The Corps never figured out what it should do with them."

"Who owns the regiment now?"

"Administratively, it belongs to the Marine Corps Support Command. Whenever a battalion is deployed on operations, it comes under the employing formation. And since Support Command is largely focused on training and logistics, the MLI has been an afterthought almost from the day the Corps stood it up."

Ryent tapped the top of his desk with the fingertips of both hands.

"Very well. Sold to the lieutenant colonel with too much time on his hands. Or I should say the colonel-designate. It's been gazetted, Zack. Congratulations. Once Jimmy puts up his second star, the inevitable domino effect starts."

"Who gets my squadron? Josh?"

Ryent nodded.

"Who else. Jory Virk takes a step up to deputy commanding officer, since he's senior, despite Curtis

Delgado's acting, soon to be permanent promotion. I'm sure you agree keeping Curtis with Erinye Company for another year or two will be in the regiment's best interests. He can comfort himself by knowing he's the modern equivalent of the primus pilus, the regiment's senior company commander."

"Oh, I'm sure Curtis will wish Jory well and count himself lucky to keep his Erinyes for a while longer."

"Good. Ghost Squadron won't be taking an operational pause anytime soon, and I'd rather we keep personnel reassignments to a minimum. Josh can decide if he wants an operations officer or whether he and Jory can split up the task between them."

"Probably the latter. Shall we call Jimmy and impart the good news he'll be commanding a four regiment division shortly?"

This time, Ryent laughed out loud.

"That's what I like most about you, Zack — the unbridled optimism. Okay. We'll do it your way. Because of the current workload, I'm sure he's still in his office."

Ryent touched the screen embedded in his desk and waited. A few moments later, a voice said, "Martinson here, Kal. Since we last spoke only a few hours ago, would asking what's up be appropriate, or should I cut the connection now, lest you ensnare me in a new scheme?"

"Zack is with me. He has an interesting proposal for you."

"Hi, General," Decker said in a droll tone. "Are you working hard or hardly working down there in Sin City?"

"Zack ensnaring me in a new scheme it is, then." Decker heard amusement mixed with resignation in Martinson's voice as his face appeared on the display. "I assume Zack laid his latest idea at your feet, and you blessed it?"

"In so many words."

"Then I'm all ears."

Once Decker finished speaking, Martinson studied both officers in turn with thoughtful eyes.

"Assuming the Corps and the Commander SOCOM blesses this, how will we deal with the training delta? MLI troopers already know much of the Tier Two basics, but there's still a significant gap between where they are now and where we need them to be so they can support Special Forces units effectively."

"Rotate the battalions through Fort Arnhem one at a time," Decker replied without hesitation. "Give them an appropriately tailored version of the SF curriculum, both individual and collective, under the supervision of the School and a designated squadron from the 1st Regiment."

"And how long would that take?"

"Two months per battalion, so a little over a year if we give the trainers a break between rotations."

"How about stationing? Will they stay at their base on Parth?"

"That depends, General. What's the stationing plan for the 2nd and 3rd SF Regiments? Or should I not ask?"

Martinson grimaced.

"SOCOM is still undecided. The factions for dispersal and centralization can't come to a mutually acceptable compromise. For now, the 2nd will remain at Fort Arnhem."

"How about this? The 1st and 2nd MLI Battalions come here to work with my regiment — they'll be the black ops Tier Two units — and take over the 2nd's current infrastructure. The 3rd and 4th Battalions stay on Parth, where the 2nd SF Regiment joins them. With four of the six MLI battalions gone, there will be plenty of room in Fort Erfoud for the 2nd. That leaves finding a base for the 5th and 6th Battalions, along with the 3rd SF."

The commander-designate of the Special Forces Division gave his soon to be deputy commander a sardonic look.

"I think Zack is telling us in a roundabout way he's ready to take command of the regiment, Kal. Don't you?"

"Considering I just told him his upcoming promotion has been gazetted, that's no surprise, sir. However, his plan is sound."

Martinson nodded.

"I agree. Let me discuss it with General Habad tomorrow and see what he says. By the way, the 3rd Regiment is destined for Cascadia. The announcement is still a few weeks off, but the Corps will expand the 7th Marine Division's existing military reservation and build a separate base for the 3rd, to be named Fort Slim."

"Make it big enough for two added light infantry battalions, and we're in business, General."

"What sort of command-and-control relationship do you propose?"

"MLI regimental HQ is an administrative headquarters, not a tactical one. Make it directly subordinate to the division and leave it with full command. Then give the three SF regimental COs operational command of the MLI battalions tasked as their Tier Two support when required. That way, you can deploy MLI units or sub-units separately from SF forces, and leave RHQ on Parth responsible for force generation, just as the School here does for the SF regiments."

Ryent nodded.

"It scans and should keep everyone happy."

"Agreed. But let me discuss it with General Habad before we let our enthusiasm run wild."

"What's your sense?" Ryent asked.

"He'll be intrigued by the idea. Some of his senior staff, less so. We three and General Habad might appreciate the capabilities the MLI delivers and overlook how more than half of its troopers are reformed and retrained convicts. But too many at SOCOM HQ have little or no experience in our sort of unconventional warfare and never saw an MLI battalion in action. But one thing I'm fairly sure of is that Marine Corps Support Command will be giddy with glee at ridding itself of the MLI, its school, and the base on Parth."

— Thirty-Three —

"Does she ever do a lick of work?" Corporal Taggart muttered as he and Sergeant Lambrix watched the *Sécurité Spéciale*'s Cascadian Sector station chief enter a posh downtown Squamish restaurant shortly after midday. They and the rest of Erinye Company had been watching Flavia DeBrito and her underlings go about their business for several days, recording every movement, every interaction, and every habit.

"Maybe schmoozing with the locals *is* her job. You can pick up a lot of good inside information by listening to well-lubricated politicians, cops, or pencil pushers. Besides, don't tell me you've never worked for an officer whom you'd rather see socializing than interfering with real Marines. Could be the deputy station chief prefers her staying away from the operations center most of the time."

"Good point. From what I saw of him, he seems like the sort who can't stand the DeBritos of the galaxy."

Lambrix chuckled.

"You're a long-distance psychiatrist now?"

"Physiognomy is real, Sarge. I don't care what they say. She looks like a big heaping handful of lah-di-dah attitude, and he strikes me as a po-faced bureaucrat who wouldn't know humor if it grabbed him by the balls. Those two types generally rub each other the wrong way. Just put both in the same cell and watch the fur fly."

"I'll pass your suggestion up the food chain. The skipper might be in an experimental mood on our way home. Of course, we'd need them alive first. They might actually be armed and dangerous and need killing."

"True." Taggart settled back in his seat and sighed. "I'm in a deeply desperate ass-kicking mood, Sarge. It's been how many weeks since our last strike? Shit, that was back on Mission Colony with the cop who wears jump wings."

"Morrow."

"That's the one. Scary lady."

"Cops who hunt other cops usually are." Lambrix saw movement out of the corner of his eyes. "Relief team is here. Back to the barn, Leroy."

**

"Not to step on your toes, Curtis, but when will you call it?" Major Ariane Redmon dropped into the chair across from Delgado, coffee mug in hand. "The longer we run surveillance, the greater our risk one of them will notice. We may not think much of the *Sécurité Spéciale* as an organization, but its members are hardly stupid or inept.

Even those working in a sector operations center will have undergone extensive field training so they can spot hostile observers."

Delgado grinned at her.

"Funny you should ask. I was just wondering the same thing. Great minds and all that, right?"

"Well," she drawled, "I'm not sure I'd call your mind great, but okay, let's go with it. So what factors are you pondering now?"

"Other than the targets finally noticing they're covered in ticks? Surveillance fatigue among my people. You know how it is. They eventually tire of the same old sneak and peek day after day and make mistakes. Small ones, to be sure, but the mistakes accumulate and wham, we blow our cover. Don't misunderstand me. The Erinyes are as good as Special Forces operators get in this universe, but they're human, and they haven't done much of their primary jobs in the last few months, what with guarding Grand Admiral Larsson on Earth."

"Any conclusions?"

He sat back and met her impassive gaze with his own.

"Their shift changes are pretty consistent, so I figure we'd strike during one of them."

"Which one? Morning, afternoon, or night?"

"That's what's still bothering me. DeBrito is a wildcard. She shows up at random times and spends most of her days playing the consummately social Commonwealth High Commission officer. Her deputy is regular as clockwork and consistently works the day shift, narrowing it down to morning or afternoon. If we can't take DeBrito at H-hour because she's in bed with the chief of police, then her deputy is our other ticket in."

Redmon let out a soft snort.

"Will you look at us, calmly discussing the abduction of two dozen federal employees."

"Who work for an agency with no legal basis for its existence and whose agents have Fleet blood on their hands. It makes them no different from cartel soldiers."

"Yeah. If you want my opinion, nab the day shift as it heads home. The deputy station chief will be tired and not paying as much attention. Infiltrate, grab the evening shift, then pick up the night shift at home."

He nodded.

"That's where I was headed. I also thought we might start a disturbance at the other end of town to draw attention away from our hit."

"Like?"

Delgado's grin returned, this time with a hint of cruelty.

"You know that cesspool the local UCF protesters call a camp in that park north of downtown? The one the local cops aren't clearing out because of reasons no one can fathom, despite the inmates constantly trying to riot?"

"Reason number one being DeBrito telling her paramour, the CPS chief, it's better for the government's image if he ignores the petty crime caused by said so-called peaceful protesters lest he be accused of suppressing free speech."

"Makes sense. Mind you, this Larow fellow still has a surprisingly good grip on the situation compared to other places we've cleared out. But I figure we might give him a helping hand, so we don't come back later and make blood run in the streets."

"What are you thinking?"

As Delgado explained his diversion plan, Redmon's smile grew wider.

"When?"

"We'll do a dry run tomorrow and execute the day after."

"Shuttles or ship?"

Delgado grimaced.

"I figure *Kobe Maru* should land a few hours before we strike. The teams can take their prisoners directly to the spaceport as they capture them. That way, once the last one is aboard, we lift and bugger off. The force protection troop can take our extra gear and sanitize this place while we move into position."

"Makes sense."

"Then, so be it. I'll draw up orders and call the ship."

**

Command Sergeant Ejaz Bassam and the rest of B Troop, dressed like the average UCF protester, approached Grendel Park from several directions in twos and threes shortly before the designated H-hour. They carried bags filled with fireworks, riot guns, gas canisters, dye-filled projectiles, and anything else that would turn the UCF camp into a cauldron of chaos.

Bassam was surprised at how easily Major Redmon and her colleague procured the items on the local black market. He was even more so when she told him her suppliers would never sell to the UCF goons after he asked why the latter weren't causing the sort of mischief B Troop intended. Apparently, even the local underworld despised the Centralist agitators.

Once near the park, the Marines dispersed to attack positions they'd reconnoitered the day before and settled in, waiting for the signal. A few sat openly on benches and under trees along the perimeter, while those with riot guns climbed on the rooftops of boarded-up and abandoned buildings, Bassam among them. Their truck was parked in an alley a kilometer away with two Marines aboard. It would take them straight to the spaceport and *Kobe Maru* once they completed their mission.

The camp, four dozen temporary shelters of every description, was calm at this time of the day, its inhabitants resting before another attempt at bringing the revolution to downtown Squamish. A faint aroma of unwashed bodies, dirty clothes, illegal narcotics, and lousy plumbing tickled Bassam's nose, and he made a face at his winger.

"Typical. Dumb fucks want a change in government but can't even keep a simple bivouac clean."

"It'll be a lot less clean once they piss themselves when we open fire."

Shortly before sixteen hundred hours, Bassam's communicator clicked three times, and he raised the device to his lips.

"Make like it's Founders Day."

Almost at once, the Marines who'd been idling in the shadows around the park pulled up neck gaiters to hide their faces, stood, and reached into the bags they carried slung over one shoulder. Out came fireworks, smoke canisters, stink bombs, and stun grenades. With practiced precision, they armed the pyrotechnics and tossed them among the shelters. Another salvo followed seconds later, then the Marines faded back into the streets and alleys surrounding Grendel Park as the first UCF thugs emerged from their tents, stunned by the unexpected assault.

That was the signal for the rooftop snipers. Anti-riot guns fired dye packs, gas grenades, and sticky bombs at the hapless, half-dressed protesters, triggering a storm of panicked screams and shouting as smoke of various colors blanketed the encampment while fireworks seemingly exploded everywhere. Each anti-riot gun fired a second time, then the remaining Marines withdrew.

Bassam and his winger were halfway to the truck when the sound of first responder sirens reached their ears. Behind them, the shouting was getting, if anything, worse as the anti-riot gas spread, triggering nausea in those who breathed it in.

The thought of what he considered useless, idle bastards puking their guts out while their eyes and mucous membranes burned like the fires of hell, made Bassam smile. Play stupid games, win stupid prizes.

At that moment, on the other side of Squamish, Harvey Zwettel emerged from the *Sécurité Spéciale*'s station house, as he did every day. He stopped on the sidewalk and studied his surroundings, then turned right and headed for his residence a few blocks away.

"There's the bastard," Lambrix muttered to his winger. "Right on time."

He and Taggart, the first in a chain of watchers, were loitering on the patio of a cafe near the unassuming two-story building, one of many housing professional offices in this neighborhood. They'd watched the evening shift enter a few minutes earlier and now waited for the day shift to come out behind Zwettel.

Lambrix touched the communicator lying on the table before him and spoke a single word to warn everyone the primary target had been spotted by the first team.

"One."

A few minutes later, it came to life with another voice, announcing the second team had him in sight.

"Two."

And so on until the snatch team, waiting at the most secluded part of Zwettel's route between his work and his residence, transmitted 'ten,' meaning the abduction was on. Now, each day shift operative exiting through that door or already on the way home would become a target for two of D Troop's Marines.

Both Delgado and Redmon were in the snatch team's car when it pulled up beside Zwettel, and they watched as two troopers jumped out, seized him, and tossed him into the rear passenger compartment. There, Redmon expertly slapped restraints on his wrists, while Delgado did the same on his ankles. The Marines climbed back in, and the car drove off at a sedate speed to circle the area.

"What—"

Redmon raised a finger to her lips.

"Please don't speak, Mister Zwettel. Just listen. My colleagues and I need to enter your lovely little hideaway, and you're our ticket in. We can do this one of two ways. Cooperate, and your hand remains attached to your wrist. Refuse, and we'll sever it. You'll probably bleed to death since we didn't bring a cauterizer or even a tourniquet. What'll it be?"

"Pound sand."

"Amputation it is."

Redmon produced a large, serrated knife from the folds of her tunic and grabbed his right wrist.

Zwettel's eyes rolled up, and he went limp.

Delgado snorted.

"Well, what do you know? He fainted with fear."

"Plan B, then." Redmon turned to the driver. "Head for the target."

"Wilco."

— Thirty-Four —

When the snatch car pulled up to the *Sécurité Spéciale* house, Delgado saw Marines from A Troop under Command Sergeant Painter strolling idly across the street, ready to enter and seize the evening shift. One of the trucks was parked just out of sight and would pull up to the service entrance, so they could load the prisoners unseen.

He climbed out of the car, followed by Sergeant Kuzek and Harvey Zwettel, who'd regained consciousness moments earlier. The man looked around nervously, aware of Redmon's needler pointed at his back. She'd told him the darts were coated in a poison that would destroy his organs while leaving him conscious of the fact he was dying. In reality, the darts would simply knock him out for eight or nine hours.

Delgado gestured at the security station embedded in the doorjamb.

"Go ahead, Mister Zwettel."

The man licked his lips, then took one shaky step forward and laid his palm on the reader. After the soft snick of latches pulling away, the door slid aside, and Kuzek stepped in as he pulled a needler from his shoulder holster. Delgado pushed Zwettel in behind Kuzek, then followed suit. At Redmon's hand signal, half a dozen Marines, dressed in casual business clothes, crossed the street, and entered while the truck came around the corner and backed up against the service entrance.

After entering on the heels of A Troop's Marines, Redmon raised her needler and shot Zwettel in the neck. He collapsed a few seconds later, out like a light. A cry of alarm reached her ears, followed by several voices shouting at the *Sécurité Spéciale* operatives to get on their knees and place their hands behind their heads. The noise level and aggressive repetition were designed to discourage any thought of resistance. When she joined Delgado at the entrance of the operations room, where the watchkeepers worked, she found them already being shackled.

A voice behind them said, "Truck's in place and ready."

"Good," Delgado replied. "Okay, folks, let's move them out of here, then ransack the place."

**

"You know what that is?" Corporal Taggart asked when a pair of Marines unceremoniously bundled the last of the day shift workers aboard one of D Troop's two cargo skimmers.

After taking their designated target off the street, he and Lambrix had watched their fellow D Troop members accost the *Sécurité Spéciale* operatives one by one and offer them a whispered choice between cooperation and death, all the while shoving needler muzzles into their sides.

"What?"

"Remember the recruit eating truck that followed us on forced marches during basic? Well, this is a spy eating truck."

Taggart seemed inordinately pleased with his wit but Lambrix gave his winger an exasperated look.

"You're enjoying this operation way too much, aren't you?"

"Makes a pleasant change from the usual take no prisoners. I may not look like it, but underneath this magnificently honed exterior is the soul of an artist."

"An artist specializing in bovine manure, no doubt. Ah." Lambrix nodded at Command Sergeant Saxer standing behind the second truck and gesturing toward the half-open cargo compartment door. "I think we've been told to load up."

"Our work here is done," Taggart intoned. "Not that I'll miss this place, mind you."

**

By the time Delgado and Redmon drove up *Kobe Maru*'s belly ramp to offload A Troop and their prisoners, along with the *Sécurité Spéciale* station's computer core, B Troop was already aboard. The ship sat at the furthest end of the cargo spaceport tarmac, near warehouses owned by the local smuggling fraternity, which was now turning a blind eye thanks to another generous payment.

First Sergeant Hak, acting as the operations coordinator, met them in the cargo hold and waited as they climbed out of the car.

"D Troop is on the way with the six day shift workers while C Troop is halfway done collecting the night shift, Skipper. One of them resisted and will need sickbay time when she comes aboard. Good thing none of them have families, otherwise it might have been messier."

Delgado nodded his thanks.

"I guess it can't be helped. What about DeBrito?"

"Still slumming at Police Service HQ. Speaking of which, it's apparently absolute pandemonium in Grendel Park. The UCF is accusing the police of attacking them for no reason, while the police are accusing one of the groups supporting sovereign star systems fed up with the UCF going unpunished for so long. At least based on the radio transmissions we intercepted. Now would be the perfect time to lift."

"I know. But we can't leave DeBrito behind."

Hak glanced at his communicator. "C Troop is six for six. We need those skimmers out of here."

They watched the car and both of A Troop's vehicles back down the ramp and veer off toward a designated parking area nearby, where their owners would fetch them the next day. No sooner were they gone than D Troop's two trucks appeared. The Marines climbed out and dragged six unconscious bodies from the cargo compartment.

"What happened?" Delgado asked when Sergeant Saxer reported his troop present and unhurt.

"A few of them found some last-minute courage and tried their luck. They'll wake up with a nasty headache for their troubles, but nothing more. Glad we brought needlers on this one, Skipper. I figure shooting the poor buggers with lethal loads wouldn't be right."

"Too easy?"

"A bit. Besides, they might be the opposition, but they're still regular human beings, unlike cartel garbage or UCF roaches."

"I hear you." Delgado gave Saxer a slap on the shoulder. "Head for the barracks. Your work here is done."

Saxer snorted. "That's what Taggart said when we loaded up after taking the last target."

Delgado, Redmon, and Hak stayed in the cargo hold until C Troop finished offloading, then headed for the compartment set aside as coordination center to wait until the team charged with abducting DeBrito reported.

**

Flavia DeBrito didn't notice the unremarkable ground car following her across Squamish as she headed home, vexed that her evening with Rupert Larow was canceled because of the riot in Grendel Park. It was degenerating into street battles between the Cascadia Police Service and the United Commonwealth Front, panicking the mayor and her staff.

So much for keeping the local UCF action to a slow simmer until conditions were ripe. If she could find out who precipitated the unfolding disaster, she'd make sure it never happened again.

The car on her tail, with two of Delgado's Marines aboard, called home so Hak could warn Destry and Sergeant Testo, waiting in DeBrito's living room, that the target was on her way.

DeBrito's private residence, in an upscale part of Squamish, was dark when she pulled into its garage shortly after sunset. The AI butler wasn't expecting her until much later, but it would notice her car's arrival. Yet, when she entered the foyer, the lights remained off, though not due to a power failure, because she saw the glow of standby indicators on various panels.

DeBrito entered the living room, one hand reaching for the controls, the other tugging at the silk scarf around her neck, and she didn't immediately notice the dark shapes sitting in two of the richly upholstered chairs facing the entrance. When the chandelier came to life, she froze, eyes wide with fear.

"Who are you, and how did you bypass my security system?" Her words came out in a strangled croak as she took in the needlers pointed at her by stony-faced men wearing business suits.

"Who is unimportant, Madame," Destry replied, climbing to his feet. "How is easy. Never trust your security to an AI butler. No matter how long they've tried, scientists never could invent an artificial intelligence capable of resisting a human mind's cunning. We've wiped it, by the way, since you won't be needing this place anymore."

Destry's needler coughed once, and DeBrito collapsed on the marble floor.

"What say we take her car and let the mob pick up our rental later," Testo suggested.

"Why?"

"We load it aboard the ship. Tomorrow, her CPS boyfriend notices she's gone, and the Traffic Control system can no longer find her car. Deepens the mystery, no?"

"We can't leave the rental here, but your idea is good. Tell you what, we'll load DeBrito in her car — you can drive — and I'll follow with ours. That way, no harm, no foul. We might need our underworld friends again someday."

"You're the boss."

Half an hour later, Testo was greeted by a look of surprise on his commanding officer's face as he drove DeBrito's elegant, expensive skimmer up the ramp.

"What gives?" Delgado asked once the operations noncom climbed out.

"A souvenir, Skipper. The previous owner is in the back, snoring. I'm sure she won't mind where she's headed."

Testo quickly explained his thinking to Delgado's visible approval while a pair of Marines carried off DeBrito.

"Maybe we can use it for target practice on the Fort Arnhem range," the latter said. "A fitting end. Where's Destry?"

"He's parking the loaner. Are we last?"

"Yup. The moment Destry's aboard, we're gone." Delgado spied a figure at the base of the ramp, jogging with an easy gait — the Naval Intelligence officer. He pulled out his communicator. "Bridge, this is Erinye Niner. Everyone's aboard. You can button her up and lift."

"And not a moment too soon," Lieutenant Commander Dien Bahn replied. "The riots are making everyone *beaucoup* twitchy. Bridge out."

Moments later, the first officer's voice echoed across the cargo bay as the belly ramp rose to seal *Kobe Maru*'s hull.

"All hands to departure stations, I say again, all hands to departure stations. We lift in five minutes. Passengers, find a flat surface and take a lie down."

As Delgado, Destry, and Testo turned to race for the Marine barracks, *Kobe Maru*'s bosun stuck his head into the cargo hold as part of a quick inspection to make sure nothing major could screw up the departure.

"With all due respect, Major, what the frack is that?" He pointed at DeBrito's car.

"War prize."

"One that isn't secured for liftoff." The bosun ran to a door marked "Cargo Handling Gear" and pulled it open. He rummaged inside and produced two restraining straps. Glaring at Delgado, he tossed him one of the straps and aimed the other at Testo. "You Marines know how to secure combat cars. Make sure this one can't move by the time we fire thrusters."

"Will do," Delgado said as the bosun vanished without a backward glance, intent on his duties during an emergency takeoff.

They finished securing the car just as the thirty seconds warning sounded. Neither of them would make it to their bunks before *Kobe Maru* lifted, and so by common accord, they dropped to the hard, cold deck, and reached for the nearest cleat. Moments later, the entire ship vibrated as the whine of thrusters spooling up reached a crescendo.

Then, a giant hand landed on Delgado's chest and threatened to squash him, but this wasn't his first full-power lift and he forced his breathing into a regular pattern. He felt *Kobe Maru* break contact with the cracked tarmac and rise on columns of pure energy. His mind's eye fancied it could see the undercover starship escape Cascadia and the increasing violence consuming the capital's northern district.

Soon enough, the giant hand eased, and after a momentary sensation of weightlessness, a familiar one gee tugged at him. He and the others cautiously stood just as the public address system sounded again.

"All hands, secure from liftoff stations and turn to cruising stations."

By the time Delgado reached the bridge, *Kobe Maru* was accelerating toward Cascadia's hyperlimit, heedless of Traffic Control messages demanding what the hell they thought they were doing.

— Thirty-Five —

"Wash." Tesser's eyes fluttered open as he felt a foot nudge him. He recognized Aleksa Kine in the gloom of a hangar lit by a few red lights. Other than the guard detail, Keres Company slept, its Marines wrapped in bedrolls, personal weapons close at hand. The soft sound of breathing, along with a few discordant snores, barely registered above the din of another heavy downpour hammering the roof.

Instantly awake, Tesser kicked his bedroll aside and stood. Kine had volunteered to take shifts as duty officer along with the company's command sergeants and her waking him meant something was happening. He glanced at his timepiece. Oh-two-hundred — not quite reveille yet. Since the cartel's truck convoy arrived a few hours earlier, it could only mean one thing.

"What's up?"

"Shuttles are landing on the Galindez hangar apron. If they stay true to form, it'll be about four hours until the convoy heads back out at daybreak."

"It's about time."

Tesser hastily put on his clothes and slipped his feet into his boots. Then, he followed Kine into the passenger compartment of the shuttle serving as a command post. There, Sergeant First Class Brantingham sat in front of a bank of displays showing feeds from the sensors Keres Company seeded around the Galindez Cartel hangar over several days.

Brantingham glanced over his shoulder and nodded politely.

"Skipper."

"Good morning, BB."

Tesser took a bench beside him and studied the displays. Four boxy, inelegant civilian shuttles hovered a meter above a cracked tarmac. Rain lashed them while hangar doors ponderously slid aside, giving Tesser, Kine, and the duty noncom an unobstructed view into a space that seemed identical to the one they currently occupied. The four cargo haulers they'd seen enter were lined up against the far wall, each beside a pile of standard containers destined for the shuttles which now threaded their way through the opening. They pivoted one-hundred and eighty degrees and settled on markers painted in yellow.

"Figure an hour to swap loads," Kine said in a soft voice as the hangar doors closed again. "The shuttles should leave immediately afterward."

"Okay. I'll go set Operation Road Warrior in motion."

Tesser walked down the aft ramp and headed for where First Sergeant Gade and the troop leaders were camped out. He found them already awake and getting dressed.

"It's on. Shuttles just arrived. One hour turnaround, then we'll let them settle for half an hour or so."

"Still raining?" Command Sergeant QD Vinn asked.

"Buckets."

"Good. That means the bastards won't pay attention to moving shadows, let alone post guards outside."

Vinn, whose H Troop would seize the Galindez hangar, checked his sidearms after stowing his bedroll — a twelve-millimeter blaster and a ten-millimeter carbine — then picked up the bag containing, among other items, his mercenary-style combat armor. "I'll run the final preps now, Skipper."

Tesser watched him join his Marines who, along with the rest of Keres Company, were silently stirring to life, as if impelled by the same instinct that told them the battle was nigh.

Command Sergeant Clayburn Knudsvig, whose G Troop would back Vinn up, hoisted his own gear.

"That's me as well."

E Troop's leader, Command Sergeant Ranit Favero, who'd drawn the short straw and therefore inherited the job of securing Keres Company's base of operations, checked his sidearms, then wordlessly wandered off to the command post shuttle, leaving F Troop's Jamal Delos to leisurely prepare. He and his Marines weren't involved with this part of the operation, but they would accompany G and H Troop to the objective.

Tesser, who knew better than to hover over his command noncoms while they prepared, joined First Sergeant Gade in the space designated as the company kitchen and made himself a cup of coffee.

Neither spoke as they watched their troopers prepare weapons, armor and other gear after clearing the floor of their bedrolls and personal items under the red lights that preserved night vision. Once Tesser gave Vinn the go-ahead, Keres Company had to be ready for immediate departure aboard *Iolanthe*'s shuttles, in case things went pear-shaped. That meant packing up the rudimentary kitchen, something E Troop would do shortly as they policed the hangar.

Tesser finished his coffee and rinsed out his cup. Then, by common accord, he and Gade dropped their personal gear off in the command post shuttle before settling in behind Sergeant Favero, now monitoring the displays.

"Everything is quiet, Skipper," the latter said without turning his head. "Scratch that. The doors are opening."

They, along with Aleksa Kine, watched the shuttles emerge one at a time, hovering a bare meter above the ground, and head off toward the landing strip where they'd lift as per Traffic Control's instructions. The hangar doors closed again, and Tesser felt a tiny wave of relief dispelling his unvoiced fear the convoy would travel in the middle of the night this time, depriving Keres Company of any chance to use the trucks as their own Trojan horses.

Tesser stood and walked to the command post's aft ramp, where he surveyed the floor. Three troops, armed and armored, were formed in ranks, waiting while Marines from the fourth policed the hangar. He nodded at Gade, and they donned their armor as well, while on his flight deck, the pilot ran through his checklist, as did the ones in the other craft. Once the lights were extinguished inside the Galindez building, Tesser started a mental countdown. When it finally reached zero, fifteen minutes later, he climbed out of the shuttle and walked over to where G and H Troops were waiting, helmet visors raised.

Both Vinn and Knudsvig game him expectant looks.

"This is it. Operation Road Warrior is a go."

The command noncoms snapped to attention, then pivoted on their heels. Vinn raised his right hand, the one holding the carbine over his head, and pumped it up and down twice. Almost at once, H Troop's formation broke apart, as the Marines split up in sections and fire teams, headed for their designated exits. Once they'd vanished, Knudsvig did the same, sending his troopers into the rain-drenched night.

When the convoy arrived, they'd counted twelve cartel soldiers, three per truck. Vinn's twenty-five Special Forces operators would wipe them out. Tesser returned to the command post and its displays, now a mere spectator, unless things went wrong. He didn't enjoy being in that situation, but his command noncoms were the best of the best and could tackle any task he set them.

Besides, Colonel Decker had shown Ghost Squadron's company commanders how he liked to work. Tell your subordinates what results you wanted, give them what they needed to do the job, then stay out of their way.

The sensors they'd placed around the objective could barely pick out Vinn's Marines moving from shadow to shadow, hidden by both the darkness and the downpour. And that meant unaided human eyes wouldn't see them. To Tesser's surprise, the smaller side door, which in Keres Company's hanger opened onto a corridor lined by empty offices, wasn't locked, and he watched one of Vinn's sections slip in.

Brief flashes lit up the night before the door closed again. Blaster fire. A sentry, perhaps? But since the company net remained silent, it probably meant said sentry fell to one of his Marines. The other two designated ingress points were barred, and the Marines used lasers to slice through the locking mechanisms in a matter of seconds.

Now came the trickiest part — taking out the cartel soldiers before any of them could call home and spoil the plan.

They watched G Troop encircle the building, covering each of the doors, ready to burst in if H Troop faced a situation they couldn't handle. But within moments, Tesser knew they wouldn't be needed. One of Vinn's Marines emerged and made the pre-arranged signal, telling them the job was done.

"Another high speed, low drag job in the bag, Skipper." Gade climbed to his feet. "Shall we?"

"You bet."

Vinn met them at the unlocked door, correctly deducing his CO would head for it, if only because of the blaster flash moments after the point men entered. Once inside, Tesser and Gade shook off some of the water beading on their armor and raised their visors.

"Building and trucks secure, Skipper. Twelve tangos dead, most of them in their sleep." He jerked his thumb over his shoulder. "Except for those two specimens who were busy goofing off together instead of paying attention."

Tesser looked past Vinn and saw two bodies lying on the grimy plasticized floor.

"The gunfire we saw."

"Yep. Poster boys for why back in the olden days, sentries who fell asleep or otherwise screwed around on duty faced summary execution."

Gade let out an amused snort.

"Then, I guess you did the cartel a favor."

"I'd rather think I did humanity a favor, Top."

"Fair enough."

"Walk us through." Tesser gestured at the corridor beyond both corpses.

Vinn turned on his heels and led them past empty offices and into the main hangar where H Troop Marines were dragging bodies into a storeroom.

"Caught ten of them sleeping. None will ever wake again. With the two sentries, that makes twelve. My folks are searching every nook and cranny to make sure we didn't miscount when the convoy arrived last night."

"Any chance they warned their superiors?"

"The twelve we shot? No way. Like I said, ten died in their sleep, and the two sentries never knew what hit them. The only way the cartel could find out before we're at their throats in a few hours is if there's a thirteenth asshole hiding in a corner somewhere, or they rigged this place to talk with home base. And we didn't find active alarms."

Tesser nodded.

"Okay. That leaves the trucks."

"We'll be checking them in a moment."

No sooner had Vinn spoken that a pair of Marines approached the first vehicle, battlefield sensors in hand, and scanned it. After a few moments, they glanced at each other, and one of them climbed into the cab, disappearing behind polarized windows. He stuck his head out the door soon after that.

"No fancy interlocks. Anyone can start and drive this thing. The navigation system is off, as are the comms. Both panels are dusty, so it doesn't look like either gets a lot of use. There is what looks like a friend or foe transponder, though. It's off as well."

"Makes sense," Gade said. "New Tasman doesn't operate a ground traffic control system, not even in downtown Hobart, nor does it have an extensive road network, and as far as the cartels are concerned, the less the authorities can track their movements, the better. That's why they prefer frontier worlds."

"Want me to test the FOF, sir?"

Tesser thought for a moment, then nodded.

"Go."

A few seconds passed before the Marine stuck his head out again.

"Standard transponder signal, encrypted, of course."

"Could be what they use to open the compound's gates and enter that garage structure we saw," Vinn said.

"Possibly. Lax security, though, if they rely on transponders instead of positive ID checks."

Gade made a dismissive shrug.

"But convenient. As far as the Galindez Cartel knows, New Tasman is a low-threat environment. We haven't hit anyone in the Cascadian Sector yet. Their complacency is our advantage."

Once Vinn's Marines checked the other three trucks, Tesser ordered them partially unloaded, so he could fit the strike force in the back and leave a little camouflage layer by the doors. But he was really counting on the Galindez Cartel being lazy and sloppy, like most criminal organizations that never faced a serious threat from either the law or competitors. And out here, on the Commonwealth's edge, that culture of impunity flowered to its fullest extent, lubricated by bribes and other forms of corruption.

Tesser checked the time. Another three hours before departure. He stood the company down, save for a guard detail covering each hangar, and stretched out on one of the flat crates they'd removed from the trucks.

"Aren't you curious what's in this?" Gade asked from atop another of the plasticized containers.

"Not enough to open them. At least not before we're back from Op Road Warrior."

The first sergeant grunted.

"Probably just as well, knowing what kind of depraved shit the cartels get into."

— Thirty-Six —

Hobart still slumbered under a wet, gray blanket when Keres Company threaded its way out of the cartel hanger aboard the captured trucks shortly after daybreak. The Marines, weapons locked and loaded, hid in the cargo compartments, save for three in each cab, including Tesser, First Sergeant Gade, and the troop leaders.

At this hour, the spaceport seemed forlorn, as if abandoned by living creatures. The automatic security checkpoint at the back gate let them through without hiccups, and they soon crossed a city that seemed unwilling to face another dreary winter's day.

"I'll be glad when we're off this dump," the Marine driving Tesser's truck muttered. "Me, I was made for sunshine, not this crap."

Tesser nodded in agreement.

"No arguments here. Thankfully, it won't be long now."

"From your lips to the Almighty's ear, sir. Let's kick ass, take names, and extract, just like it says in the good book."

"Oo-rah." Sergeant Bjorn Hennes, Tesser's winger, gave the Marine a friendly thump on the shoulder.

With Hobart's outskirts behind them, the convoy left the main north-south road and turned inland on a secondary that served the lumber and mining industries. It also led to the headquarters of the Galindez Cartel, tucked away in its own valley, far from prying eyes. Not long afterward, they reached the final turn off, signaling the cartel's compound lay behind one last crest. Tesser felt his tension increase.

They weren't exactly going in blind, not after a week studying the compound, watching the routine of its inhabitants, and analyzing *Iolanthe*'s scans — visual, electronic, and infrared — from orbit. The latter gave them a good idea of the interior layout, including sensors and weapons emplacements. But he didn't know what to expect once the trucks were inside the large parking structure between the main entrance and the rest of the compound.

The truck reached the top of the incline, and there it was, the Galindez Cartel's headquarters, laid out under a glowering sky that threatened yet another miserable downpour. Tesser saw nothing move, but it was still early, not to mention chilly and damp.

He reached out and switched on the friend or foe transponder, knowing those in the other trucks would do the same momentarily. They covered the last kilometer downhill to where a closed gate cut off the road, in what seemed like a few heartbeats. This would be the first test. They'd not seen any live guards admit ground vehicles, so the theory that the transponders served as electronic keys was a good one.

And the assumption proved right. When Tesser's truck was a few meters away, the heavy metal gate slid aside and the door to the large, flat-roofed garage beyond opened as if by magic. As they drove into the gloom, he spotted well-marked unloading bays with four empty spots where white lights beckoned.

The driver swung his vehicle around in front of the first open spot and backed into it as if he'd done this a thousand times. The other three followed suit. So far, they hadn't spotted a single human, and when Tesser glanced at Sergeant Hennes' handheld sensor, it showed only four side-by-side life sign clumps.

"Kind of eerie if you ask me," Hennes said.

"Just another early morning in a low-threat environment where they don't even worry about the police." Tesser lit up the company net. "Go, go, go."

Almost as one, the back of the trucks opened and Marines in mercenary armor streamed out, spreading across the vehicle hangar, weapons at the ready.

"Sensor contact," a voice said over the radio. "Four humans approaching the inner door."

"Weapons free."

Moments later, a shout echoed across the building.

"Hey! What the—"

Plasma carbines coughed, abruptly cutting off the cartel soldier's words as he and his mates died instantly. Within seconds, a lugubrious siren cut through the chilly morning air.

"I guess they know we're here," Hennes said, eyes looking for any threat to his commanding officer as they made their way into the compound on F Troop's heels.

When they cleared the inner garage door and emerged on a small central plaza surrounded by one and two-story buildings, cartel soldiers clutching weapons, a few still pulling on clothes, spilled through doors everywhere, driven by the urgent klaxon. Remote weapon stations rose from their domes at the four corners, their gunners seeking targets.

A streak of flame and a loud whoosh caught Tesser's attention as a Marine from F Troop fired a disposable bunker-buster rocket at one of the RWS emplacements, destroying it outright. Three more, one also from F Troop and two from G Troop took out the remaining systems, while the rest of the Marines mowed cartel soldiers down in windrows.

Keres Company's overwhelming firepower against half-awake, not remarkably disciplined, and in most cases scared and confused men, briefly struck Tesser as unfair. But then he recalled one of Colonel Decker's many pithy sayings — if you're in a fair fight, you screwed up somewhere along the line.

However, not every cartel soldier was panicking, as evidenced by gunfire coming from second-floor windows on two sides. The Marines' armor and quick reactions kept them from the worst of the plasma and railgun slugs. Still, a few would sport spectacular bruises.

Then, teams from each troop entered their designated target buildings. The remaining tangos wouldn't last in the face of room-clearing grenades and rapid plasma carbine shots.

Within a few minutes, F and G Troops reported the side structures secure. H Troop was still fighting its way through the main house where the boss and his closest underlings lived, and where the cartel kept an operations center. It proved a more challenging proposition, something akin to a final redoubt behind armored walls and doors with automatic weapons covering the hallways. Two of Vinn's Marines were injured, and Tesser told him to back off. Leaving as little visible damage as possible wasn't worth more casualties.

"I'll blow a way in from the outside, so make sure you're well away."

"Acknowledged. We're heading for both wings. You can go ahead."

Tesser ordered a pair of Marines with disposable rocket launchers to take aim at the building's outer wall after figuring out the operations center's approximate location. He marked the desired point of impact with a laser.

"Ready, rocket one."

"Ready," the first Marine replied, launcher held steady on his right shoulder, its own aiming laser merging with Tesser's.

"Fire."

"Firing now."

A whoosh followed by a streak of flame, then almost at once, the detonation of impact. When the dust cleared, a ragged hole marred the formerly smooth facade. Through it, they could see a front room with furniture tossed about.

"This is your aiming point, rocket two." Tesser's laser pointer lit up a spot on the inner wall.

"Ready," the second Marine said.

"Fire."

"Firing now."

Delgado was rewarded by another streak of flame followed by a detonation that sounded slightly different. When the impact site became visible, Tesser saw a small, neat, fist-sized opening in a thick metallic wall. Within seconds, they heard screams, proving the people within were injured.

Since F Troop was closest to the main building, Tesser called Command Sergeant Delos on the company net.

"Two-two, this is Niner. Push a few grenades through that hole."

"Roger." Delos turned to the section waiting behind cover near the left-hand side building. "You heard Niner. Go."

"Roger."

The Marines, moving by fire teams, ran to the main house, up the stone stairs, and vanished inside. After a few seconds, Tesser could see two of them through the large opening in the facade as they cautiously approached the hole. When the first was right next to it, he armed the grenade in his hand and shoved it through.

Five seconds later, a dull thump echoed across the yard, followed by a resurgence in the screaming. A second grenade followed the first, then a third, and the human voices tapered off until Tesser heard only the low sobs of mortally wounded men merging with the Infinite Void.

Tesser called Vinn and gave him the go-ahead to try again. This time, his Marines made it unscathed and set explosive charges on the operations center's door.

"A couple are still breathing," the latter reported shortly after that, "but it won't be for long, even with emergency medical care. Between the bunker-buster and the grenades, it's a meat grinder in here. We're giving them mercy shots from the first aid kits."

"Understood. Look for the computer core. I'm on my way." Tesser glanced at First Sergeant Gade. "F and G Troops can go ahead and turn the place inside out. Load anything that might interest another cartel in the trucks and spread the death cards."

The cards, fifty-two aces of spades per pack, each bore the logo of the Kiryu Cartel, a stylized chrysanthemum with the cartel's name in kanji script on the back. Criminal organizations often dropped death cards on their victims after a hit to claim responsibility. They considered the act a show of strength and confidence.

SOCOM imitated the practice by using cards with cartel markings as a way of sowing confusion. Whoever found the bodies of the Galindez commanders and soldiers would immediately blame the Kiryu, hopefully triggering a war between the latter and any Galindez remnants still capable of fighting.

"Roger that, Skipper."

Tesser and Hennes entered the main house and quickly found the operations center's entrance. Vinn wasn't exaggerating when he called it a meat grinder. Blood spatters covered the walls while a dozen men lay in contorted poses on the floor, their bodies shredded by shrapnel. Marines occupied several workstations, pulling up data and transferring it to memory packs, seemingly oblivious to the surrounding carnage.

Vinn called Tesser over and pointed at one body.

"If I'm not mistaken, that's what's left of the Galindez Cartel's *presidente*."

"Looks like it."

Tesser pulled a pack of death cards from a pouch on his combat harness, broke it open and dropped one on the cartel boss' charred chest, then distributed another eleven among the corpses scattered around the operations room.

"Found the computer core," one of the Marines said, pulling a shiny polymer block the size of an adult man's head from a niche in the armored wall.

"Good. QD, finish your search of the building and take everything another cartel would back to the trucks."

"Will do."

After one last glance around, Tesser left the operations center and exited the main house, Sergeant Hennes at his side. Taking this place and eliminating its inmates with no one else on New Tasman being the wiser was the straightforward part.

The local *Sécurité Spéciale* station would be a tougher nut to crack. Fortunately, its inhabitants were creatures of habit, especially the one they'd identified as the station chief, a man who enjoyed fine food and drink several nights a week, mostly by himself.

"Casualties?" Tesser later asked when Gade walked up to his truck and reported the company ready for extraction.

"Dembe and Capelli. Nothing penetrated their armor, but both suffer from cracked ribs, severe bruising, and potentially internal injuries. Nothing life-threatening from what the medical sensor says, but I'll be glad if we wrap things up tonight and send them to *Iolanthe*'s sickbay. Their armor is toast, by the way. Completely non-serviceable, but it did the job. Other than that, the usual bruises for those who didn't duck fast enough. All in all, not bad, considering we counted ninety-six dead tangos. It doesn't look like anyone escaped."

"What's our haul?"

"Plenty of anonymous cred chips issued by two dozen of the largest chartered banks; precious metals and gemstones; explosives, weapons, and battlefield electronics, a lot of which went walkabout from Fleet supply depots. I'd say we're bringing back a few million for the black ops fund. We'll need two more trucks. And maybe we should take the *presidente*'s personal skimmer." Gade pointed at a sleek, low-slung ground car parked away from the trucks and utility vehicles. "It'll serve the snatch team better than the cars Aleksa found or one of these ugly crates, especially in the part of town our target frequents. Why don't you ride it back? I'm sure Bjorn will be glad to drive."

— Thirty-Seven —

Warned by a brief radio transmission via *Iolanthe*, E Troop made sure both the cartel and Keres Company's hangar doors were partially open to receive a convoy twice as big as the one that left a few hours earlier. The luxury car and the trucks carrying the confiscated items peeled off to the latter and the original four trucks to the former.

Once back in the cartel hangar, Tesser's Marines reloaded the items taken off during the night and parked them precisely the way they had been, hoping it would create another mystery — trucks but no crews. And when someone finally found the bodies, hopefully weeks, if not months later, they would be decomposed to the point where the cause of death was no longer identifiable.

Tesser climbed out of the car under Aleksa Kine's amused gaze.

"Prize of war. We'll use it tonight instead of a truck or one of the clunkers you bought."

She nodded approvingly.

"A good idea. What's with the additional cargo haulers?"

"Also prizes. Negotiable items for the black ops fund and military gear that should never end up in cartel hands." He caught Gade's eyes. "Let's apportion the loot between the shuttles now, Top. The pilots can load it the way they want."

This time Kine snorted.

"Loot. Well, you certainly look villainous enough, Wash. So do your people."

Then, she noticed two Marines being helped off a truck. "Casualties?"

"Dembe and Capelli. Automatic fire covering the cartel operations room corridor hit them. Nothing life-threatening, though they would probably feel like shit right now if not for painkillers. You should see what their armor looks like. But the cartel leadership is gone, along with its local muscle — twelve next door and ninety-six at the compound. Whoever gets there first will find a Kiryu death card on each body. Hopefully, a little gang warfare in this sector will thin the buggers out and leave the *Sécurité Spéciale* with fewer assets."

"Then, we roll in and pick off the rest."

Tesser chuckled.

"You sound less and less like a cop and more like the rest of us. Are we assimilating you?"

Kine shook her head.

"No. I'm still a cop, and eventually, I'll go back to being one full-time. But my experience at the hands of the Saqqa Cartel and what I've seen since makes me believe there's no choice but to take the law into our own hands if we want to stave off a descent into corporate and Centralist sponsored chaos."

"You know, either the Corps or the Navy would probably take you on as an intelligence officer at rank, based on your experience. Keep that in mind if the idea of going back to enforcing weak or useless laws, or not enforcing them, depending on political interference, makes you feel queasy. We're in this mode of action for the long haul."

"I'll keep that in mind when I receive orders reassigning me as a criminal intelligence analyst in a Sector HQ. That's pretty much the only job I'll find at this point."

"Or speak with Assistant Commissioner Morrow. She might offer you a position with the Political Anti-Corruption Unit. Didn't you mention she was one of us and a pretty cool sort?"

Kine scoffed.

"Yes, she's a good egg, but working the rest of my career as a Professional Compliance Bureau investigator doesn't sound appealing right now."

Tesser let out a bark of laughter.

"Only because you're a law-breaker by helping us clean up on New Tasman. Are you afraid you'll spend the rest of your career wondering whether your own colleagues will arrest you?"

"I was a law-breaker before this mission, Wash. Before I joined Ghost Squadron, even. My virginity is long gone."

"If Miko Steiger can enter the Intelligence Branch as a Marine Corps warrant officer, you can as well, considering you're a graduate of the basic Pathfinder course and wear jump wings these days. In the meantime, you're a cop, so I'll ask, are you still ready to go through with facilitating an abduction?"

"I'm your best bet at not startling the target, and I have experience with real-life role-playing."

"Okay. Let's hope he heads into town tonight so we can wrap this mission up and go home."

"It's been three days since his last foray into what passes for gastronomy around here, so chances are good."

**

The day passed quietly, with no signs someone discovered their raid on the cartel complex — at least judging by the radio traffic on the Constabulary regiment's operational net, which Keres Company had monitored since their arrival. Nor did the satellite *Iolanthe* placed in geosynchronous orbit pick up any activity at the site.

Shortly before sunset, the usual evening patrol headed out to observe the *Sécurité Spéciale* compound from across the harbor and make a note of its inmates' comings and goings. Less than two hours later, they sent the message Tesser hoped for — the station chief was taking a leisurely stroll downhill toward the ritzy waterfront district now that the rain had stopped.

E Troop, designated as the snatch team and door kickers, quietly prepared. At the same time, Aleksa Kine reviewed the abduction procedure one more time with the four

Marines who'd be traveling with her in the late cartel *presidente*'s fancy car.

Whenever the station chief took a gastronomic stroll, he made it a three-hour affair, so Kine and E Troop took their time getting into position. A lengthy loiter in a part of town where the wealthy lived and played wouldn't do.

Shortly after twenty-three hundred hours, Kine, now wearing a smart business suit, strolled past the restaurant identified by the evening patrol and saw the target enjoying a post-prandial coffee. A middle-aged woman with a pinched face sat across from him.

Both wore the sort of self-satisfied air Kine often witnessed on the faces of men and women who felt entitled to their luxuries. With any luck, the food and drink, and life in a low-threat environment would dull their situational awareness.

She flicked on her communicator. "Our friend has a friend. If they go home together, it'll be Plan B."

"Roger."

When she walked past the restaurant again, this time away from the harbor, Kine saw the target and his companion shrugging on knee-length overcoats. She made a quick hand signal, alerting the Marines in the ground car parked further uphill that it was on. She glanced over her shoulder in time to see the stocky, middle-aged man with a distinct paunch usher his friend through the restaurant's front door.

They shook hands and the woman headed off toward the harbor while he took the same winding road as usual and walked with a steady pace, eyes on the slope ahead.

A relieved Kine raised her communicator to her lips. Dealing with the woman could have made the abduction messy.

"The friend left. Plan A is back on."

By now, he would have noticed the tall, slender woman a few dozen meters in front of him, seemingly headed in the same direction. The car, which didn't look out of place in this district, still sat among more of its kind, silent and unremarkable, in a nightclub parking lot. Kine, by shortening her steps, allowed him to slowly close the distance between them until a bend in the road hid the harbor district and, more importantly, hid them from casual strollers.

Upon reaching the designated spot where trees on either side formed a green canopy that filtered out the city lights, Kine stumbled, as if her foot caught on something and fell. She let out a high pitched, though not particularly loud shriek, the sort caused by surprise and sudden pain. The target, who was only half a dozen meters behind Kine at that point, ran up to her.

"Are you okay? Do you need help?"

She looked up at him with a strained expression.

"Yes, please. I think I injured my ankle."

The car, silent, its lights off, came gliding up behind him unnoticed as he bent over to help Kine stand. He grabbed her by the forearms, and she held on to his. The car stopped, and a pair of dark-clad figures emerged just as Kine came to her feet. The *Sécurité Spéciale* officer released her arms, and she could see by the expression in his eyes that he sensed something was off, so she wrapped herself around him, sobbing.

Just then, one of the newcomers reached out and stuck a dermal injector against his neck. It hissed, and he went limp a few heartbeats later. The two Marines grabbed his sagging body as Kine let go and dragged him into the car. She jumped in behind them, then pulled a communicator from her tunic pocket.

"Fish."

"Trawler on its way," Command Sergeant Favero's voice replied, indicating that the truck with the rest of E Troop was headed for the *Sécurité Spéciale* house.

"Okay." Kine nodded at the darkened hillside. "Let's see if sleeping ugly's hand will open the magic gate and let us in."

As they approached the property, she saw a dark shape coming from the other direction. It slowed to a crawl the moment the driver spotted them turning into the driveway. The car stopped under the gate's sloping roof, its rear driver-side window level with the automated security station's biometric reader. The window dropped, and the *Sécurité Spéciale* officer's arm came through, held by one of the Marines. His palm connected with the reader, and almost at once, the metal gate slid aside.

The car's driver waited until the truck was behind them, then sped forward to make sure it got through before the security system slammed the gate shut. The trick worked. Within moments, they were driving up to the darkened mansion. When they stopped by the front porch, the Marines with Kine dragged their prisoner out of the car and again used his limp hand to trick the security system.

It obligingly unlocked the door, which slid open silently. E Troop's Marines streamed through and spread out, looking for life signs on their handheld battlefield sensors.

Several minutes later, they reappeared, carrying five limp bodies which they unceremoniously dumped into the truck's rear compartment, along with the sleeping station chief.

"No resistance," Sergeant Favero reported in a soft tone. "We caught them sleeping. They'll wake up in the brig and wonder if they've crossed into another dimension. My people are looking for their computer core right now. If you want, I can leave with the prisoners and my people except the four inside. They can ride back with you."

Kine thought for a moment, then nodded.

"Go. I'll take care of the car."

She watched them leave, the main gate obligingly opening as it sensed a previously admitted vehicle approaching to exit. That was the problem with automated security systems. Artificial intelligence would never replace human cunning. Ten minutes passed before shadows emerged from the house.

"Got it. We can leave."

The four Marines piled into the car while Kine shut the front door and made sure it was locked. Then, they, too, passed through the main gate and headed for the spaceport.

As they neared the hangar, its doors opened to reveal dark shapes outlined by red battle illumination, and the car sailed through. Sergeant Hennes, wearing his armor, waved them to one side and pointed at where Kine should park the car beside the purloined trucks, now empty.

Two shuttles still sat with their aft ramps open, one waiting for the last E Troop members, and the command shuttle waiting for Kine herself. The others were buttoned up, ready to lift. And once they left, no trace of Keres Company's sojourn would remain.

Kine and her four passengers climbed out and wordlessly headed for their assigned craft, Hennes hard on the Constabulary warrant officer's heels. Once aboard the command shuttle, Hennes poked his head into the flight deck compartment where Tesser sat beside the pilot.

"Good to go, Skipper."

"Excellent."

As Kine strapped in beside a pile of containers seized from the cartel, she heard and felt the thrusters spool up. Then, she sensed movement when the shuttle lifted to hover a meter off the ground as it led the flight through the open doors and out onto the darkened tarmac.

"You want me to contact Traffic Control?" The pilot asked Tesser.

"Nope. We lift and good luck at stopping us."

"Roger that, sir."

Sixty minutes later, the flight landed on *Iolanthe*'s hangar deck, having ignored the imprecations of the ground controllers until the latter gave up as they passed ten kilometers altitude. The moment the space doors closed, the Q-ship broke out of orbit. It accelerated toward the hyperlimit, with six unconscious *Sécurité Spéciale* operatives in its brig and the detritus of the Galindez Cartel in its wake.

— Thirty-Eight —

"Bauchan swallowed the bait, sir." Talyn said after taking a seat across from Admiral Kruczek's desk. "Warrant Officer Steiger thinks he plans on making the Deep Space Foundation his own and not just rely on it as eyes and ears where he has none. If so, the possibilities for our subverting the *Sécurité Spéciale* are endless."

A predatory smile lit up the Chief of Naval Intelligence's face.

"Well done, Admiral. Well done indeed."

"Sir?" Talyn cocked a questioning eyebrow at her superior. "Are you trying to tell me something?"

"Your promotion to rear admiral came through effective today. I thought we might gather your division and a few SOCOM friends this afternoon so they can watch me pin a second star on your collar. Oh, and Colonel Decker is on his way from Fort Arnhem. Shall we say fifteen hundred hours?"

"Certainly, sir. And thank you."

"Thank yourself, Admiral. Your performance since taking over from Admiral Ulrich has been nothing short of exemplary."

"Yes, sir. But I meant summoning Zack so he can witness my promotion in person."

"I'm sure Colonel Decker would never forgive me if I'd done otherwise, and I rather like him. He's a fine officer and a thoroughly decent, honorable human being."

"Agreed on every count, sir. And he's a delightful life partner too."

"Then make it official, already. You wouldn't be the first rear admiral to marry a Marine Corps colonel. Besides, give it a few years, and he'll be wearing a star."

Talyn's eyes narrowed. "And you're trying to tell me something else, right? The Special Forces Division promotions came through, didn't they?"

"Yes. Major General Martinson is about to call Colonel Decker and Brigadier General Ryent and set a date for the change of command ceremony. No doubt shortly after your partner's current command is back."

"Which will be in a few days."

"What happens with the *Sécurité Spéciale* operatives?"

"If they haven't already, *Iolanthe* and *Kobe Maru* will meet in interstellar space. Erinye Company transfers across to *Iolanthe* while its prisoners join the ones taken by Keres Company in *Kobe Maru*. Then the latter will head for Parth and hand the lot of them to our people running the special rendition site."

Kruczek nodded. "How long will we hold them?"

"Anywhere between six months and a year, I think. As long as it takes for the Deep Space Foundation to embed itself with the *Sécurité Spéciale*. The captives will not know for sure Naval Intelligence took them, and the rendition site is sterile. We won't interrogate nor mistreat them either. And since their organization doesn't officially exist because it wasn't created through legislation, isn't funded by a proper line item nor subject to Senate oversight, Bauchan can't well ask us for their whereabouts. And much less accuse us of breaking any laws. The *Sécurité Spéciale*'s very creation violated the law, and he knows it. And eventually, it'll belong to us."

**

When Hera Talyn entered her office, she found Decker studying the pictures hanging on the walls. As soon as he heard her, the Marine turned around and came to attention.

"Congratulations, Admiral. I knew you'd finally become respectable, even though you hang around with me and my unwashed, unshaven, and unmannerly buddies."

"At ease, you irritating Marine, and give me a hug."

They embraced, then she said, "Kruczek asked me just now why we don't make it official, which means our relationship isn't a bar to further glory as flag officers of our beloved Armed Services. Did you speak with Jimmy yet?"

"He called just as my aircar was landing. I'll see him and Kal after the CNI does his thing so we can sort out the formalities."

"When do you put up your third pip?"

"The night before the change of command parade, as per tradition. Although I'm already getting paid as a full colonel." Decker chuckled. "Do you remember when we first met?"

"How could I forget?"

"Did you figure back then you'd become a rear admiral and run intelligence's Special Operations Division, and I'd take command of the 1st SFR as a full bull?"

"The way you looked on that beach, seconds from a horrible death? No. Nor did I see us where we are now when you returned from the trans-Coalsack and came back into the Service as a chief warrant officer to team up with me. I guess we've led something of a charmed life together, haven't we?"

Decker let out a bark of laughter.

"If you call courting death at every turn for years charmed, then sure."

"We're here, in good health, and with all our parts intact. And we have each other. How about it, Marine? Want to visit the chaplain?"

"Now?"

She glared at him.

"No. Once things are calmer after you take over from Kal."

"You know it'll be a regimental ceremony at that point, right?"

Talyn winked at him.

"I'm counting on it."

"Oh well, in that case, I'll see to drawing up plans for a new Pegasus Club."

"Considering who'll be present, I'm sure your Marines will behave decorously?"

Decker gave her a suspicious glare.

"What do you mean?"

"Do you think we can afford to disappoint our respective superiors by not inviting them? Yes, the Regiment and School are family, our only one beside Saga, and that family is raucous. But they'll be on their best behavior around a bevy of admirals and generals because they won't want us to look bad."

He met her eyes in silence for a few moments.

"Why the sudden desire to get hitched? I'm for it, make no mistake. And so is Saga."

She shrugged.

"Your taking command of the regiment means our days gallivanting across the galaxy are truly over. We might as well celebrate the obvious fact we'll always be together, even when duty keeps us a few hundred kilometers apart."

"I suppose in a couple of years, I'll be working at division or even SOCOM HQ, and that means we can finally live together when I move here."

"Now you're getting it. Once it's official, I'll ask for proper married flag officer quarters, and in due course, we can build our own house, somewhere south of here, perhaps on the shores of the Middle Sea, where we can eventually retire."

Decker let out a snort.

"You're really thinking this out, aren't you?"

"Neither of us will serve the Fleet forever, and I can't think of a better place to retire than Caledonia. In a few decades, of course. But having a holiday home in the meantime isn't a bad idea either. Somewhere we can spend time away from the clamor of duty, invite those close to us for a stay, and if Saga ever becomes a mother, we can watch your grandchildren play."

When she saw the strange expression in Decker's eyes, Talyn asked, "What?"

"The idea of watching grandchildren play seems weird, but in a really wonderful way." She knew there was more to it but didn't insist. He would tell her when he was ready. "Just don't drop hints I'd like my daughter to produce offspring, okay?"

She raised both hands, palms facing outward.

"Promised. The thought never even occurred to me."

"What thought?" A female voice asked from the door. "Or should I not ask?"

Decker turned around, and a big grin split his face at seeing his only daughter. He stood.

"Never mind, honey. Come and give your father a hug."

She stepped into the office and saluted.

"Lieutenant Saga Decker reporting as ordered, sir."

Talyn returned the salute.

"At ease."

Decker embraced his daughter, then said, "I figured it would be nice if Saga witnessed your promotion, doubly so now that we decided."

Saga's eyes widened.

"You're getting married?"

Talyn smiled at her.

"In a few weeks, yes. We decided we'd bow to the inevitable."

"What she means," Decker growled, "is that the Chief of Naval Intelligence suggested we bow to the inevitable. But not a word to anyone until we make it public."

A mischievous smile, so much like Decker's, crossed her finely chiseled features.

"Mum's the word, dad."

"Oh God," Talyn groaned theatrically. "She inherited your dubious sense of humor as well."

"Of course. It's a reminder we Deckers aren't for the faint of heart."

**

At fifteen hundred hours precisely, Decker, standing by the door, spied Admiral Kruczek, accompanied by General Habad, Vice Admiral Ulrich, and, wearing his second star for the first time, Major General Martinson in the corridor. Hera's officers and noncoms currently on Caledonia were present, including the Camp X instructors, making the space feel rather crowded.

As Kruczek crossed the threshold, Decker called out in his best command sergeant voice, "Atten-SHUN. Chief of Naval Intelligence on deck."

The room fell silent as everyone stiffened and faced the door.

"At ease." The CNI and Admiral Ulrich headed for the front of the room where Talyn waited while Habad and Martinson stayed with Decker at the back.

"Congratulations," Habad murmured. "The Commandant approved your idea of assigning the MLI to the Special Forces Division. He wondered why it took a Special Forces officer commissioned from the ranks to find a proper role for those orphaned battalions. Please have a draft plan for their training on my desk by Monday. I'd like the first rotation in eight weeks with the battalions assigned to Fort Arnhem going through last, so we can finish expanding the infrastructure."

"Yes, sir."

There was no time for further discussion as Kruczek launched into the usual promotion speech praising Talyn's long career as a Navy officer before pinning a second star on her tunic collar. After the applause died away, well-wishers wanting to shake her hand beset Talyn. The three Marines stayed at the back and continued their discussion about the Marine Light Infantry Regiment, SOCOM's newest Tier Two unit.

Decker was last to congratulate the newly minted rear admiral, though he did so with admirable restraint instead of picking her up and planting a fat, wet kiss on her lips.

The gleam in Talyn's eyes, however, promised an appropriate rematch that evening.

— Thirty-Nine —

"Britta. Please sit." A visibly preoccupied Bauchan watched her sweep into his office, elegant as always and smiling with unfeigned joy at seeing him.

"You seem like a man with a problem." She sat on one of the chairs across from him and frowned. "I recall getting at least a fond hug upon arrival, if not a peck on the lips."

"My apologies." He rose and came around his desk, arms outstretched, and surprised her with a passionate kiss when she climbed back to her feet. "I should never let work come between us."

"Kind of hard to do, considering we're professional allies as well as lovers. Let's just promise we won't let anything, clothes included, come between us tonight." Steiger gave him a lascivious wink.

"Done." He led her to the settee group by the antique fireplace.

"What's eating at you, darling? And how can I help?"

"Do you recall telling me trouble was brewing in the Cascadian Sector between the Kiryu and Galindez Cartels because the former wishes to replace the latter and control the trade in illegal goods?"

"Yes."

"I have, or perhaps it would be more exact to say I had assets using the Galindez Cartel as unwitting soldiers in our fight against enemies of the Commonwealth. The Galindez Cartel's headquarters on New Tasman was attacked a few days ago — news just reached me this morning — and destroyed. The cartel itself has been decapitated. My assets on New Tasman vanished shortly after that, turning the star system into a blind spot. Worse yet, almost at the same time, my assets on Cascadia itself, those running the node that coordinated activities in the sector and served as the intelligence clearinghouse, were abducted by persons unknown. In both cases, the attackers stole computer cores before destroying sensitive equipment. It means until I can re-establish a new node, my ability to keep tabs on the Cascadian Sector will be limited, since there are no direct links between assets in the various star systems and here."

Steiger made a face.

"Ugh. Do you believe the Kiryu Cartel is responsible for your people on Cascadia as well?"

Bauchan shrugged.

"I'd blame both on the Fleet if it weren't for the Kiryu death cards found on Galindez Cartel bodies. In any case, we no longer have a reliable window into the Cascadian

Sector," he paused for a second or two while his eyes met Steiger's, "unless the Foundation has it covered."

"Not as well as the Rim Sector, but yes. Our people are operating in both affected star systems. I'm sure my superiors would be happy to share resources with you. Let me send a message and warn them of incoming intelligence-gathering requests."

Bauchan gave her a weak smile.

"Thank you, my dear. Will everything be funneled through you, assuming the Foundation agrees to become a de facto arm of the Commonwealth executive's intelligence and security cadre?"

"For now, yes. But I expect Cimmeria will want direct lines of communication, especially if this new relationship becomes permanent." Steiger was pleased she could keep any sign of jubilation from her voice and expression. Her mission was succeeding beyond anyone's wildest expectations.

"Oh, I'm hoping it will become one for the ages." Bauchan's smile strengthened as if he saw a victory of his own on the horizon. "A marriage between two like-minded organizations that share a single goal."

Steiger smiled back while wondering whether he planned to subsume the Deep Space Foundation and make it an unofficial arm of the *Sécurité Spéciale*. If so, the irony would be almost unbearable — Andreas Bauchan laying the foundations of his own agency's demise by embracing an avatar of his most dangerous and hated enemy.

"So am I, my dear."

**

"How does it feel being married to the man who rules over this shining domain?" Decker, whiskey glass in hand, waved at a brightly lit Fort Arnhem, where the wedding reception was still going strong.

He and Talyn had slipped away with two glasses and a bottle of Glen Arcturus shortly before midnight and climbed the small promontory separating the fort proper from the training area. There, the aptly named Observation Post's gazebo and benches offered visitors a place to rest and admire the scenery. Both still wore the mess uniforms they'd donned for the reception after a formal military wedding attended by half the flag officers on Caledonia and the entire Special Forces community. But this late into the evening, they'd undone the stiff, gold braid-encrusted collars.

She wrapped her arm around his and squeezed.

"Not much different from when we climbed out of bed this morning, honey. We've been a couple for so long that the burst of spousal pride for my newly minted colonel happened when you took over the regiment two weeks ago."

"It was a nice ceremony, wasn't it? You sitting with the other flag officers, looking adorably regal. I won't even ask how much that admiral's sword cost."

"More than you'd expect. The regiment did you and Kal proud. Everyone will remember that day for a long time."

"The flypast by *Mikado*'s gunships was a delightful surprise."

Talyn gave him a smug look as she raised her glass.

"You're welcome."

"Today was just as wonderful. Who'd believe my Ghost Squadron rogues could manage such a perfect sword arch?"

"I'm sure Josh had something to do with it. He wouldn't think of honoring his best friend with anything other than the highest standards."

"His best friend and the finest NILO who ever served with Special Forces. Caelin Morrow showing up for the wedding was another pleasant surprise."

"She was in the sector when I sent out the invitations. I gather being an assistant commissioner in the Political Anti-Corruption Unit gives her extra pull in making travel changes on the fly."

"No doubt. And we're about to get one more surprise, darling." He nodded at the crowd forming below them. "Our absence has been noted, and our whereabouts tracked."

"Your Marines are reconnaissance specialists among their manifold skills."

"And our Constabulary friends good at tracking fugitives. Between the lot of them, they could clean up our part of the galaxy in no time."

"Let's just hope they can sing as well as they can hunt the enemy." She pointed at Lieutenant Colonel Bayliss, Commanding Officer, Ghost Squadron, and Major Curtis Delgado, Officer Commanding Erinye Company, as they organized part of the mob into a large choir, Saga Decker and Caelin Morrow among them. "It looks like they cooked something up for us."

"We may be serenaded with one of the regiment's more salacious drinking songs, their words suitably altered for the circumstances. Grin and bear it, my dear admiral. Grin and bear it."

They raised their glasses in salute as the first voices rang out with a heavily modified and rather lewd version of *Blood Upon the Risers*, Zack Decker's signature song. By the time they hit the chorus, Decker and Talyn were roaring with laughter, as were at least half of the guests.

When they finally regained a measure of self-control, Decker wrapped his arms around Talyn and kissed her like never before to cheers that echoed off the fort's many buildings and the promontory.

Below them, Major Delgado nudged Lieutenant Colonel Bayliss and, over the din of applause, asked, "Do you think we surprised our newlyweds?"

"Yep. No doubt about it." Bayliss let out a loud snort. "Knowing Zack and Hera, they'll make that version of *Blood Upon the Risers* their official wedding song just out of sheer devilment."

A pop sounded from the other side of the installation, followed by dozens more as fireworks shot into the crystal clear night air — a suitable finale to a day like no other for the Special Forces family. Two legends had finally united.

And the Pegasus Club was still standing.

About the Author

Eric Thomson is the pen name of a retired Canadian soldier who spent more time in uniform than he expected, both in the Regular Army and the Army Reserve. He spent his Regular Army career in the Infantry and his Reserve service in the Armoured Corps.

Eric has been a voracious reader of science fiction, military fiction, and history all his life. Several years ago, he put fingers to keyboard and started writing his own military sci-fi, with a definite space opera slant, using many of his own experiences as a soldier for inspiration.

When he's not writing fiction, Eric indulges in his other passions: photography, hiking, and scuba diving, all of which he shares with his wife.

Join Eric Thomson at http://www.thomsonfiction.ca/ Where you'll find news about upcoming books and more information about the universe in which his heroes fight for humanity's survival.

Read his blog at https://blog.thomsonfiction.ca

If you enjoyed this book, please consider leaving a review with your favorite online retailer to help others discover it.

Also by Eric Thomson

Siobhan Dunmoore
No Honor in Death (Siobhan Dunmoore Book 1)
The Path of Duty (Siobhan Dunmoore Book 2)
Like Stars in Heaven (Siobhan Dunmoore Book 3)
Victory's Bright Dawn (Siobhan Dunmoore Book 4)
Without Mercy (Siobhan Dunmoore Book 5)
When the Guns Roar (Siobhan Dunmoore Book 6)
A Dark and Dirty War (Siobhan Dunmoore Book 7)
On Stormy Seas (Siobhan Dunmoore Book 8)
The Final Shore (Siobhan Dunmoore Book 9)

Decker's War
Death Comes But Once (Decker's War Book 1)
Cold Comfort (Decker's War Book 2)
Fatal Blade (Decker's War Book 3)
Howling Stars (Decker's War Book 4)
Black Sword (Decker's War Book 5)
No Remorse (Decker's War Book 6)
Hard Strike (Decker's War Book 7)

Constabulary Casefiles
The Warrior's Knife
A Colonial Murder
The Dirty and the Dead
A Peril so Dire

Ghost Squadron
We Dare - Ghost Squadron No. 1
Deadly Intent - Ghost Squadron No. 2
Die Like the Rest – Ghost Squadron No. 3
Fear No Darkness – Ghost Squadron No. 4

Ashes of Empire
Imperial Sunset (Ashes of Empire #1)
Imperial Twilight (Ashes of Empire #2)
Imperial Night (Ashes of Empire #3)
Imperial Echoes (Ashes of Empire #4)
Imperial Ghosts (Ashes of Empire #5)
Imperial Dawn (Ashes of Empire #6)

Made in United States
Cleveland, OH
17 November 2024

10707970R00203